NOVÁ VLNA

Dreaming of Autonomous Vehicles

Miloslav (Miles) J. Breuer:
Czech-American Writer
and the Birth of Science Fiction

Jaroslav Olša, Jr.

Published by:
Space Cowboy Books
61871 29 Palms Hwy.
Joshua Tree, CA 92252
www.spacecowboybooks.com

In collaboration with:
Nová vlna
Letecká 6/658
Praha 6, the Czech Republic
kosmas.cz/nakladatelstvi/6552

ISBN: 979–8–9896308–6–8 (Space Cowboy Books)
ISBN: 978–80–53048–08–8 (Nová vlna)

This book is dedicated to "Mr. Sci-fi" Forrest J. Ackerman (1916–2008),
the founding father of the Los Angeles Science Fantasy Society,
a life-long science fiction enthusiast, collector, and editor,
and a personal friend of Miles (Miloslav) J. Breuer.

And to the creators of Waymo, the first true self-driving car.

Contents

Acknowledgments:

This book could not be possible without the help, support and previous research of science fiction editors and publishers, namely Ivan Adamovič, Michael Ashley, Everett F. Bleiler, Richard Bleiler, John Clute, Jim Emerson, František Hlous, Ondřej Neff, Michael R. Page, Zdeněk Rampas, Michaela Rampasová, Robert Silverberg, and Jan Vaněk jr., as well as researchers and experts on Czech-American history, namely Ivan Dubovický, Martin Nekola, David Muhlena, Miroslav Rechcígl, Jr., Cecilia Rokusek, Danielle Sigler, and Michaela Tydlitátová.

Because I feel a deep sense of gratitude for the people who have supported me during the researching and writing of this book, I would like to express my debt to Miles J. Breuer's descendants, who shared with me information, documents, photographs, and manuscripts, namely granddaughter Christine Dale, grandsons Ian Neligh, and Dave Neligh, and the great grandson Alexander Sonn.

These institutions also deserve my gratitude:
Briscoe Center for American History at the University of Texas, Austin
Libri Prohibiti library, Prague
Los Angeles Science Fantasy Society, Los Angeles
Museum of Literature, Prague
Náprstek Museum of Asian, African, and American Cultures, Prague
National Czech and Slovak Museum and Library, Cedar Rapids
National Museum, Prague

*Illustration by Frank R. Paul
for "The Inferiority Complex"
(Amazing Stories, September 1930).*

The 20th century saw a boom in science fiction literature, with authors following in the footsteps of genre pioneers such as Jules Verne and H. G. Wells. In 1920, Czech author Karel Čapek published his famous drama *R. U. R. Rossum's Universal Robots*, in which the term 'robot' was coined. Moreover, in places such as Germany, France, Italy and Scandinavia, utopian and technologically-oriented novels and novellas began to gain favour with readers, the works often describing fantastical inventions or trips to the other planets and beyond. Meanwhile, in the United States, Hugo Gernsback, editor of the monthly magazine *Science and Invention*, began to conceive of a publication that would exclusively feature science fiction tales, which he initially labelled as 'scientifiction.'[1] This led to the founding of monthly pulp magazine *Amazing Stories* in 1926, albeit Gernsback was soon faced with a shortage of authors. For its first nine issues, *Amazing Stories* contained reprints of classic stories from the likes of Jules Verne, H. G. Wells, and Edgar Allan Poe, also supplemented by more modern works from writers such as Edgar Rice Burroughs and Abraham Merritt, both of whom were already publishing their works in other pulp magazines.

Only in subsequent years did *Amazing Stories* feature a new generation of writers. In 1928, Jack Williamson, whose career as a science fiction writer would span three-quarters of a century, published his first story in the magazine. A year earlier, *Amazing Stories* featured a story by David H. Keller, one of the pioneers of early technological science fiction. However, the very first person in this wave is the now largely forgotten author Miles J. Breuer. His story "The Man with the Strange Head," featuring a dead man stuck in a still operational human-like machine, was published in the January 1927 issue.

Miles J. Breuer was born to Czech parents in Chicago, studied in Texas, lived in Nebraska and died in California. At the turn of the 1920s and 30s, Breuer's readers viewed this author, who was supposedly 'discovered' by Gernsback, as a major star of the science fiction genre. Unusually popular as an author in his time, Breuer wrote stories of a four-dimensional nature (i.e. parallel or alternate universes), but was also the first science fiction author to utilize the concept of the dilation of time.

However, Breuer's career as a writer began long before *Amazing Stories*. Indeed, his first genre story in English was published two decades prior. Writing as 'Miloslav' – the Czech version of his name – Breuer had already published numerous stories in the Czech language as well. Moreover, his early stories featured numerous innovative ideas – in 1924, in his Czech-language story "Vyšší tvor", Breuer was the first to conceive of a world featuring self-driving cars. But this story was soon largely forgotten, leading most historians to point to Breuer's later expanded version of the story, novel *Paradise and Iron*, published in 1930 in the magazine *Amazing Stories Quarterly*, as the true source of this idea.

From Bohemia's Kutná Hora Region to the Heart of Czech America

During the second half of the 19th century, North America saw a wave of immigration from Central Europe. These arrivals, numbering in the hundreds of thousands, were largely poor, with limited educations, and, unsurprisingly next-to-no knowledge of the English language – albeit with a very strong desire to make better lives for themselves. During these times, cities such as St. Louis, Missouri and New York became key centres of Czech settlement, followed by the agricultural regions of Iowa, Nebraska and Texas, which saw entire Czech settlements emerging. But it would be the city of Chicago, Illinois that, by the end of the 19th century, grew to become the largest Czech community in the United States, with a population exceeding 150,000. By the end of the 19th century, the city was still only home to a relatively small number of educated Czech immigrants – with most struggling to break through language and cultural barriers.

One exception was Charles Hugh (Karel Hugo) Breuer[2] (1866–1946), who arrived in the United States at the tender age of ten. His family lost almost all their possessions in the wake of flooding in the village of Malešov not far from the town of Kutná Hora in Central Bohemia. This led them to try their fortunes in the United States. First, older brother Hynek Breuer left for the New World in 1874, followed the next year by younger brother Alois Breuer, and then the year after that father Karel Breuer[3] took the rest of the family to New York. It was here, in the Big Apple, that the family began working as cigar-makers, a common occupation for Czech immigrants at that time. Gradually, however, the Breuers began spreading into fresh corners of the United States – with Hynek Breuer heading to Kansas, and subsequently to Oklahoma, where he ended up owning a foundry and machine shop. Meanwhile, Alois Breuer settled in Minnesota, while sister Matilda Breuer's fate remains something of a mystery following a trip to Anoka, Minnesota in search of work.

The Breuer parents settled in New Prague, Minnesota, on a farm situated half-way between Czech and German settlements, where young Charles H. Breuer began attending school. The result was that Charles learned excellent German and English, while also learning Czech through home study, including reading the books in his father's native language library. The family – despite being far from wealthy – also subscribed to several Czech-American periodicals, and so Charles "learned to write Czech relatively well with the help of his siblings."[4] Charles completed his schooling at the age of sixteen, when,

Novoroční dárek.

Povídka z pruskofrancouzské války. Přeložil Karel H. Breuer.

I.

Kočár, tažený dvěma bujnými oři, na jehož kozlíku seděli kočí a sluha v zelených livrejích, jel rychle jednoho letního odpoledne starým městem Saint-Jean-Sur-Loir. Celá ekypáž ale byla poněkud již sešlá, což nasvědčovalo, že její majitelé nevládnou přílišným jměním. Tmavé úzké uličky tohoto města byly dnes plny života; velké náměstí před kathedrálou bylo přeplněno rozličnými vozy, kočáry, elegantními ekypážemi a deštníky, pod nimiž se ukrývali obyvatelé města před palčivými paprsky slunečními. Na širokých stupních kathedrály stáli dva pánové v bílých vestách, majíce též deštníky v rukou, živé rozkládajíce rozčilenému množství o posledních událostech v Paříži—o možnosti války, neb dnes byl den výročního trhu v městečku. Bylo to v prvním týdnu července 1870.

V kočáru seděly čtyry osoby; přední místo zaujímala stará, nápadně bledá dáma, černě oděna, podle níž seděl starší již venkovský abbé, který bez nstání k ní hovořil a naproti těmto seděli dva mladí mužové, velmi elegantně oděni, tak že se zdálo, jako by byli připraveni na nějakou vznešenou návštěvu neb slavnost. Jeden z těchto mladých pánů se zdál býti jaksi zádumčivým a smutným. Ačkoliv byl velmi příjemného zevnějšku, že se téměř hezkým zváti mohl, nebyl daleko tak příjemný jako jeho bratr, který se stále usmíval a někdy i zažertoval. Snad byly žerty jeho dráždivé anebo zlomyslné, ale tolik jest jisto, že se bratru jeho nikterak nelíbily, neb se stával čím dále tím zasmušilejším, temný mrak vystával načele jeho a odpovídal mu stále řidčeji. Ku příkladu, když projížděli náměstím, upoutali oni dva pánové na stupních kathedrály stojící pozornost veselejšího bratra, který proho-

Ludvík, bratr Karlův, když byli právě minuli zahradu, v níž hrála hudba úryvek z nějaké nejnovější opery.

„Vždyť budeme pak mít peníze," pravil Karel mrzutě, „ona může žíti kde si přeje a já také — já budu žít, kde si budu přát."

„Může též být, že se jí bude v Mesnilu lépe líbit než v městě."

„Já myslím že ne. Já tuším, že by raději žila v Trouville a Biarritzu, s malými přestávkami v Paříži. Čím bezčí je, tím budu radši, čím méně ji budu viděti, tím šťastnějším budu. Osoba, která by s námi chtěla bydleti na našem statku, osoba, vychovaná panem Duvalem, jest nestálá a nevydrží dlouho na jednom místě."

„Pan Duval jest dobrým katolíkem; jest to řádný a vážný muž. Já se obávám, že jest slečna spíše tuze vážnou," pravil Ludvík.

„Ne, ne; v tomto případu bych ji nikdy za manželku nepojal," pravil Karel, hrabě z Mesnilu.

Ludvík se jen usmíval, byl již na mrzutou povahu svého bratra zvyklým. Mrzelo ho to též, že jest bratr jeho pořád tak zasmušilým a zádumčivým, přece se ale smál jeho výstřednostem. Tento ubohý Karel byl jedním z nejpříčinlivějších mladých studentů Francie. On byl pro své studie tuze zaujat, že nemyslel na nic jiného a zlobil se, když byl ze svého dumání vytrhováм svým veselým bratrem. Pakli nebyl zahloubán ve svých knihách, zajisté bys jej byl nalezl na některé ze stinných pěšinek domácího parku, neb v lese kolem zámku se prostírajícím. Obyčejně nosil na rameně ručnici ale nikdy nic nezastřelil. U večer obyčejně se probral ze svých hlubokých myšlének a bavil matku rozličným podivín-

One of many Charles H. Breuer's translations published in contemporary Czech-American press.

as he later wrote, "the teacher no longer had anything new to teach me."[5] After that, he worked on his father's farm, also learning to operate steam engines.

Some time in 1885, Charles read that August Geringer,[6] the most renowned figure in the world of Czech-American publishing, was seeking a new editor for his Chicago-based publishing house. Charles proposed his services and was soon offered the job. By the end of that spring, he was already working as an assistant editor at the Czech-language daily *Svornost* (The Concord).[7] Specifically, Charles' job entailed selecting and rewriting interesting news of potential interest to the Czech community from Chicago's various English- and German-language periodicals. The number of qualified journalists among the Czech-American community at that time was small, especially for the number of Czech-language periodicals being published. This soon led Charles H. Breuer to expand into the literary arena of Geringer's publishing behemoth, fifty years later noting that "during my time there, I translated countless compelling novels from German and English, for example *'Boj o miliony,' 'Gabriela,' 'Matka a syn,' 'Číslo 99,' 'Dcera anarchistova'* and many others."[8]

At the same time, Breuer began to take an interest in completing his education, attending evening high school classes, and also taking a greater interest in Czech cultural events such as theatrical performances, concerts, and the activities of Czech Sokol gymnastic club.[9] Indeed, as a journalist working for the most notable Czech-American publisher, Breuer later remembered that he

DR. K. H. BREUER.

was almost universally not only warmly welcomed but given cost-free entry to such events.

In February 1887 Charles H. Breuer married wife Barbora,[10] who less than two years later, on January 3, 1889, in the Czech Pilsen quarter of Chicago, bore him a son, Miles John (Miloslav Jan) Breuer. By this time Charles H. Breuer ended his two-year stint at *Svornost*, after "consulting with my wife and concluding that Czech journalism in the United States had no future and lack the opportunities for to excel oneself that are available in other fields not limited to targeting one nationality."[11] Breuer then spent a short time working at a local courthouse, and even began studying law, albeit soon realizing that much more money was to be made as a land broker in the ever-expanding city of Chicago. "I was doing well in this field and making good money,"[12] he later recalled. However, a bad investment into the second most popular Chicago--based daily, *Chicagské Listy* (Chicago Paper)[13] followed, leading Breuer to lose a fortune.

Breuer's restless soul soon led him, his wife and two kids to Arkansas.[14] Alas, they did not like the land made available to them and so continued to look for fresh pastures. Ultimately, Breuer accepted an offer from Nebraska-based Czech publisher Jan Rosický,[15] who had began publishing the monthly *Hospodář* (The Farmer).[16] "I went straight to Omaha and assumed my post, and my wife soon came out to see me, thus enabling me to begin a new chapter, albeit still as a journalist, in Omaha. I worked at both publications, meaning both *Hospodář*, and also *Pokrok Západu*,"[17] Breuer later recalled.[18] The Breuer family resided in Nebraska for a number of years. But because Charles H. Breuer continued to "think about something more permanent, given that I viewed Czech journalism as something more transitory, and

Národní tiskárna (National Printing Co.) –
seat of all Czech-language periodicals published in Omaha, NE.

CHAS. H. BREUER, M. D.,

Physician & Surgeon,

HALLETSVILLE, - TEXAS.

Offic at N. Morris Drug Store.

A portion of private residence (Ellis homestead) fitted up for a hospital.

---

that it would not be sustainable long-term,"[19] he once again began to look for fresh opportunities.

In 1892, Creighton Medical College was founded in the city of Omaha. This led the 26-year-old Charles H. Breuer, along with a journalist colleague, to sign up for a course, albeit continuing to hold their existing jobs at the same time. And so, "for three years, as was the length of a medical course at the time, we slogged it out. The first year, we still helped out in the editorial office; but the second and third were so difficult that we had to leave journalism behind."[20] Right after graduation, Charles H. Breuer began practicing medicine in the then 100,000 strong Omaha. For the first generation of European immigrants to the United States – both Czechs (numbering several thousand in Omaha by the start of the 20th century), as well as Slovaks and more numerous Germans – a doctor who spoke their native tongue would have certainly been a godsend. Alas, after a mere year and a half, the Breuers, now numbering five, thanks to the addition of a second son, Roland,[21] were on the move again. This time, the destination was Texas, a state which was then home to roughly 40,000 Czechs. At first, the family settled in the town of Seguin, but soon discovered that this area was mostly populated by German immigrants. Consequently, at the start of 1897, after only a few weeks in Seguin, they shifted to the nearby community of Hallettsville, which had a much larger Czech population. Here, Charles H. Breuer opened a medical practice as well as a pharmacy, which he immediately began to promote in the local Czech--language Catholic weekly *Nový Domov* (New Home).[22] But the Breuers did not stay put long in Texas, either. Indeed, by the spring of 1899, the family is recorded as residing in Colorado Springs, Colorado. And it was here that his wife Barbora gave birth to their third son, Senn Edwin.[23] Alas, "even though the wife was happy here, the medical practice was not successful."[24] One possible factor is that the entire state at this time only housed around 150 Czech families; the result being that the Breuers once again uprooted in search of fresh pastures.

Miles J. Breuer – Literary Beginnings

As noted, Charles H. Breuer believed that Czech-language journalism lacked a future in the United States. Despite this, he remained an active figure in the journalistic arena in the Midwest. Nor did he lose sight of his former contacts in Chicago. In 1897, Breuer began writing reader-friendly articles on various ailments and their treatment, first in *Hospodář*, and then subsequently in other Czech-language periodicals – mostly near his current place of residence, as well as frequently in publications of the Chicago-based Geringer publishing house. Breuer managed to make a good living as a doctor, also motivated by a keen patriotic duty to his country of birth, still seeking to promote its culture and traditions, organizing Czech events, and bringing up his children in a similar vein.

Eldest son Miles J. Breuer[25] made his first contribution to Czech-American journal in the spring of 1895. Writing in the "Omladina" (youth) section of the Chicago weekly *Amerikán* Breuer wrote: "I am only six years and three months old. Since January, I have been attending an English school and reading from the second Chrestomathy. [...] I am [also] learning Czech from the first Chrestomathy [published] by you, but I don't know it very well yet."[26] Despite continually changing schools – and only attending American schools – the Czech language remained close to his heart. Indeed, Miles was an avid reader of Czech books from childhood.

In 1900, the Breuers again returned to Nebraska and settled in the small town of David City, in the heart of a large community of Czech immigrant farmers around a hundred kilometres from Omaha, and 70km from Lincoln, the capital of Nebraska. This barely 2,000-strong town had a strong influence

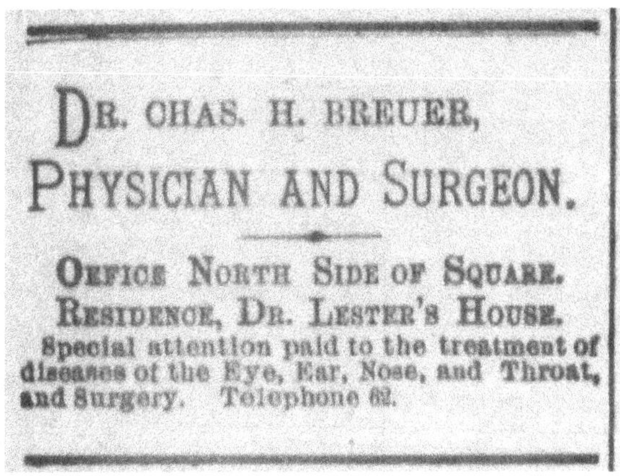

Advertisment in English-language press in David City.

Legend of the Stars.

In those very long gone days of old
As little Indians are told
In the sky, there was nothing there
But the moon, big and little bear,
And big dipper and milky way,
That is what the Indians say.
The man in the moon got to think,
That he would like to have a drink
Of milk out of the milky way,
Not thinking if he might or may
So the dipper in hand he took,
And with a bold defiant look,
Not thinking about the great bear,
Or thinking if the bear would care,
He slowly and carefully filled it.
But the big bear growled and he hit
The dipper hard against his chin,
There wasn't anything left in
It, but was all spilt in the sky,
As seen to-day by you and I.

Miles J. Breuer.

on eleven-year-old Miles, despite the mere few months stay. "From this time, [Miles] has memories of a David City library, where he first became acquainted with the works of H. G. Wells, French writer Jules Verne and British author H. Rider Haggard, going on to feverishly seek out and read all their works."[27] Moreover, David City also became the first place – via the local press – where Miles later, in November 1900, was able to publish his English-language poem "A Queer Thing,"[28] and then in February of the next year, the space-themed "Legend of the Stars."[29]

Indeed, the year 1900 was also a notable one for the elder Charles H. Breuer. At the start of the year, the newly established Knihovna Americká (American Library) in Omaha began to publish the first parts of Breuer's academic opus *Nemoce Koňské* (Horse Illnesses). In October of that year, the local press reported that he had installed a large X-ray machine in his surgery, just five years after this device was invented. Reportedly, this was the first such machine to be available in Nebraska's rural communities, and allegedly the largest device of its kind west of Chicago, as noted in the local press, which devoted an entire column to this marvel.[30] Media interest in Charles H. Breuer was something of a mutually beneficial arrangement – Breuer knew how to present a compelling story, while the media was glad for the simultaneous advertising revenue received by Breuer that publicised his medical practices.

For Breuer's insatiably curious son Miles, the futuristic devices in his father's surgery proved irresistible. Thus, it is no surprise that even "in his boyhood, [he] spent much time in his father's laboratory helping him – not [helping with the] practice of medicine, but rather with his correspondence with others."[31] All the while, the father would undoubtedly have been proud that his son was following in his father's footsteps.

The head of the family evidently had nomadic life in his blood, because the Breuers ultimately did not stay long in David City. Soon Charles H. Breuer was looking for fresh opportunities for commercial success, later writing: "I was not yet contented, as I sought to operate a well-equipped sanatorium with

numerous beds."[32] This time, Breuer headed to Omaha, aiming to build his own hospital intended for Czech patients. And soon in a (likely self-penned) advertisement article in the daily *Pokrok Západu* Breuer was praising the benefits of his Omaha Sanitarium (Sanatorium) for Czech patients: "When they come to a good American [facility], they often struggle with the language and have to seek out an interpreter, which can be very problematic, especially for women with various illnesses."[33] In order to emphasize the benefits of the sanatorium versus the competition, aside from a list of cured illnesses, Breuer also boasted of the availability, during treatment, of "Czech cuisine."[34]

"The Czech sanatorium and hospital"[35] was situated in a large house in a picturesque spot in Omaha, and was outfitted with the latest modern medical instruments, as noted in *Pokrok Západu*: "The sanatorium houses a large static electric device with X-rays and an ozone inhalation device, as well as a light therapy device, galvanic, faradic and other electrical machines, inhalation cabinets, gym, operating rooms, massage rooms, etc."[36] This time, however, Charles H. Breuer evidently overestimated his own strength, because "he was unable to carry out all needed work by himself, but negotiating the services of other practitioners proved to be uneconomical."[37] All of which led the family to move once again – this time, back into the bosom of the Czech-American farming community in Crete, Nebraska, not far from the capital, Lincoln. Here, Breuer opened a small hospital with an X-ray machine – and managed to stay in the town for almost four years.

For Miles J. Breuer, Crete would be a place that he recalled with fondness years later. With increased frequency, he began to visit his father in the hospital, where he "acquainted himself with the basics of medicinal practice, thus even while still a boy, he was able to give out provisional advice 'until my dad

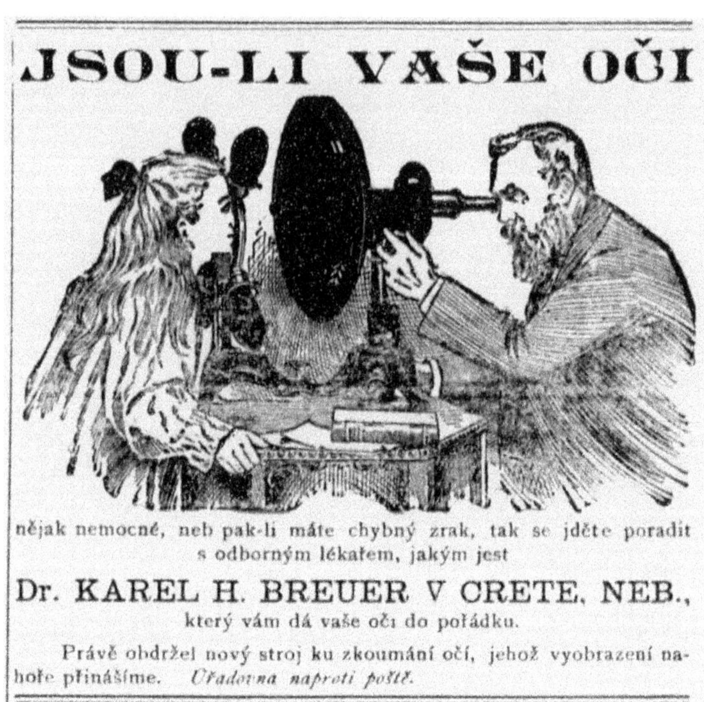

Charles H. Breuer worked also as an optician.

returns' which was often more than sufficient."[38] Charles H. Breuer once again decided to relocate his medical practice in 1905, to the town of Wilber, just 20 kilometres south of Crete. According to local press reports, he then "purchased three land plots […], where he intends to build a new hospital. The plans, courtesy of the Chicago-based architect Hulla[39] are now ready and this week work begins on digging the foundations. The construction is welcomed by Mr. Jan Daniel, a Crete-based Czech builder, who has already built many fine buildings here."[40]

In May 1906, Miles J. Breuer completed his studies in Crete. The local papers then covered his first contribution to the world of science fiction, noting that: "Last Friday, the graduating class of our high school organised a farewell theatrical performance, [at which] the student Milouš [sic] Breuer presented a 'class prophesy,' meaning a look into the future, in which he allowed himself to be transported […] into the future, and then told us what he saw and which male and female pupils had derailed their lives and what the town of Crete will look like 14 years hence."[41] Alas, the text itself appears lost to history.

The completion of high school studies in Nebraska apparently came at a fortuitous time, in light of the fact that Charles H. Breuer, as a result of his wife's poor health, had decided to uproot – this time back to Texas. This also suited Miles, who "in spite of his varied interests […] spanning the theatre, music (piano) and writing, decided […] on a medical career."[42] In the autumn of 1906, Karel H. Breuer opened his medical practice in Yoakum, Texas.[43]

KRAJANÉ! Jsem jediným českým lékařem v Texasu, který koná sám všecky operace na lidském těle a léčí všecky těžké choroby. Já konám všecku práci sám a neposílám nemocné k jiným, jak po mnoholeté mne znáte, mám v tom vzácnou zkušenost.

Moje privátní nemocnice jest zařízena dokonale, mám všecko potřebné zařízení, mám české ošetřovatelky a asistenta, který mluví česky, takže se cítíte jako doma.

Krajané! podporujte krajana, který se mezi Vámi usadil a hleďte si udržeti jedinou českou nemocnici v Texasu a podporujte ji, posílejte své nemocné do ní a nenechte se závistníky přemlouvat.

Pakli potřebujete operaci neb léčení, nedbejte na přemlouvání a přijeďte ke mně a budete poctivě obslouženi. Když chcete ke mně přijeti, nikdo Vás nemůže od úmyslu toho zdržovati. Hlásáme svůj k svému, tedy to také konejme. Když přijedete do Waco, vezměte si u nádraží kočár a nechte se dovézti do nemocnice číslo 10005 North 5th St. aneb přijďte do soukromé úřadovny čís. 324 Austin St. Dr. Karel H. Breuer.

Dr. Karel H. Breuer
český lékař a operatér
Léčí všecky nemoce a koná všecky operace. Má spojení se všemi nemocnicemi v Houstonu a ve dvou má české ošetřovatelky
Zvláštní pozornost věnuje operacím a ženským nemocem
V lehčích případech udílí poradu poštou a pošle léky, jež sám připravuje ve své laboratoři. Když přijedete do Houstonu venku si u nádraží omnibus a ukažte rozkovi dole udanou adresu. Večer se nechte dovézt do Tremont Hotelu a oni vás ráno ke mně dovedou.
Dr. Karel H. Breuer, Room 11. Fox Bldg. 317½ Main St. Houston, Tex.

Znamenitá příležitost
pro českého lékaře neb lékárníka.
Národní Lékárna v Cameron, kde ordinuje český lékař Dr. Breuer, jest nyní na prodej. Jest to ve velké české osadě, kde jest sta krajanů; jest vedle českých obchodů v české čtvrti. Jsou tam lidé navedení a dělá se dobrý obchod. V okolí žádný jiný Čech nedrží léky.
Když se prodá hned, tak se dají dobré podmínky. Český lékař neb lékárník nalezne zde vzácnou příležitost. Hlaste se hned pod adresou:
NÁRODNÍ LÉKÁRNA,
Cameron, Texas.

Dr. Chas. H. Breuer,
český lékař a ranhojič,
Yoakum, Texas.
Specialista v léčení nemoci očí, uší a nosu, nemocí ženských a všech operacích.
Má zařízenou soukromou českou nemocnici k léčení těžších případů, kde mohou být krajané pohodlně obslouženi. Připravuje své léky sám a zasýlá je všude kde třeba. V mírnějších případech udílí poradu poštou a zašle léky.
Úřadovna ve Weagemanově budově; telefon 111. Obydlí druhý dům západně od Opera Housu; telefon 142.

PŘESTĚHOVÁNÍ.
Tímto oznamuji svým přiznivcům, že jsem se přestěhoval z Taylor, Texas, do Austinu, Texas, hlavního města státu Texas. Po dni 1. června, budu připraven uvítati své přiznivce v mé nové zařízení office v čísle 400 Congress Ave., v Austinu. Moje úřadovna se nalézá v čísle 400 Congress Ave., nahoře v prvním poschodí u zadu, jen jeden block od nádraží, na levé straně ulice směrem ku kapitolu. Tam mne snadno každý nalezne, kdyý jest to blízko nádraží. Nyní mám zařízenou pohodlně a nemocní, kteří potřebují do nemocnice, mohou jíti do kterékoliv nemocnice v městě a já budu mít všude české ošetřovatelky, aby se mohli krajané domluviti. Kdo tedy bude potřebovati mé lékařské pomoci, ať již nejede do Taylor, ale přímo do Austinu. Krajané kteří přijedou ve dne, mohou jíti pěšky přímo do mé úřadovny, však kteří přijedou večer neb v noci, mohou jíti přímo do HOTELU HAIGLER, v čísle 211 Congress Ave., jen půl blocku od nádraží, na hlevní ulici směrem k městu, kde mám smluveno, že budou krajané lacino a dobře ztravováni. V hoteltu jest také jeden krajan zaměstnán, s nímiž se mohou český domluviti a nemuseji se nechat po městě v drožkách vozit, neb mne z hotelu hned zavolaji telefonem, kdyý někdo přijede.
Dr. Karel H. Breuer,
český lékař,
400 Congress Ave., Austin, Texas.

Wherever Charles H. Breuer established his practice in Texas, he widely advertised in local Czech-American press.

Formative Years in Texas

In 1906 Miles J. Breuer began his studies, gradually incorporating chemistry, physics and mathematics, at the University of Texas at Austin. He graduated five years later, becoming the first Czech in Texas to gain an M.A.,[44] also becoming a member of the Phi Beta Kappa fraternity.

Miles' years at the University of Texas were also formative in a creative sense. He immediately partook in university literary life, soon becoming one of the most active contributors to various local publications. Moreover, he continued to write short poems and stories – to such a voluminous degree that they filled almost every issue of the now largely forgotten literary monthly *The University of Texas Magazine*.[45] In the autumn of 1909 Breuer first appeared as the magazine's associate editor, evidently holding the position for the next two years.[46]

Miles J. Breuer's first poem in the pages of *The University of Texas Magazine* appeared in December 1907, with a total of 35 works ultimately published there. He also wrote prose, publishing 18 stories between the spring of 1908 and spring of 1912. The first stories are of a genre-type nature, less-than-compelling horror stories titled "The Night and the Demon Fear" and "The Power of Darkness." More than twenty years later, Breuer significantly rewrote the second of these, publishing it as "The Unknown Hand at Gergy." Alas, being published in a student literary magazine meant that most

of his other stories did not reach the wider public. However four of Breuer's works from this time, all with a fantastical motif, did find an extended literary life. "The Will and the Way" from 1910 is the story of an engineer who overcomes his own death to save a town from flooding. Ten years later, the story was translated into Czech as "Vůle a cesta." Also in 1910, "The Flaw in the Premise," tells the story of a man who discovers a device that can peep into the future. Evidently Breuer had further plans for this tale, because exactly twenty-five years later a significantly reworked Czech-language version was published under the similar title "Háček v předpovědi." Accordingly, it is impossible to rule out the existence (and publication) of an English-language reworked version somewhere. However, neither of these science fiction stories ever found their way into the pages of any pulp magazine[47] – even though the second story matches the tone and content of the kinds of stories being issued at the time in these publications.

At least two of Breuer's early works ultimately found their way to science fiction readers. The first (Breuer's fourth fiction ever published), from the spring of 1909 is called "The Stone Cat." It tells the story of a mad scientist who eliminates his enemies by the use of a liquid that turns them into statues, only to have his invention turned against him. Seven years later, the story was published in a slightly updated Czech version (as "Kamenná kočka"), and then, in 1927, a significantly reworked English-language version under the same title found its way into Gernsback's *Amazing Stories* – the second of Breuer's works to be published here.

Another early story was "The Man without an Appetite" about a man who had discovered a way to survive not with food, but photosynthesis. Initially published in March 1910, it had a slightly more complicated path towards reaching science fiction readers. Breuer evidently liked his own story so much that he undertook a significant post-publication rewrite for a 1916 Czech-language version as "Člověk bez hladu." The English-language version of this rewrite only reached readers in 1963, when science fiction editors Groff Conklin and Noah D. Fabricant reached out to Breuer's first wife Julia, seeking some kind of story with a medical theme. "She found the following remarkable tale in her husband's papers," the editors later wrote in the introduction to their *Great Science Fiction About Doctors* anthology. Presumably Julia Breuer gave the editors a text in English, most probably unpublished manuscript, as she wrongly recalled that "it was probably published in some science fiction magazine about 1924 or 1925, but I do not know."[48] In response to queries about whether the reworked English version was ever published during Breuer's lifetime, this remained unanswered even by the two anthology editors – who reached out to readers at the time on this point;[49] and even sixty years later we still have no answer.

In any event, Miles J. Breuer did not limit his writings to his university magazine, and evidently sought to achieve further success with his stories. In April 1909 his first professionally published (and certainly paid) work was issued, namely "The Adventures of the Bronze Mahadeva." This detective story, which borders on the fantastic, was issued in the today highly collectible and rare *10 Story Book*,[50] Chicago-based pulp magazine. In March and April of that same year, it was published in numerous regional newspapers

Founding members of Čechie club. Standing from left: E. E. Křenek, future farmer, Joe Kopecky, future medical doctor, and Louis Mikeska, later moved to New York. Sitting from left: Miles J. Breuer, and C. H. Chernosky, future noted Texan lawyer, and an important personality of Czech-Texan life in the first half of the 20th century.

from New Jersey to Kansas, and some editions are even found from later years.[51] Therefore, it cannot be ruled out that Breuer succeeded in publishing additional stories in other hitherto undiscovered periodicals.

Little documentation has been uncovered about how the first readers – fellow students and teachers – reacted to Breuer's early tales. But these stories were certainly read across the United States, in light of the fact that the university magazines of the time were extensively shared among universities and their respective literary clubs. Alas, no commentaries or reviews have hitherto come to light.[52] It can also not be ruled out that in line with the times, Miles J. Breuer received other literary rewards beyond those for his short poems. Such poems, unlike his later stories, were issued from 1910 to 1913 in the University of Texas' most prestigious publication, the yearbook *Cactus*. The status of Miles J. Breuer as a decorated university poet is also attested to by his being named "class poet" in 1911, which was even covered by a number of Texas newspapers.[53]

By his early 20s, Miles J. Breuer was already an accomplished author, having published a good dozen of his stories in English. Despite only learning English at school, his abilities to express himself in this language from a relatively early age vastly exceeded those he had in his native Czech language. In 1926, the greatest chronicler of early to mid 20th century Czech-America, the New York writer and banker Tomáš Čapek, wrote that "all that is born in America, belongs to America – belongs to it in the statistical, linguistic and ideological sense."[54] However, this was only half-true in the case of Breuer and his siblings. Indeed, Miles J. Breuer was fortunate to spend his formative school and university years among Americans speaking English, while also, as noted in *Hospodář*, "he spent his adolescence in the company of fellow Czech youth, recalling their songs and dances, as well as their theatrical plays, in which he also had a hand. At the time, he read numerous Czech books there, including novels of both a social and historical nature."[55]

At the start of the century, only a tiny number of Czech-Americans attended universities in Texas, because Czech "compatriots in Texas, largely of a Moravian and Silesian background, and farmers by occupation, only sent [...] very few of their sons and daughters to university,"[56] noted the University of Texas' professor Eduard Míček[57] two decades later. For example, in the school year 1909–10, aside from Miles J. Breuer only four other Czechs studied at the university.[58] To promote the country of their ancestry, they occasionally met, and later on founded "the association and club 'Čechie' on 23 October 1909, in order to learn the Czech language, Czech songs, poems, history and so on. "[59] Miloslav J. Breuer became the club's first chairperson, de-

Announcement of Czech-Slavonic Day in Waco, TX.

livering his own lectures on literature during monthly meetings. A year later, the students sought to have Czech taught at the University of Texas, albeit without success. But Čechie would continue to function until well after the Second World War.[60]

Miles J. Breuer's relationship to the Czech language, as well as to Czech literature and culture would continue to deepen in Texas. In 1909 he evidently established a Czech theatre in Hallettsville;[61] and a year later he assisted his father Charles in organising a Czech-Slavonic day in Waco, serving as the greatest demonstration of the strength and significance of the Czech community in Texas in the early 20th century.[62] Moreover, Miles also partook, from afar, in the activities of Komenský (Comenius Club) at Omaha University (now the University of Nebraska – Omaha), which published the monthly *Komenský* (Comenius) which continued up to 1918. Despite publishing only one poem in this periodical (in English), in 1911, Miles also contributed the important article "Proč máme zůstati Čechy?" (Why Should We Remain Czechs?), in which he levelled criticism at those Czech immigrants and their children who sought only assimilation into America: "I do not know why they think that if a person remains Czech, that they cannot know English and educate themselves in the American manner. […] Indeed, it is precisely those who maintain their Czech nationality that help create the best possible [US] citizen."[63] Breuer also added that it was important for "our youth to learn the Czech language, history, literature and art."[64] It is therefore little wonder that he translated two stories by František Herites[65] and Alois Dostál[66] from Czech into English for *The University of Texas Magazine*, as well as two poems by Vítězslav Hálek[67] and Svatopluk Čech[68] (one of these for *Komenský*). Moreover, notable Czech motifs appear in several of his earlier stories, for example the horror story "The Ghost of the Big Hussar" (1910), or his poem about first Czechoslovak President T. G. Masaryk. Sister Libbie references Miles' efforts to fuse Czech and American culture thusly: "my brother and I wrote [for *The University of Texas Magazine*] often transcribing [i.e. retelling] a Czech folktale or translating a Czech story or poem."[69]

Accordingly, it is also of little surprise that Breuer wrote both in English and in Czech. In the summer edition of the Czech-language weekly *Obzor* (Horizon),[70] published in Hallettsville, Texas, Breuer presented his story "Sestřička" (Little Sister),[71] which serves as a kind of exception to the author's hitherto uncovered written works. For the story offers a more 'social' sketch of the lives of Texas-based Czechs, naturally replete with voluminous sentimentality, as was common in Czech-American literary works of the time. Specifically, the tale tells the story of two sisters and a male suitor. "*Arabeska z texaského života*" (A Short Story of Texan Life), as the subheading of the story noted, very much reflected the contemporary trends of Czech-American literature of the times, both in terms of its content, and its relatively poor quality. It cannot be ruled out that Miloslav J. Breuer (as he signed his name in all his Czech works, be them prose, poems or articles) wrote other similar stories during this period, especially given that a series of three similarly descriptive works later published in *Bratrský Věstník* (The Fraternal Herald)[72] appear to originate from the same era.

Immediately upon graduating, Miles J. Breuer decided to continue his education, applying to study medicine in 1911 – albeit, the respective University

Miles J. Breuer (upper left)
in the University of Texas yearbook.

of Texas facility was situated in the port city of Galveston rather than Austin. At the time, this served as the only institution of its kind for gaining a medical education in Texas. But Breuer soon began to lament what he saw as the less--than-adequate quality of education there. And so, in 1913, he successfully applied to one of the top American medical colleges of its day, namely Rush Medical College in Chicago. And it was here, two years later, that he earned another master's degree.

The evidence suggests that upon his arrival in Chicago, Miles J. Breuer switched to writing works in the Czech language. Indeed, the conditions in the city were ideal and supportive. Chicago was, after all, a centre of Czech-American literature. And Breuer soon joined the circle of friends of publisher August Geringer along with his close collaborator, the editor-in-chief and noted Czech-American author F. Jaromír Pšenka.[73] At the time when Miloslav J. Breuer began to write in Czech, the Czech-American community was by and large a very strong and cohesive group. Czech-language publications were still on the up, with the number of readers growing during the 1910s, and with the number of Czech native speakers in the United States rising to 622,796 by 1920.[74] According to the historian Tomáš Čapek in 1910 eight Czech-language dailies were being published in the United States, with another eight published twice weekly; add to that, thirty-two weeklies, three bi-weeklies, and twenty-three monthlies.[75] Accordingly, Miloslav J. Breuer made every use of a decade replete with plenty of opportunities to have his Czech-language works published.

Practicing Medicine in Nebraska

When Miles J. Breuer graduated from Rush Medical College in Chicago, the family returned to Nebraska, where his father, Charles H. Breuer, was opening a new hospital in the capital city of Lincoln. In 1915, advertisements for this hospital feature the names of both father and son, who "carried out internal medicine and diagnoses, while [Charles H. Breuer] mainly carried out operations."[76] The combined medical facility was situated at 1115 O Street in the centre of Lincoln, but soon relocated a few doors down to the newly built ten-storey Security Mutual Building. The latter was also the first in the city to have an elevator and housed numerous prestigious doctors and lawyers as well as medical laboratories.

Along with Miles (later the five-years-younger Roland, a fellow medical school graduate, also joined the team), Charles built a facility that boasted exceptional, for its time, medical equipment and facilities. Indeed, it was "one of the finest laboratories of its kind in Lincoln […] a complete clinical and pathological laboratory for diagnosis. Here they have much delicate and expensive equipment for experimental work." The period magazine also adds

Miles J. Breuer in his laboratory in a photo from the contemporary Czech-American press.

Miles J. Breuer with his wife Julia Breuer.

that in addition, the Breuers, "keep their own animals for using in serum work, and [the] manufacture of vaccines."[77]

Miles J. Breuer married soon after arriving in Nebraska. His wife Julia,[78] was likewise a child of Czech immigrants, being born in the town of Table Rock south of Lincoln, and was evidently selected as a partner by Miles' parents.[79] Less than two years later, Julia gave birth to daughter Rosalie;[80] four years later, this was followed by a son, Stanley;[81] and five years thereafter, by a second daughter Mildred.[82]

At this time, Miles J. Breuer began contributing to *Bratrský Věstník*. The monthly was headed by a notable Czech nationalist and pro-independence figure, the journalist and later Czechoslovak consul in Omaha, Stanley Serpan.[83] The magazine was published by Západní Česko-Bratrská Jednota (Western Bohemian Fraternal Association), the largest Czech life insurance association in the United States. First headquartered in Omaha, Nebraska before relocating to Cedar Rapids, Iowa, *Bratrský Věstník* served as a key news source for its members, as well as offering numerous pieces of practical health and medical advice. Often such articles were penned by either Charles or Miles Breuer; in addition, the magazine featured entertainment, stories and serialised novels. By the end of the First World War, the magazine had an unusually large circulation of around 20,000.

From 1916–18 five of Miles J. Breuer's stories were published in *Bratrský Věstník* alone. In the first year, this comprised "Kamenná kočka" (The Stone Cat) and "Člověk bez hladu" (The Man Without an Appetite),[84] a previous English-language version of which had been published in *The University of Texas Magazine*. The third published work, "Hladové morče" (The Hungry Guinea-Pig), published in 1917, also had a fantastic motif. It tells the story of an inventor, who creates a giant pig, before losing control of the creature, which embarks on a destructive rampage across the city. Another fantastic story was published in *Bratrský Věstník* in the spring of 1923, namely "Případ učené hlavy" (The Boffin's Story), in which a physically slight scientist fatefully manages to create a huge version of microscopic organisms.

Breuer's fantastic stories were typically of a short nature, in principle with only brief exploration of science-themed ideas. They could be characterised as 'what if…?' tales in this respect, with at least two written by the end of the first decade of the 20th century. It is of little surprise that such proto-science fiction stories as "The Stone Cat," "The Hungry Guinea-Pig" and "Případ učené hlavy" (published in English as "The Inferiority Complex") were among the first of Breuer's works to be published a decade later in Gernsback's *Amazing Stories*.[85]

Moreover, *Bratrský Věstník* also published an additional two non-fantastic stories by Breuer that featured Czech protagonists, namely "U radiografa" (Visiting the Radiographer) at the start of 1918 and subsequently "Zrak pana Plachého" (Mr. Plachý's Vision), which in many respects served as follow-ups to the Czech-language "Sestřička" published years earlier.[86] Although *Bratrský Věstník* was primarily targeted at Czech-speaking readers, it also offered content in the English language, reflecting the fact that many second-generation Czech-Americans struggled with the language of their parents. Breuer remained prolific, offering Serpan several English-language works – in this case detective stories. At the end of 1918

Kamenná kočka.

Povídka od dra. Miloslava J. Breuera.

Četli jste o tvrdých českých palicích. Události o nichž jste četli, měly za jeviště půdu českou, a za kulisy chalupy některé české vesnice. Já, jenž jsem českou vlast nikdy nespatřil, budu vyprávěti o tvrdé české palici v době drsné přítomnosti, v nesmírném moderním městě bzučícím obchodem a vědou; a nebudou v něm sedláci a panímámy, nýbrž lidé, již měli mysle cvičené a ruce obratné ve svém oboru pokročilé vědy, a žili způsoby a zvyky vzdělané a složité společnosti.

Myslím, že v den, kdy ukazoval doktor Blažek mně a mladému Koenigovi kamennou kočku, bylo posledně co jsem spolu s Koenigem navštívil laboratoř, a vůbec naposledy, co jsem Koeniga viděl. Jak jsme otevřeli dvéře, na odpověd' dra. Blažka našemu zaklepání, ohlížel jsem se po velké, jasné světnici, neboť mi nijak nechtěla připadat známou a všední. Měla vzevření vzdušnosti a světlosti, se třpytem slunce na nesčíslných skleněných věcích a lesklém kovu různých barev. Koenigovy oči však rychle přelétly světnicí a stanuly na druhém konci, kde pracovala slečna Vlasta, neboť obyčejně když jsme našli dra. Blažka pracujícího ve své laboratoři, jeho dcera Vlasta mu pomáhala.

Měla na sobě sbíranou zástěrku s ohrnutými rukávy; slunce vrhalo lehký odlesk s jejích hnědých vlasů, a jak byla nahnuta nad stolkem s očima sklopenýma nad svou prací, přebírajíc jemným dotknutím bílých prstů tenké, pavučině podobné parafinové stuhy, byla skutečně půvabnou Minervou mezi třpytícími se sklenicemi a nástroji. Když jsme vešli, zvedla oči a spatřivše Koeniga, kynula mu na prozdrav. Koenig váhal, ohlédl se po světnici, a konečně následoval mne ke stolu, u něhož seděl u práce dr. Blažek. Doktor nás roztržitě pozdravil, vyzval abychom se posadili, a pracoval dále. Vyndával kapacími trubičkami tmavé tekutiny různých odstínů z řad zkoumavek a kapal je na červené kusy, podobné syrovému masu, na Petri-mističkách, načež tyto zčernaly a scvrkly se, a píchal do nich zubatou jehlou. U lokte mu stál drobnohled, a vedle něj poznámková knížka s nesrozumitelnými symboly.

Title page of Bratrský Věstník (1916).

31

Miles J. Breuer in his army uniform before his tour of duty in France.

the story "The Death Clandestine"[87] was published, followed half a year later by "The American Ghost" – neither of which have a known Czech version. Around the same time, the academic publication *The American Journal of Clinical Medicine* published Breuer's detective story "Sherlock Holmes Gets Busy" – which also lacks a known Czech version.

The First World War ultimately curtailed Breuer's literary and medical careers for two whole years. In 1917, he joined the US Army, and following training at Fort Riley, Kansas, and Des Moines, Iowa, Breuer became an army doctor with the rank of first lieutenant in the medical corps at Nebraska Base Hospital Number 49 stationed in France.[88] Breuer managed to avoid frontline service, by instead working as a pathologist and later heading a serological laboratory. However, in the summer of 1918, the hospital at which he was working was located in Allerey, near the Swiss border. Only a few weeks later, the facility received thousands of injured from the August Meuse River-Argonne Forest offensive, which led to the deaths of 26,000 American troops. This meant that the Nebraska facility in France, designed to offer 1,000 beds, had to treat around 5,000 wounded.[89]

During the war Miloslav J. Breuer availed himself of the opportunity to learn French. Evidently, a private female teacher was utilised in this respect, as suggested by his only known spy-themed story, titled "Dva franky za hodinu" (Two Francs per Hour).[90] The protagonist is an army doctor, who

Inside the barracks of the US army hospital in France.
Man in the glasses in the middle is most probably Miles J. Breuer.

takes regular classes with a female French teacher – one who ultimately turns out to be a top German spy. Breuer's time in the army offered more than just literary inspiration, however, also affording him priceless hands-on medical experience in fields spanning surgery and even bacteriology. These wartime experiences then led to the authoring of his first medical paper, of which dozens more would be published in both academic and popular magazines in the ensuing decades.

Upon his return to the United States at the start of 1919, Breuer promptly returned to his medical practice. At the same time, he once more started supporting Czech students and their work as part of the Komenský club at Omaha University.

The Earliest Science Fiction Stories

The years 1922 and 1923 would prove to be critical both for the development of American science fiction, and for Miles J. Breuer as a soon-to-be top genre author. This coincided with Hugo Gernsback publishing a special issue of his popular *Science and Invention* magazine which focused solely on science fiction stories. The resulting positive reception from readers then convinced Gernsback that a publication focused only on science fiction could indeed enjoy commercial success. Moreover, at the same time the pulp magazine *Weird Tales*[91] was launched, featuring fantastic tales spanning the genres of fantasy and science fiction – the magazine was an instant hit with the readers, but a failure financially.[92]

Around this time, Breuer wrote his first expanded science fiction story set in the future, the novella "The Fatal Ray." The evidence suggests that the story was already complete by 1921, because its contents were covered by the weekend supplement of *The Lincoln Star* daily in December of that year.[93] This was after the story had already been presented by Breuer to the local medical association. Meanwhile, the novella was published almost concurrently in both English and Czech. First in English in serialized form in the summer of 1922 in *The American Journal of Clinical Medicine* (a publication that rarely published fiction stories at all).[94] Subsequently, at the end of the same year, *Amerikán Národní Kalendář* almanac for the year 1923 followed suit, Czech version was faithfully translated as "Osudný paprsek."[95] Breuer by all accounts valued this work, because in 1926 he again published it in English in the first volume of the academic quarterly *Social Science*,[96] on whose editorial board he also sat.

The protagonist of "The Fatal Ray" is, naturally, a medical doctor from Lincoln, Nebraska, who finds himself in his home city in the year 2075 after using an untested analgesic, leading him to 'hibernate' for 150 years. The future proves highly enticing for the doctor, especially its stunning medical advances, as demonstrated by a fellow top doctor from the 21st century. "The Fatal Ray" illustrates Breuer's inspiration from the works of H. G. Wells and Jules Verne, and their respective depictions of the human future: "We were on the roof of the hospital, on the south side of a little tower-like structure, and about three hundred feet above the street. Two hundred feet away were the roofs of the buildings on the opposite side; great, graceful structures of a bright, glassy material. The one just opposite had a dozen huge white columns in a row, and, further down, a greenish, translucent edifice was a wonder of great interlacing arches. Hundreds of enormous buildings of different

"'Lincoln!' I gasped."
Illustration by B. Butler for "Osudný paprsek" (Amerikán Národní Kalendář, 1922).

35

degrees of gleaming translucence, in tints of pink, blue, green, and gray, were spread before us, with domes, porticoes, huge statues, and graceful little towers. All of them harmonized in size, style, and tint. I noticed also that each building became narrower from its foundations upward, with a tendency toward a pyramidal shape, so that, above, there was more room among the buildings than on the ground, with the result that the streets were well lighted. Away to the north, there was a general decrease in size, while to the south and east, they grew higher and more splendid, until in the distance, apparently the center, they were surmounted by a huge, bright shaft, towering into the heavens high above the rest. That tower—I had never seen it, but I recognized it, and it made my heart glad. It was the new Capitol building. [...]

The street looked like a river, crowded with people in light tints of various colors, and very few people in dark shades. Streams of them poured swiftly by into the distance. At first it puzzled me, and then, in a moment, I understood. The street itself moved in longitudinal sections, each half in an opposite direction, at slow speed near the edges, while the middle sections, which were also the highest, moved so swiftly that they seemed a continuous stream of changing and blending tint."[97]

Indeed, Breuer evidently openly spoke of his literary inspirations with friends, because in a major article, on the occasion of his fiftieth birthday, an anonymous author wrote: "The style of these – specifically these – authors is something he successfully emulated. But the benefits of a scientific, medical and bacteriological education was something that these novelists lacked; this meant [Breuer] gave his novellas the kind of scientific foundation that Wells and Verne never could, despite many of their predictions having already come true to some degree."[98]

The story, typical for its day, also contains one other quintessentially important Breuer element – fear of how human society will evolve in the future. Indeed, the influence of Wells' novel *When the Sleeper Wakes* (1899) on Breuer's vision of the future in "The Fatal Ray" is highly evident. Despite the main protagonist being enthralled by the unbelievable discoveries and newfound opportunities in the realm of medical science, he is also aghast at the concurrent social development that he sees. Because in the future "each person is rated with respect to hereditary characteristics, and given a color--badge."[99] This means that the protagonist himself must be subjected to tests in which the: "rating examination took several days. They apparently had careful records of my family, before and after my generation; and I went through an amazing course of physical and psychlogical tests. Incidentally, I learned that I was only imperfectly adapted for the practice of medicine, and, ideally so, for pure scientific research. I came out with a blue badge."[100] The result is that he cannot marry the girl with whom he has fallen in love, who has been designated a purple badge. Several days later, the police even come and quiz him, learning from his girlfriend that: "They say you will have to go to a special school; that you can not be trusted at liberty in the community until you have had a proper education. They said that the people in your time were barbarous, murderous, and ignorant, and that you are already planning murder. They seem to be afraid of you."[101]

The protagonist then realises that his future is bleak, given that: "In order that undesirable characteristics might be weeded out of the race, only persons with the same color badge could marry each other, except in cases where they cared to permit themselves to be sterilized by means of X-rays, in which case they received a white badge. There were not many of these. There were seven other colors, so arranged that desirable dominants would overcome undesirable ones, and desirable recessives would reinforce each other. By this method, the human race had not only eliminated most of its insanity, feeble-mindedness, syphilis, tuberculosis, congenital anatomical deformities, but had purified itself of many physical and mental traits, which, though not actual disease, were a source of far more individual suffering than the deprivations imposed by the marriage regulations."[102]

Shortly thereafter the main character visits his girlfriend:

"'But what terrible thing is to happen to me? I haven't done anything. A school? I'd like to go to school.'"

<u>Osudný paprsek.</u>

dr. Miloslav J. Breuer,
Lincoln, Nebraska.

I.
Pokus.

Cestující jednatel od vyrabitelů lučebnin přišel právě když já jsem prozatimně obstarával řízení nemocnice, za nepřítomnosti ředitele, dra. Penrose. Byl vzorem uhlazené zdvořilosti, a mluvil s pravou vědátorskou zdrželivostí; avšak následkem jeho vylíčení o novém uspavajícím prostředku, a výstřižků a otisků z pověstných časopisů lékařských jež mi ukázal, jsem byl přesvědčen že tuto příležitost nesmím nechat ujít. Byl bych se rád poradil s doktorem Penrosem, ale tento se měl vrátit až za dva dny; a lučební jednatel mi pravil že je mu nutno opustiti Lincoln ještě ten samý večer. Dovolil jsem si tedy právo koupiti několik krabiček.

Czech-language manuscript of "Osudný paprsek" (1922).

"'But they will shut you up and keep you there, like they do retroverts. Adults do not train like children…'"[103]

Which leads him to the realization that: "It was a sort of prison-before-the-crime to prevent its taking place."[104] Consequently, the protagonist seeks to escape, only to wake up contented in his less-than-perfect and backwards early 20th century existence – where the story concludes.

In "The Fatal Ray" Miles J. Breuer only lightly touches on (and warns against) the theme of an emerging totalitarian society, which forcefully implements so-called "good" decisions on the subjects under its power. Breuer then offered an even stronger warning in his novella "Vyšší tvor" (The Superior Being), first issued in Czech by *Bratrský Věstník* in a three-part serialized form in the autumn of 1924, and two years later in English as "The Superior Race" in the magazine *Social Science*.

In terms of modern science fiction "The Superior Race" represents one of the first warnings against the danger to humanity posed by the rise of modern technologies. In the story, Breuer foresaw the danger posed to humanity by robots,[105] or more specifically what we today call artificial intelligence. The nameless protagonist is from Galveston, Texas and sets out in the footsteps of the inventor and millionaire Jan B. Kašpar (John B. Kaspar in the English version), who disappeared along with his family in Chicago forty years earlier. When the protagonist manages to smuggle himself aboard the missing inventor's ship, and reaches a faraway island in the Caribbean, he finds a sort of a paradise: "a city in which all the buildings and all the streets […] so harmonized into one unified and beautiful whole. Not only was each separate building a work of art, but it was a harmonious part of whole which was a work of art. There were no ugly structures; neither were there any ugly people, toiling in rags. Even in the people themselves, I saw only beauty, and culture."[106]

On the one hand, he finds that Fortune Island is a utopian civilization, where people do not have to toil, and as the protagonist observes, "the genial men, charming women, and pretty children occupied themselves with light athletic amusements, tennis, golf, and similiar games […]. Dancing seemed to be especially in favor; everywhere people were dancing."[107] But on the other hand, he hears from all sides that "Our first duty is to the machines,"[108] because, "all around there was an astonishing amount of ingenious and complicated machinery for doing all the rough work."[109]

Before long, the protagonist decides that aside from the comfortable do-nothingness of The City of Beauty he also wishes to visit the nearby City of Smoke, which contains the machines that bring the people on the island their comforts. But Kašpar issues words of warning: "Those that have tried it

Beginning of the first part of "Vyšší tvor" (Bratrský Věstník, September 1922).

have never returned. And, they are getting harder and harder to deal with…"[110] The protagonist soon discovers that the cryptic "they" are in fact intelligent machines, and that people have no choice but to guard them.

The machines' inventor himself concedes that "[we] suddenly realized that we had created a race of beings, independent of us and working for us. As soon as we installed the mechanical memory, the machines made independent progress, rapidly and steadily. Without our help, they increased, not only in power and ability, but in numbers."[111] Kašpar begins to fear his own inventions, "these cold brains of steel and electricity might reach a point in their logic where they would see it to their interest to throw off their bonds of slavery to us, and become a source of real danger to us."[112]

But the third generation of island settlers has let down its guard, and Kašpar notes that "'Watching the Machines' was once a prerogative of the masters: now it is a symbol of slavery. The City of Beauty is the slave and the City of Smoke is the master, a master without a living soul!"[113] Which left him little choice but to build "a dozen small machines, completely independent of all human assistance, [to] take the places of the watchers of the machines. They are able to handle the dials and switches, and they carry wax dummies of human appearance."[114] Alas, it is soon shown that "the machines in the City of

Smoke intend some sort of vengeance. [...] I fear that by this time they have carried away a number of people."[115] Moreover, "the machines practice vivisection on their captives; they are studying life, which they do not have, and which they desire,"[116] adds Kašpar.

"The Superior Race" concludes with the protagonist standing up to the machines. But he soon realises the futility of this gesture and decides to flee together with his girlfriend whom he met on the island, the granddaughter of the inventor Kašpar. She bids adieu: "Farewell, my wretched people. How long you will last, I do not know. And you, terrible monsters! How soon will we see you again, persuing us -?"[117] The story ends with a fatalistic declaration: "These are not vain words. They are constantly learning, constantly progressing, with astonishing rapidity. Their intelligence grows, but they have no feelings, no hearts. And they are immortal; worn parts can be replaced, and the individual never dies."[118]

"The Superior Race" is also the first literary work to describe what today we call autonomous vehicles, or self-driving cars. Both the 1924 Czech-language version "Vyšší tvor" and the English-language "The Superior Race," published two years later, ended up largely forgotten in subsequent years. Thus, it has become accepted wisdom that "driverless cars duly appear in science fiction for the first time on the pages of Miles Breuer's [novel] *Paradise and Iron*,"[119] the significantly expanded version of "The Superior Race" published in *Amazing Stories Quarterly* in 1930.

In the original version of the story, Kašpar describes how autonomous vehicles were invented: "I was mainly interested in the perfection of automatic machinery. Already, during the past few years, I had worked out an automobile that automatically supplied itself with fuel, oil, water, and air, when these ran low. [...] The next step was to make the driving of a car more of an automatic matter. The discovery of the selenium reflex enabled us to construct a car that automatically avoided obstacles. The whole principle of the vision of these machines, by means of which they see sufficiently for the purposes of their activity, depends on the sensitiveness of selenium toward light, which increases its resistance to the electrical current. The next step was the construction of a machine for which it was possible to lay out on a dial, an entire trip ahead, and then send it on alone to accomplish it. This step did away altogether with the necessity of a chauffeur or driver. [...] You can follow, as I tell it to you, how we progressed in the working out of an almost living organism from an ordinary automobile; but at the time it was not nearly so apparent to us...."[120] Kašpar then adds that, "In the course of time, we made use of these same principles in other classes of machinery. We made a truck which we could send after the desired freight, without a driver, which automatically

A half dozen motorcycles were approaching, coming on like the wind.

I see the wisdom of your reasons. At least I can say that I am very much interested."

"Besides," Kaspar said, "you, yourself, are in considerable danger. By your very act of following me on board the ship, then by your deeds that night in the dock, and again on the river with the logs, and above all, that night at the pavilion, you have attracted attention to yourself as an unusual person and an undesirable one to the reigning powers. I knew you would, the first time I talked to you that evening on the ship, before we had gotten out of sight of Galveston. They are after you and they may get you at any moment."

"If I can judge by what I see," I replied, "they'll have to hustle harder than they ever hustled before if they want to catch me. They won't find me letting myself be carried away like a sheep. And if they do get me, I'm going to get in a few good licks first, and I'd like to start right now. Just give me a few hours to get this business studied up and straightened out. Then I can get you people started to working properly, and you'll lick them whether I'm with you or not. I've watched this business, and I've got it figured out already that your adversaries have all the possible material advantages, but that somehow they lack the personal equation; they do not seem to know how to follow up their opportunities."

Cassidy was delighted and he wrung my hand.

"I knew you would be valuable to us," he shouted.

"Well, I've got something for you right now," I continued. "When you said that you needed young men, you said a mouthful. I know a young fellow who belongs right here, and you'll never be complete without him."

Self-driving motorcycles in Hans Waldemar Wessolowski's illustration for Paradise and Iron (Amazing Stories Quarterly, Summer 1930).

loaded and unloaded the goods."[121] The protagonist also describes the driving experience: "We sat down, and the vehicle started off, very smoothly and silently, and raced swiftly through the darkness. I sought in vain for the driver; one of the young men, a red-headed, Irish-looking fellow, moved a hand on a dial and from that moment, neither of them paid any attention to the machine."[122]

Meanwhile, the novel *Paradise and Iron*, enabled Breuer to expand on his concept. The story's protagonist describes his first drive: "I walked all around the curious vehicle, and I finally decided to get into the car. [...] So I climbed in and sat down, with a queer feeling at the complete absence of the steering wheel and gear-shift levers. However, on the dashboard were a great many dials; and something was ticking quietly somewhere inside the machine."[123] This driverless journey has clear echoes of those vehicles used today by firms such as Waymo, which as of early 2025 operates in its first four cities:[124] "Then there was a 'clickety-click' and a whirr of the motor, and the car moved gently away from the curb. It swerved out into the street, gathered speed, and then turned to the right around a corner. It slowed down for two women crossing the street, and avoided a truck coming toward us. It gave me an eerie feeling to sit in the thing and have it carry me around automatically [...] I examined the dials on the instrument-board closely. There were ten of them, and they had knobs like the dials on a safe-door, or like the tuning dials on a radio receiving set. Some of them had letters around the periphery and others had figures. I looked for something that said 'stop' or 'start', but there was nothing of the sort, nor even any words of any kind. There were a number of meters, but a speedometer was the only one whose use I recognized. The whole proposition looked about as impossible to me as a Chinese puzzle."[125] Breuer also imagined the importance of the vehicle having access to a detailed map: "A little pointer travelled on a chart all the while, to check up the setting as well as to assist in determining directions and distances from a map when these were unknown to the driver. The study of this map provided me with much subsequently useful knowledge of the island and the cities."[126]

And autonomous vehicles are far from the only novel idea in "The Superior Race"; indeed, Czech science fiction editor Michaela Rampasová has also found what she claims are sections that precede Isaac Asimov's famous 'Three Laws of Robotics,' namely the following: "We feared that these cold brains of steel and electricity might reach a point in their logic where they would see it in their interest to throw off their bonds of slavery to us, and become a source of real danger to us. We therefore intentionally saw to it that each machine remained to some extent still dependent on human assistance. Of this service, for which the machines depended on human beings, there remains only a sort of superficial inspection. But they cannot be without it; they cannot do any work or carry on any activity without it; the necessity was built into them when they were manufactured. It is like an instinct in animals. These machines live their own lives, care completely for themselves, as well as for us, do all our work, feed us, etc., but they cannot do without our 'watching'."[127]

In any event, what is without doubt is that both versions of the story offer "some of the first glimpses into the dystopic world of automatization and robot operated social systems [and] foreshadow many of the tropes of later SF by exploring the dystopia of robotic machines (the loss of human interaction, the potential obliteration of humankind by machines and the horror of total robotic manufacturing)."[128] Indeed, in all of these thematic areas, Breuer's imagination surpassed the times in which he lived.

Nor did Miles J. Breuer stop thinking about the future of the human race in subsequent years. In original versions of both "The Fatal Ray" and "The Superior Race" Breuer's protagonists escape and choose to return back to their own less advanced world. However, in the much more controversial, largely forgotten novella "The Legion of the Fittest" the author tells the story of an educated minority of the global population, which decides to take fate into its own hands and to change the future of mankind. In this hitherto longer of Breuer's works (around 14,000 words), published in the quarterly *Social Science* in 1931, the author freely explores a fascination with the idea of a society comprised only of the intellectual elite. The central figure is the secret 'Legion,' organization based on the traditions of the Sokol, Czech gymnastic movement, and comprised of an ever-shrinking minority of the smartest and most educated in the population. The Legion plans to implement serious social changes in society from the end of the 20th century, because "the constantly decreasing 'constructive' minority could not long continue to carry on its back the burdens of the rapidly increasing dependent majority."[129]

In "The Legion of the Fittest" Breuer makes it perfectly clear that he has little faith in technological progress bringing about an improvement in man's circumstances. Right at the start of the tale, he ponders on the contemporary science fiction output of the time, which he sees as excessively focused on the supposed wonders of technology solving all the world's problems. The unnamed protagonist of the story, which is set in the 23rd century, has a mocking attitude towards an "ancient" book published back in 1931: "This book, paper-covered, with a brilliant front cover, contains a story in which cities three hundred years to come are pictured as huge, crowded, complex hives, staggering mechanical marvels, with all their inhabitants under the fearfully high pressure of an intense and strenuous civilization. Interplanetary travel and

THE LEGION OF THE FITTEST

By Miles J. Breuer

I. The New World

I have before me a book published in 1931, just three hundred years ago, which sets forth very well the fantastic ideas of that time as to just what the world would be like today. That was just about the time at which scientific attempts at prophesying the future had their beginning; but these attempts during the first half of the twentieth century, still had about them more of imaginative fancy than of scientific accuracy. It is interesting how well agreed both fiction and philosophical essays were in the essentials of their prophesies, and how all human prophets at the time neglected a factor that upset all their deductions.

This book, paper-covered, with a brilliant front cover, contains a story in which cities three hundred years to come are pictured as huge, crowded, complex hives, staggering mechanical marvels, with all their inhabitants under the fearfully high pressure of an intense and strenuous civilization. Interplanetary travel and atomic power are common events—in the story. It is quite typical of the prophecy-stories of the time; its staggeringly huge buildings, its great machines as vast and complex as its social order, its illogicalities of human motive and human behavior, ludicrous as they seem to us now, seemed to them, not only reasonable, but probable, yes, inevitable. For the first fifty years of the century, their ideas of their future were like that.

134

Their reasoning process was correct as far as it went; but they had only scratched the surface of the knowledge of data on which to base prophetic reasoning.

For, look at our world today! I sit here writing at an open window, my fingers sliding lightly and without effort over the keys of my machine. The window is large, so large that the pink glow of the setting sun bathes me from head to foot, bringing out little orange and purplish reflections from the ridges of the silken folds of my soft robe. My chair is large and comfortable, so that I may partly recline as I write. The room is large; compared with the tiny rooms of the buildings that remain from the twentieth century, it is large as a hall; and through the wide door, I can see into my bedroom, which is just as large. The marble walls, the silk rugs, the allegorical tapestries all blend into restful effects. Had I had to live in one of the "living-rooms" of the age of which I write, with its crowded confusion and its clash of color and form, its merciless lighting, I should have—well, I suppose I should have behaved just as illogically as did the people of that time.

Out of my windows, I can see between two great columns, over my garden with its yellow roses and pink oleanders, and its gray fronds of hanging moss among the deep green billows of laurel and magnolia. Then comes the street; several people in soft colors and flowing robes stroll leisurely in the direction of

First page of "The Legion of the Fittest" (Social Science, 1931).

atomic power are common events – in the story. It is quite typical of the prophecy-stories of the time; its staggeringly huge buildings, its great machines as vast and complex as its social order, its illogicalities of human motive and human behavior, ludicrous as they seem to us now, seemed to them, not only reasonable, but probable, yes, inevitable. For the first fifty years of the century, their ideas of their future were like that."[130]

"The Legion of the Fittest" offers a description of future world events starting in the 1930s, and describes the preparations for and final successful execution of an ultimately successful revolution by the mid-21st century. The future centre of this new world turns out to be Omaha, Nebraska – a city obviously well known by Breuer. In the 21st century, right before the beginning of a global revolution, Omaha is described thusly: "Of the two million inhabitants of Omaha and environs, 400,000 were wards of the community: 40,000 insane, 28,000 in the penitentiary, 148,000 orphans, and so on through blind, deaf-and-dumb, feeble-minded, orthopaedic hospital, isolation hospital. Charitable Employment League, *et cetera*. As in most other places, the taxation to support these institutions was a terrific burden; and a great many possible producers were tied up as attendants and thus kept from doing useful work to support the community."[131] After victory of a revolution, however, it has become "a little town of about ten thousand people, north of the old site, near the river," with the author adding that "the old city was a mass of ruins, overgrown with weeds and vines, and infested with birds and rabbits."[132]

The main ideological figure of the future global revolution is an American by the name of Harry Brandivere, a professor of social psychology at Tulane University in New Orleans. He claims to be a descendant of the fictional Václav Branidvor, a courtier of the Bohemian king and Roman Emperor, Charles IV.[133] Václav's descendants were supporters of Hussite commander Jan Žižka,[134] and as Protestants, they were forced to flee to America following the ascendancy of the Catholic Hapsburgs to the Bohemian throne in the 17th century. And so another descendant, Charles Brandivore, became a person who "fought for, as a colonel, under George Washington."[135]

The revolution, which occurs following decades of mid-21st century political upheavals, is described by Miles J. Breuer as a perfectly prepared operation, where the liquidation of the majority of the earth's inhabitants was carried out successfully: "it went off like clock-work [...] long hoarded secrets of the Legion were utilized: thermite rockets that burned holes through stone walls, earthquake bombs that shook down huge buildings, and especially the terrible 'cyalase' shells which liberated a catalyctic agent that produced a chemical combination of the nitrogen of the air with the carbon of the carbon-dioxide, resulting in cyanogen, and killing instantly every living thing with which the gas came in contact."[136] The revolution began in Nebraska: "In four hours, Omaha was four-fifths a mass of wreckage, only five thousand people were left alive, and these were Legionnaires."[137]

And then the revolution quickly went global: "In a few days the war blazed out in Europe. Naples went first. […] In a few hours there was nothing left of Naples but three thousand Legionnaires. Manchester, Breslau, Lisbon, Marseilles, and Athens all blew up on the same day, two weeks after the Omaha uprising."[138] Within a mere few years, "the morons were all exterminated, and reconstruction began."[139]

Nor does Breuer forget to describe the new post-revolutionary utopia: "For today, our world is simple. That vast mass of countless cities and towns, with their teeming swarms of inhabitants, is gone."[140] Elsewhere, he adds the following details: "Now, there is space, beauty, harmony, peace. There are no tall buildings, except an occasional graceful tower. The buildings blend with the landscape and seem to belong there. There are no crowding masses of humanity, rushing pell-mell over each other. People's faces are serene and their movements leisurely and graceful; and the little groups and occasional individuals, fit harmoniously into the entire scene. There is no ugly machinery in evidence; true, our wants are supplied by machinery, much more completely than ever before in the world's history; but the machinery is either concealed and silenced, or modulated into the general scheme so that it adds to the beauty rather than detracting from it.

On the whole, we have made no staggering advances in science during the past two hundred years; the brutal subjugation of Mother Nature, so thrillingly described in the science fiction of the twentieth century, is just a little out of harmony with our ways of thinking. But, we have no poverty, no illness, no unemployment. We have no courts nor wars nor strikes; no prisons, no insane asylums, because there is no one to put into them.

The whole world is a happy, leisurely, comfortable garden. It is inhabited only in the areas where the climate is permanently agreeable. The population of the world is ten million people; it might almost be said that they all know each other. There is no government, with the exception of local boards to look after housekeeping problems. Our lives are pleasantly spent, in the search for knowledge, and in being of service to each other."[141]

But this does not mean that Breuer personally identifies with or condones the events or measures he describes. Indeed, he notes that the Legionnaires "were horrified at their own work, after they had stopped to contemplate it. But they had been sworn to carry it out."[142] And by the end of the story, the characters express increasing frustration with the new order, with one descendent of the hero of the revolution lamenting that the revolution merely brought a new form of dictatorship – and Breuer ends the tale similarly to his others, with the protagonist fleeing the nascent new world, in this case to live in the earth's remaining uninhabited areas.

The period during which "The Legion of the Fittest" was published was replete with notions of law and order and even of the positive potential of eugenics, with notable adherents including future British Prime Minister Winston Churchill and author George Bernard Shaw reflecting the allure of this trend. The problems associated with societal development were something that Miles J. Breuer also explored in a journalistic sense, contributing numerous articles in, for example, *Social Science* quarterly, including "The Race Between Civilization and Catastrophe" (1925), "The Outlook for a World Peace" (1928) and "The Need of a New Racial Habit" (1928). Alas, Breuer's vision of a successful global revolution that leads to the extermination of a majority of the world's inhabitants – specifically, "seven-eighths of the population [who were] every degree of parasites upon the remaining eights,"[143] is an admittedly very extreme idea – and one which was entirely discredited through the eugenics-inspired horrors perpetrated by the Nazis. The work, in which a global revolution is carried out through the calculated extermination of several billion people, and "the two and a half million Legionnaires were all the people left on earth, among the great wastes of ruins"[144] would today be viewed very differently than in the ideologically and economically turbulent era of the early 1930s. The novella was by all accounts also received with controversy during its publication. And despite being viewed as one of Breuer's more interesting works, "The Legion of the Fittest" was never published in any period pulp science fiction magazine. Moreover, despite having the most specifically "Czech" elements of the author's science fiction works, no evidence has yet been uncovered that it was ever published in Czech.

The three novellas ("The Fatal Ray," "The Superior Race," and "The Legion of the Fittest") authored by Breuer in the 1920s – all of which were published in English – could have easily placed Breuer among the top pre-pulp-magazine-era American science fiction authors of his day. But that would likely have required these stories not being published in a magazine so far removed from this genre, namely the Kansas-based quarterly (still in publication to this day) *Social Science*.[145] But back in the 1920s, the publication was just getting started, and the first two of Breuer's stories were published in its inaugural year, in issue numbers 2 and 3 in 1926. The third story was then published in its pages five years later. But Breuer would soon seize the chance to make a more significant mark in the world of science fiction.

Miles J. Breuer – Star of the Pulp Magazines

Miles J. Breuer wrote and published his first science fiction stories at a time, during the 1920s, when this emerging genre was still largely unknown to the wider public. At the very same time, editor Hugo Gernsback was considering founding a monthly publication that would exclusively contain stories that popularized science and scientific advances. These plans were revealed to the public in late 1925, with numerous literary periodicals of the day featuring advertisements seeking out new authors. When the first issue of *Amazing Stories* hit the newsstands in April 1926, Gernsback included a publisher's note on the kind of literature he wanted to see within the magazine's future pages: "By 'scientifiction' I mean the Jules Verne, H. G. Wells, and Edgar Allan Poe type of story – a charming romance intermingled with scientific fact and prophetic vision."[146] By coincidence, he was looking for exactly the kind of stories that Breuer was already trying to craft.

Evidently, Miles J. Breuer was not a reader of Gernsback's existing popular magazine of the day, *Science and Invention*.[147] After all, he would have likely offered Gernsback some of his stories earlier; and given their quality, it's equally likely they would have been accepted for publication. One can only speculate as to whether Breuer was enticed by Gernsback's newspaper advertisements, or whether he only decided to submit his offerings upon holding an early issue of *Amazing Stories* in his own hands. What we do know is that the January 1927 issue (published in December 1926) contains Breuer's story "The Man with the Strange Head," which only a few weeks earlier had also appeared in a Czech version published under the faithfully translated title "Muž se zvláštní hlavou" in *Amerikán Národní Kalendář* almanac for the year 1927.

The story is about a man whose attached body is a radio-powered autonomous prosthesis – one which continues to 'live' even after the original head, the last truly biological part, has died. "The Man with the Strange Head" proved popular with readers, and thus additional Breuer works were soon forthcoming in *Amazing Stories*. In September of the same year, the magazine issued a significantly reworked version of one of Breuer's older stories, namely "The Stone Cat," initially published in English as far back as 1909 (and also in Czech as "Kamenná kočka" seven years thereafter). Despite the September 1927 issue of *Amazing Stories* also containing "The Colour Out of Space," arguably the most famous H. P. Lovecraft[148] story, as well as an ongoing serialisation of H. G. Wells' *The War of the Worlds*, the magazine's

The MAN with the STRANGE HEAD
By Dr. Miles J. Breuer

Anstruther leaped upon the hold-up man; the driver said he heard Anstruther's muscles crunch savagely, as with little apparent effort he flung the man over the Ford.

940

Illustration by F. S. Hynd for Miles J. Breuer's first contribution to the Amazing Stories (January 1927).

cover also enticed buyers with the name of Miles J. Breuer – evidence that Breuer's first story had so enthralled readers that his name was now a selling point for the entire magazine.

Hugo Gernsback's new publication desperately needed a staple of new science fiction authors, especially those able to write short stories. Indeed, back in 1926 Gernsback was already lamenting that upon founding *Amazing Stories* he received many submissions, which, alas, were mostly novels that were not appropriate to publish in light of their length. Instead, the publisher sought works up to 10,000 words long, adding that: "We receive an increasing number of letters, asking if we are in the market for short stories, and to these we wish to reply in the affirmative. We can not get too many real short scientifiction stories."[149] That would undoubtedly have been a godsend for Miles J. Breuer. Likely without Gernsback being aware, Breuer had a large number of already completed stories, and the fresh publishing opportunities (now for remuneration – it is almost certain that his stories published in *Bratrský Věstník*, or *Social Science* were most propably unpaid) would certainly have given the author a fresh impetus for writing even more works. Thus, within the space of a few months, Breuer became one of the most influential authors of the budding science fiction genre, which, in 1927, was undergoing a process of "self-exploration, with science fiction feeling its way, seeking its parameters, and trying to understand its own identity."[150]

Gernsback and Breuer shared not just an admiration for H. G Wells, but the former also found in Breuer's works an ideal example of what he was looking for, namely science fiction stories that exemplified a genre designed to popularise science through the use of literature. Miles J. Breuer also impressed with his own scientific/medical background; and, along with author David H. Keller[151] was among the few early *Amazing Stories* authors who could sign themselves with an 'M.D.' (*Medicinae Doctor*), undoubtedly giving their stories extra gravitas and impact in the eyes of readers.

In December 1927, *Amazing Stories* published Breuer's third story, "The Riot at Sanderac," in which a crazed scientist uses an inaudible sound to cause mass murder. By this time, it was clear that the budding genre had yielded its first, hitherto unknown author. "It's fair to say that Breuer was Gernsback's only genuine discovery of 1926,"[152] genre historian Michael Ashley[153] would later observe.

Other stories would follow. In 1928, Miles J. Breuer had two stories published; the subsequent year, six stories were published; and over the next three years, his name appeared sixteen times authoring both short and longer-form works. When examining the names of authors whose stories appeared during the first five years of the existence of science fiction pulp magazines, Breuer without question ranks among the most prolific. Within *Amazing Stories* reprints of the works of H. G. Wells held the top spot (more than thirty, spanning almost all of the author's fantastical works). Moreover, more than a dozen stories from the pen of Jules Verne were also published. American author and zoologist A. Hyatt Verrill[154] had more than twenty of his existing works published, followed by David H. Keller, Edmond Hamilton[155] and Miles J. Breuer, each with more than a dozen. Lower down the list in terms of volume we find another new writer Jack Williamson[156] and today largely forgotten science fiction authors such as S. P. Meek[157] and Harl Vincent.[158]

The favorite topic of Miles J. Breuer's early stories were gigantic animals and new life forms, such as in "Případ učené hlavy" (1923), rewritten as "The Inferiority Complex" (1930). In terms of the most common themes of Breuer's brand new mid-1920s stories, the fourth dimension features prominently. 1928 saw the publication of "The Appendix and the Spectacles" about a surgeon, who manages to enter the body of a patient through the fourth dimension, and thus successfully remove a malfunctioning organ, all without even touching the patient's skin. A year later, Breuer published "The Captured Cross-Section," in which the protagonist seeks to rescue a girl who has been abducted by a being from the fourth dimension. In the story, Breuer concludes that even if we were able to enter the fourth dimension, we would in any event still perceive it only in three-dimensional terms, and only be able to see a confused jangle. Conversely, in "The Book of Worlds" (1929) the pro-

Both Czech-language ("Případ učené hlavy," 1923) and English-language
("The Inferiority Complex," 1930) versions of the story
about gigantic microscopic life are accompanied by Breuer's photographs.

tagonist uses the fourth dimension to look into the future. He sees both his contemporary world as well as a parallel future, which shocks him to such an extent that he decides to destroy his time machine.

Unlike the majority of Gernback's other authors, Breuer's stories were far removed from pure adventure tales. All the more so, Breuer also had a keen interest in psychology, along with questions surrounding the future development of mankind. Indeed, British science fiction editor Walter Gillings[159] notes that these are "some of the most intriguing tales that appeared in the early volumes of *Amazing Stories*."[160]

In 1929's "Buried Treasure" Breuer transports readers to the 31st century – a place in which people no longer have emotions, at least only up to the moment when they discover some long-buried bottles of alcoholic beverages from hundreds of years ago. Psychology also plays a significant role in the aforementioned short story "The Fatal Ray" (published in Czech as "Osudný paprsek"). In the summer of 1929, Breuer's existing work was published in new sister publication *Amazing Stories Quarterly* in a significantly reworked form, doubled in length, under the title "Rays and Men." The novella is an example of a new approach by Breuer to his own older works. Specifically, those themes for which Breuer had an affinity and which also fit into to Gernsback's Wellsian conception of science fiction would thus be polished up afresh. Specifically, Breuer expanded the middle section of his old text,

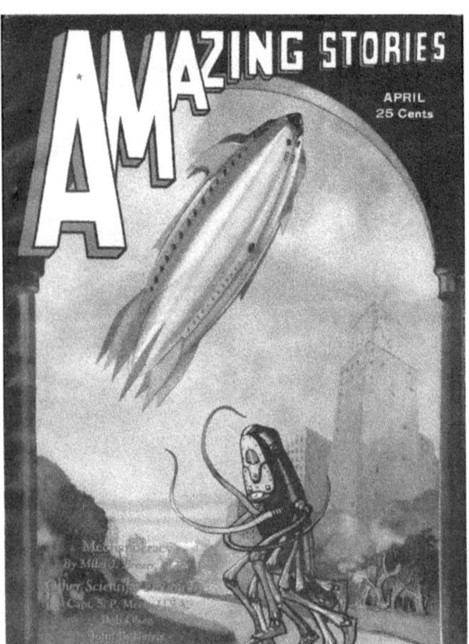

adding new descriptions about futuristic medical approaches,[161] as well as more details on life in Lincoln, Nebraska of the future and how the city and people operate. The beginning and end of the former story remained essentially unchanged, with only the setting changing, moving significantly into the future, namely to the year 2180.

Early in 1929, Hugo Gernsback went bankrupt, with *Amazing Stories* taken over by creditors, now headed by a provisional editor-in-chief, the inventor, writer and former editor of the noted periodical *Scientific American*, T. O'Conor Sloane.[162] The new editor had little interest in making major changes at the magazine, writing in his first editor's note in May 1929: "It is a pleasure to us to be able to state that some of our better known authors, such as Dr. David H. Keller, Dr. Miles J. Breuer […],[163] are going to stand by *Amazing Stories* and will continue as contributors to the Monthly and Quarterly."[164] Sloane also expressed a clear desire to continue to work with Breuer, adding: "The Fourth Dimension, which is after all to be regarded as a mathematical conception, has been very ingeniously used by some of our writers."[165]

Meanwhile, Hugo Gernsback was far from finished, and in June 1929, he published the first issue of his new science fiction magazine, *Science Wonder Stories*.[166] A month later, this was followed by another pulp publication, *Air Wonder Stories*;[167] and in October an additional Gernsback's publication, *Sci-*

ence Wonder Quarterly, appeared at newspaper stands. The following year, in 1930, Breuer offered Gernsback a story involving space travel, "The Fitzgerald Contraction" which was indeed published in *Science Wonder Stories.* It describes the landing on Earth of a space vessel with visitors from the Moon. During a trip beyond our galaxy, their spaceship almost reached the speed of light and when after a mere several days they returned back to the Solar System, they found their civilization vanished as hundreds of thousands years having elapsed on the Moon, thus they had to land on Earth,[168] The end of the story significantly expounds upon the titular physical phenomenon at play – today referred to as time dilation. According to science fiction author Robert Silverberg[169] this is the first such story to deal with this phenomenon.[170]

A sudden boom in science fiction publishing was a direct result of Gernsback's pioneering work. The growth of the genre had been entirely his work but "the expansion of science fiction publishing […] could not have gone unnoticed by Gernsback's fellow publishers, who were increasingly seeking to specialize and tap a rich vein of commercial popularity."[171] Thus next Breuer's story published in 1930, namely "A Problem in Communication," which focused on a religious cult, appeared in another new science fiction periodical, *Astounding Stories of Super-Science,*[172] which was launched by William Clayton,[173] publisher of a wide range of pulp magazines.

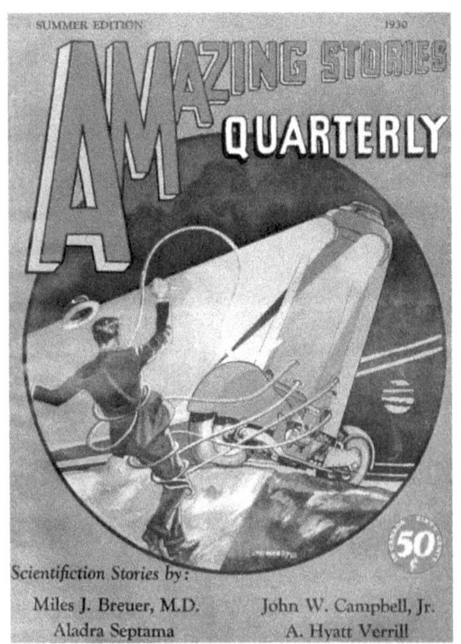

Covers by pulp magazines with stories by Miles J. Breuer.
On the left, cover by Leo Morey for Paradise and Iron.

In the same year, Breuer's hitherto most ambitious work was published, a novella based on a significantly reworked version of his 1924 older work "Vyšší tvor" (aka "The Superior Race" /1926/).[174] The theme of the future development of civilization, along with its respective technical and also social development, was a lifelong passion for the author. This is also evident in Breuer's contemporary academic articles as well as the selection of books to be reviewed in the *Social Science* quarterly, which also published an English-language version of "The Superior Race." A new version, titled *Paradise and Iron*, and carrying the subtitle "Novel of an Ultra Machine Age" formed a large part of the summer edition of *Amazing Stories Quarterly*. The former text was more than expanded in this case, and new story elements were also added to the second part of the novel. While the former Czech and English story merely sees the protagonist have several tense encounters with self-driving and self-thinking vehicles, in *Paradise and Iron* the protagonist discovers that people on the island are beginning to "fear these cold brains of steel and electricity without feelings, without sympathy,"[175] because "we are beginning to realize that we have not only the individual intelligences of the various machines to deal with – of course there are machines of various grades of intelligence, ranging from no intelligence at all, to brains so vast and powerful that your mind can hardly grasp the conception."[176]

Moreover, the inventor of self-driving vehicles, Kaspar is convinced that "they have reached a point in their logic where they can perceive that the thousands of us in the City of Beauty are of no real good to them; that in fact we consume too much of their time and energy. It must be plain to them that we are frail and helpless before their mighty strength. It looks, from various indications, that they have begun to decide to throw off their bonds of slavery to us."[177] How many other science fiction writers, prior to 1930, were already reflecting on the dystopian aspects of what today we term artificial intelligence? The answer is very few. Breuer's dark vision of humanity's future continues, as Kaspar notes: "There is a complex 'social organization' in the City of Smoke that I am not quite clear about. [...] There is a chief ruler, a sort of 'king' of the machines."[178]

Both of Breuer's versions have a completely different ending. The former version saw the protagonist weighing waging a battle for the future: "Can I not return, and lead them in a war against the machines? Could I not arouse them [i.e. the people on the island] to action?"[179] But the granddaughter of the inventor thwarts such plans: "Do not think of it! I know that it is not possible. [The people on the island] fear too much for their poor soft bodies against iron beams and chains. They have no courage, no bravery. At this moment they tremble under the threats of the machines that are searching for you for their

Paradise

and

Iron

CHAPTER I

A New Kind of Ship

WHY anyone so old as Daniel Breckenridge, my grandfather's brother, should keep on working as hard as he did, was a mystery to me. He was about eighty-four; and a million little crinkles criss-crossed on the dry, parchment-like skin of his face where it was not covered by his snow-white beard. But he still went briskly about his duties as shipping manager of a great ship chandler's establishment at Galveston.

Just now he whispered sharply to me, and drew me by the arm behind some bales of canvas in the depths of the vast shipping-room.

"Look! There he is!"

He seemed to be trembling with intense excit[ement] as he pointed toward the great sliding doors.

There, watching the men loading up a truck a pile of goods consigned to some ship, was an old just as old and snowy and crinkled, and just a and active as my grand-uncle himself. I looked blankly for a moment. He was an interesting old man, but I saw nothing to set me off a-t with excitement. But my old grand-uncle clutch arm.

292

¶ *It is a far-fetched vision, perhaps, to think of a time when the thought-machine, which now can be worked with very little supervision, might some time get to a point where it can make suggestions for its own improvement—mathematically figured out improvements, of course—but it is not impossible. And if and when that happens, who can forecast the future of mechanical progress? In this complete novel, Dr. Breuer gives us, in good literary style, a wealth of absorbing elaborations on the possibilities of the machine age, which makes the story one of unusual scientific interest.*

The City
of
Smoke

By
Miles J. Breuer, M.D.
Author of: "The Gostak Distims the Doshes," "The Stone Cat," etc.

Illustrated by WESSO

d John Kaspar, the Mystery Man!" he whispered

t suddenly galvanized me into action. I took
ore good look at him, and got into motion at once.
you think you could hold him here somehow until
my outfit?" I asked. "I'll be back in ten minutes."
s now my turn to be tense and thrilled.
will take them longer than that to load up the
" he said; "but hurry."
ook hands with him hastily but fervently, know-
at I might have no further opportunity to do so,

and then dashed out after a taxi. While my taxi is rushing me off to my room, I can explain all I know about John Kaspar, the mysterious octogenarian.

Forty years ago, back in the days when the gasoline industry was just being opened up, John Kaspar was the richest man in the world. His father had been a manufacturer of automobiles in Ohio and, foreseeing the importance of gasoline, he had bought up half a county of the most promising oil lands in East Texas. Before his death, oil was found on every acre of it. The son John, the old man at whom we have just been looking, was not interested in becoming a financier; he was working out some original ideas in automobile design. There were some wildly headlined newspaper clippings in my grand-uncle's collection, about John Kaspar's having thrown a reporter bodily into the ash-can because the poor fellow had made his way into Kaspar's shop and was looking too closely at some marvelous new invention on an automobile.

vivisection."[180] Consequently, the pair flees the island and heads back to the normal world.

In the expanded version, the protagonist takes a stand against the machines.[181] Specifically, he manages to take out the "king of the machines," thus bringing down the entire robotic civilisation. This saves the people on the island, but soon leads his girlfriend to ask: "'But what are the poor people going to do?'"[182] And the protagonist, who does not necessarily approve of the earlier hedonistic way of life on the island, answers: "'They'll have to do some work. [...] That will be terrible. [...] This is going to mean a tremendous change in living conditions, which means privation and suffering. [...] They'll have to hustle for a bare living first – plant grain, kill meat, keep the city clean. Only after they have learned this and become accustomed to it, will they have time to study machinery. [...] There is not enough left to be of any immediate use. When the people learn to understand and repair and operate some of the machines, then there might be some service, of a sort. But they won't have time for that for a while.'"[183]

The novel *Paradise and Iron* undoubtedly offers a far more rewarding reading experience than the former Czech or English short story versions. Indeed, Breuer managed to take the essence of the original and add several exciting new scenarios concerning encounters with the dangerous world of machines; the work was also subjected to considerable revision and editing. But despite this, *Paradise and Iron* still remains a jazzed-up version of the original short stories, one subject to the kind of overhaul common for stories being published in the pulp magazines of the day – indeed, the hand of the author's editor is also heavily present.

For Breuer, 1930 represented a peak in terms of his output as a science fiction author. He published a record eight works, including his most famous story "The Gostak and the Doshes." In the story, the protagonist travels, via the fourth dimension, into a parallel universe. Here, he finds a world in which the seemingly meaningless political slogan, "the gostak distims the doshes" suddenly appears in the media and bizarrely manages to affect the behaviour of the populace. The story's protagonist seeks to find out the meaning of the slogan, asking his host, a university professor, for clarification. Although, this hardly helps:

"'The gostak!' he exclaimed. 'Hurray for the gostak!'

'But what is a gostak?'" asks the protagonist.

"'Not a gostak. *The* gostak. The gostak is – the distimmer of the doshes – see! He distims 'em, see?'

'Yes, yes. But what is distimming? How do you distim?'

'No, no! Only the dostak can distim. The gostak distims the doshes. See?'

'Ah, I see!' I exclaimed. Indeed, I pride myself on my quick wit. 'What are doshes? Why, they are the stuff distimmed by the gostak. Very simple!'

'Good for you!' John slapped my back in huge enthusiasm. 'I think it wonderful for you to understand us so well, after being here only a short time. You are very patriotic.'

I gritted my teeth tightly, to keep myself from speaking."[184]

The reader soon discovers, that no one in this alternate universe seems to mind not knowing what a gostak is, or what the doshes are supposed to do. Soon, the meaningless slogan ends up sparking a war between the nations. The story met with such an enthusiastic response that the letters in discussions columns of *Amazing Stories* saw a passionate months-long debate over its meaning. Moreover, it remains to this day Breuer's most reprinted story in genre anthologies. As a "story of mass psychology, totalitarianism, and the misprision of language [it] still holds considerable relevance."[185] And in today's age of fake news and social media manipulation, the story may be even more prescient than when Michael R. Page, the editor of the first English-language selection of Breuer's stories, wrote the above commentary.

The following year, 1931, sees Breuer's peak prolific writing era slowly coming to an end with the publication of six science fiction stories. These included the murder-mystery from the future, "On Board the Martian Liner." Moreover, Breuer also embarked on a collaboration with the "first lady of pulp science fiction" Clare Winger Harris,[186] yielding the story "A Baby on Neptune." Previously, Breuer had described Harris' story "The Miracle of the Lily" as "the best story published in *Amazing* [*Stories*] up to that date."[187] A year later, Breuer published "Mechanocracy" set in the 26th century, in which the world is fully taken over by machines – a fact passively accepted by humanity, because any attempts at resistance by humans is met with instant euthanasia. This would turn out to be Breuer's final truly notable work.

All of the above-referenced stories serve to affirm an opinion expressed by fellow science fiction writer Jack Williamson, that "Breuer had far more competence than most beginners [and] had he given it his whole time, he might have done a greater volume of more memorable work."[188] Not only that, but Breuer's sense of imagination, his innovative ideas, and also his mining of the latest scientific concepts for use in science fiction, truly serve to rank him as one of the key figures of the genre's early period. Alas, by the end of the 1930s, Breuer had practically disappeared from the scene as a science fiction author.

Illustration by Leo Morey for "Mechanocracy"
(Amazing Stories, April 1932).

Building the Modern Science Fiction

In his publisher's note in the first issue of his new science fiction magazine, editor Hugo Gernsback wrote: "How good this magazine will be in the future is up to you. Read *Amazing Stories* — get your friends to read it and then write us what you think of it. We will welcome constructive criticism — for only in this way will we know how to satisfy you."[189] Not long after Breuer's stories began to be published in *Amazing Stories* he also became an avid contributor to the magazine's "Discussions" columns playing a notable role in popularizing a new literary genre and also engaging in debates about his own stories and those of other authors. In particular, his medical background led Breuer to throw cold water on many outlandish ideas from his contemporaries. For example, in a letter from September 1929, Breuer took issue with a story by Jack Barnette,[190] namely "The Purple Death." In particular, Breuer objected to the author's apparent ignorance of the field of bacteriology, as well as his inability to properly understand the use of a microscope and noted: "I think it is wrong for writers to play with subjects they do not understand."[191] When Barnette responded apologetically,[192] Breuer was quick to extend a hand of friendship: "You have excellent and original ideas," he noted in a letter published three months later, adding: "I should be more than delighted to be of friendly and complimentary service to you in helping with the technical points of any of your stories which involve such technical matters as I am familiar with."[193]

Such initiatives led to Breuer becoming more than a mere 'author' – but rather he also became an advocate for the genre, helping to shape its future direction. Indeed, his eleven short critiques and commentaries published in *Amazing Stories* between 1927 and 1931 often focused on the nature of 'scientifiction' and included lists of authorial dos and don'ts. In these letters, "we see how Breuer worked to shape the discussion of science fiction, first by offering a definition and insisting that it have literary quality, and then by praising other writers whom he saw as successfully following through on these demands."[194]

Breuer put many of his ideas on the nature of science fiction into an introduction piece titled "The Future of Scientifiction"[195] published in the summer edition of *Amazing Stories Quarterly* in 1929. This key text serves as something of a manifesto for the newly emerging literary genre. In the article, Breuer lets it be known that he believes that the science fiction has a great future ahead of it, and is set to become a critical component of the development of human civilization; moreover, people will soon realize that *Amazing Sto-*

The Future of Scientifiction
By Miles J. Breuer, M.D.

The outstanding characteristics of every period in human history have been reflected in the literature of that period. Fiction, especially, is more free to concern itself with the everyday life of the common man, than is any other form of literature. In ancient times the hero of the common man was the warrior and the orator, and the epic poem, which is the fictional type of the ancients, contains nothing but war and oratory — unless it be love, which is common to all ages. The fiction of the Middle Ages is distinguished by religion and chivalry; that of early modern times, when men broke out of their narrow corner in Europe and explored the world, is distinguished by adventure and romance. In recent fiction, what do we find as the preponderating element? Industrialism, politics, finance. What men do in real life, they do in books.

Science in fiction is not new. I saw an account of a trip to the moon by one Cyrano de Bergerac, written in the sixteenth century. There must be older examples. But, stories of that type, like Mrs. Shelley's "Frankenstein," were few and far between; and certainly found a limited reading public.

Few men know or care anything about science. The average reader is not a student; he reads the familiar things that come easy.

It is only in recent years that Science has begun to invade the everyday life of the everyday man. Up to yesterday, science was a thing set apart; it dwelt in the sacred laboratories, which none but the initiated few might enter. Who wanted to write about it? Still less did anyone want to read about it? Today, science does for the common man in his daily life more marvellous miracles than the mightiest monarch of old could command. Did Solomon or Caesar ever ride as luxuriously as does your grocery clerk every Sunday in his Ford? Not only does the humblest of us have in his own home and under his hands such things as the radio, the electric washer, vacuum cleaner, refrigerator, the modern automobile; not only does he daily see such marvels as the airplane, the talking picture in colors, the wonders of surgery, of printing, of the phonograph, of telephony — but new things are constantly coming to remind him of the vast and thrilling possibilities of what is yet to happen.

The average man has ceased to wonder at the miraculous accomplishments of science; it is all a part of his everyday existence.

Not merely the material impedimenta of science, but the thought and method of science are becoming part of the life of the people of this nation. The lives and efforts of a constantly increasing percentage of them are becoming involved in science in one way or another. A hundred years ago the proportion of people that came into intimate contact with it was insignificant. Today, who shall say what proportion is constantly occupied in one way or another, directly in the service of our mistress? All the way from the men at the head of great research organizations and teaching in the high institutions of learning, through engineers, medical men, manufacturers, on down to the humble repair man who "services" your radio or "finishes" your Kodak prints, science catches the many in her net. All these people live with science, and more or less for science. In one way or another they think science. Their number is great, and it is constantly and noticeably increasing.

Is it unreasonable, therefore, to predict that an increasingly large part of our country's population will want science served up with their fiction, rather than war or chivalry or exploration? Is it far-fetched to suppose that the fiction-writer's imagination, which, to please the reader, has heretofore exercised itself on the heights of Olympus and in the African jungles, with black magic and the Wild West, will soon for the same reason have to delve into the atom, press out past the confines of the solar system, and deal with intricate apparatus? If war comes next to love in the writings of men, when everyone is occupied with war, will not science come next to love when everybody lives by science and almost everybody works with science?

Scientific fiction as a fine art is truly new. Rarely does any fine art spring fully developed from the brow of its goddess. Years, decades of painful evolution will yet be necessary before Scientifiction can take its seat at the banquet, fully recognized by her sisters, Drama, Historical Romance, the Novel, etc. Scientifiction of today is not yet perfect; and those of us who write it recognize that fact better than does anyone else. When we attempt to wed two such dissimilar personalities as Science and Literary Art, it is but natural that there should be a period of adjustment before conjugal life is perfect. But the point I make is, that progress is being made, right now.

Amazing Stories is a pioneer. Our Magazine is ineradicably down in history as the leader with the far-flung vision. A hundred or a thousand years in the future, men will point back to it as the originator of a new' type of literary art. In the meanwhile, the art is spreading. Scientifiction is gradually creeping into general literature. Old writers are turning their attention to it; new writers are developing. Above all, public interest is increasing.

There is a great, fallow development going on at the present moment. Some day the public will wake up to an intense, conscious interest in Scientifiction. Just as in the past in the realms of war, exploration, or mystery, so it will be in science: man will use fiction to express his pride in the deeds he has done, and his dreams of the things he wants to do and has not yet accomplished.

(1929)

*Symbol of "scientifiction"
used in early issues of Amazing Stories.*

ries had been at the vanguard of "scientific fiction as a fine art."[196] The respective issue would be an important milestone, both for science fiction, and for Breuer personally, as it also contained the author's first long-form science fiction story, namely the aforementioned novelette "Rays and Men," enlarged version of his stories "The Fatal Ray" aka "Osudný paprsek."

There were three texts which helped make a mark in the wet cement of the emerging science fiction genre. The first was the introduction by Hugo Gernsback in the inaugural 1926 issue of *Amazing Stories*. Two subsequent articles, very much in the spirit of Gernsback, also helped set the standards, namely "Scientifiction, Searchlight of Science"[197] by the then budding writer Jack Williamsons published two years later in the autumn issue of *Amazing Stories Quarterly*, and, of course, Breuer's text. But "while Williamson's essay has become a landmark in the discussion of the attitudes of early science fiction, due to his position as a major figure in the field for nearly eighty years," Breuer's text was soon largely forgotten, despite the fact that "Breuer's essay is just as significant in articulating and defining the genre in the early days,"[198] notes Michael R. Page, adding that these essays "despite their crudeness [are] the foundation of science fiction criticism."[199]

Less than a year later, Breuer returned to the subject in another of his published letters. He began by praising a story from author G. Peyton Wertenbaker[200] titled "The Chamber of Life," which he described as "a really first-class piece of scientifiction; one that ranks with the good literature of the day,"[201] adding that such quality efforts emerged in the pages of *Amazing Stories* only "every now and then."[202] Breuer then went on to offer his take on how a quality science fiction story should be written: "Scientifiction, primarily, must entertain. In that way it differs from science which may or may not entertain; for the principal function of a scientific article is something far different from entertainment. But in order that a short-story [...] with a scientific foundation be entertaining, it has to fulfill some other rather stringent and difficult requirements." He also added how science fiction should not look like: "Some sort of a raving fancy, a wild, incoherent hodge-podge of machinery, or of stunts with rays or hypnotism or impossible apparatus, or some melodramatic adventures in the middle of South America or on Venus, among some caricatures of beings who express the inconsistencies of the author's psychology rather than any scientific principles – these things cannot possibly be entertaining to a person with an orderly mind, a scientific training and a taste for good literature,"[203] he wrote in 1930.

In another letter published in July 1928 *Amazing Stories*, Breuer sought to empathise with those readers who had yet to develop a taste for science fiction, and who had found much to criticize in this emerging genre, feeling such stories to be "'too dry,' 'too much mathematics,' 'too much stuff that doesn't mean anything,' 'too much theory,' and so on, all mean that the stories have a tendency to lack a modern literary quality."[204] And because he sought to build up a readership that would itself produce new writers, Breuer advised the existing authors and editor Hugo Gernsback that: "I don't care how much science you put in, if the stories conform to modern literary standards, the above criticism will not occur. Let your stories have plot and unity of impression, and the general reader will like them, in spite of the science. [The Reader] will buy the magazine by the million."[205] Breuer evidently had a strong interest in guiding science fiction through its teething troubles…

Mentor Breuer
and His Apprentice Williamson

The letters published in *Amazing Stories* and other similar magazines that emerged in the late 1920s and early 1930s helped to mould this emerging genre, as well as to lay down the roots for active readers to become members of science fiction fandom. And because space was limited in pulp magazines for the exchanges of such views, 1928 saw the emergence of two of the world's first science fiction clubs, namely in Alabama and Illinois. A year later, these clubs joined forces with the Chicago-based Science Correspondence Club, whose members set about creating a lively forum for the exchange of ideas and viewpoints on science fiction. Despite Breuer living away from these new centres of science fiction fandom, he managed to stay in touch with his readers from his home in Nebraska, thanks also to his contributions in the fanzine *Cosmos*.[206] Evidently, Breuer served as a strong motivating force for his colleagues, as "he had fans then, and his name on magazine covers."[207] Indeed, the twenty-year-old aspiring writer Jack Williamson noted that and when "one of his letters invited correspondence, [...] I was soon in touch with him,"[208] he recalled a half century later.

Indeed, the youngster from New Mexico – a similar science fiction 'backwater' as Nebraska, which was home to the twenty years senior Breuer –

*Young Jack Williamson
in contemporary illustration.*

would become something of a pupil of the Czech-American author. Williamson then published a single work in *Amazing Stories* and one would have been hard pressed at that time to predict a literary career spanning almost six decades. By all accounts Williamson viewed Breuer as an experienced scientist and author: "I was impressed by his relative skill and success. Trying hard to learn the rules, I asked him to collaborate with me. He wrote that his medical practice kept him too busy for a full-time collaboration, but he did agree to accept me as a sort of student apprentice."[209]

Williamson adds that Breuer "was the instructor, I the student." He then expounds upon how his own writings looked: "I did most of the plotting and writing while he made suggestions for improvement – and they were excellent. [Breuer] had a sound knowledge of the fundamentals of fiction, and of what constituted good writing."[210]

At the point when the new Breuer—Williamson team began working together, the situation behind-the-scenes began to change dramatically. Hugo Gernsback went bankrupt and the magazine was taken over by the new management. At first Miles J. Breuer and Jack Williamson both decided to

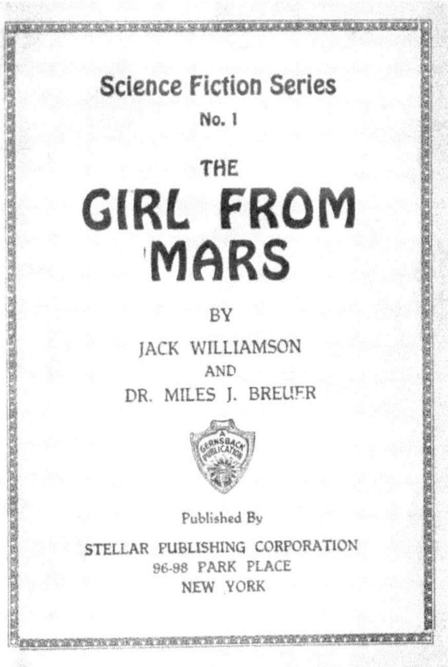

stay loyal to their first editor and thus the first fruit of their collaboration, a manuscript titled "The Egg from the Lost Planet"[211] was accepted by Hugo Gernsback, whose new publishing house Stellar Publishing was able to offer an improved deal over the former *Amazing Stories*. In October 1929 Gernsback filled the market with no less than six so-called science fiction chapbooks. These included the aforementioned text, albeit re-titled to *The Girl from Mars*.[212] This decidedly average work nonetheless made its mark in the history of the genre – the thin, 24-page publication represented the first collection from the newly founded *Science Fiction Series*, with Breuer and Williamson's joint work becoming the first 'book' in the world to be labelled on its cover and title page as being a work of 'science fiction.'

At that time, both authors were already hard at work on their hitherto largest joint effort, the novel *The Birth of a New Republic*. Williamson recalls that Breuer came up with the original idea, claiming that "if history repeats itself [...] the colonization of the moon and its war for independence could recapitulate early American history."[213] The writing team's work practices, however, proved somewhat chaotic: "Looking back, I'm astonished at how rapidly I could write in those early days, "[214] – indeed, the writing only took from October 1929 to the subsequent February. Despite the fact, that "the original manuscript seems to have disappeared, along with [...] working papers and the carbon copy,"[215] we can learn a little about how the writing team worked

Illustration by Hans Waldemar Wessolowski for "The Birth of a New Repubic"
(Amazing Stories Quarterly, Winter 1931).

thanks to Williamson: "In our joint efforts, I did most of the actual writing, sending story drafts to him for comment and criticism."[216]

Soon Gernsback's successor T. O'Conor Sloane lured Jack Williamson and Miles J. Breuer back as the practice in the past when all the authors of

Amazing Stories have been underpaid and payments often delayed, was forgotten. *The Birth of a New Republic* with great cover artwork by Leo Morey[217] and interior illustrations by H. W. Wesso[218] was thus published in the winter issue of *Amazing Stories Quarterly* in January 1931. Narrated by an old man living on the Moon some 70 years after the fight for Luna's independence has begun in 2325, the novel is full of exciting action, descriptions of battles and spy-related operations. Although successful with readers, the book was not immune from criticism. One noted fan and occasional science fiction author, Robert W. Lowndes, offered the following feedback: "It's a good story, but, as one reader complained, is a retelling of the break of the American colonies from England and the war that followed. Not only are elements and incidents repeated, with slight changes to allow for Lunar conditions, but many characters' names are too similar to their historical counterparts [...] In one instance, the character who is the equivalent of Benjamin Franklin is referred to as 'Franklin', and neither authors nor editor caught the error."[219]

Notably, back in its day, the novel inspired a future major science fiction figure, author Robert A. Heinlein.[220] According to Williamson, Heinlein "has confessed his debt"[221] and thus revealed that *The Birth of a New Republic* served as an inspiration for his celebrated 1966 novel *The Moon Is a Harsh Mistress*, which went on to win the coveted Hugo Award for the best science fiction novel of the year. Regardless of this, *The Birth of a New Republic* was soon largely forgotten, and only received second edition in a small print run in 1981, followed by a third edition in 2021, when a modern-day reviewer described it as "a very pleasing blend of realistic sci-fi, wartime action, espionage and even romance," adding that "it is actually a pretty impressive affair, overall."[222]

For Jack Williamson, collaboration with Miles J. Breuer represented a formative experience. Moreover, Williamson allowed himself to be convinced by Breuer of the need to write truly 'science-based' stories instead of merely fantastic tales in the style of the then popular Abraham Merritt.[223] Alas, Williamson's collaboration with Breuer ended as quickly as it began – with efforts to rekindle the writing partnership in the late 1930s (see below) amounting to nothing. The writing partnership proved intense, but short-lived – and the pair only met in person on a single occasion, when Williamson visited Breuer in Nebraska in 1931. According to the visiting writer, Breuer "had seemed youthful, vigorous, and happy enough."[224] None of them knew at that time, that the literary careers of both writers were on a divergent course, with Williamson quickly becoming a star of the science fiction scene, and Breuer, conversely, fast disappearing from the literary scene.

Sliding into Obscurity

Between 1929 and 1932 Miles J. Breuer was undoubtedly at the peak of his literary career, publishing more than 25 stories in various American pulp magazines. During this period, we also find Breuer's final story to be published both in Czech and English. In May 1932, *Amazing Stories* issued "The Perfect Planet," with the same story published only a few months later in Czech-language *Amerikán Národní Kalendář* almanac for the year 1933 under the title "Světoborný nález Majka Gruntoráda" (The Epochal Discovery of Majek Gruntorád). In the story, the somewhat maladjusted youngster Matěj (Majek) Gruntorád (in the Czech version); namely Gus Kersenbrock (in the English version); accidentally discovers "an interplanetary flier" in the Nebraska dunes, "whose occupants had perished in their first attempt to get about on Earth."[225] Inside the ship the protagonist discovers a mysterious gaseous substance that improves the mental capabilities for several days before returning the user back to their previous state. This discovery enables Matěj to transform himself from a poor, dumb nobody into a wealthy and successful businessman, also winning the heart of his beloved Kačenka (aka Kitty in the English version), whose heart the successful rival Thompson has also been pursuing.

This decidedly average tale is nonetheless of interest as the only of Breuer's works to be published in both Czech and English simultaneously, albeit with both versions differing from each other markedly. One can hardly expect that the editor of the Czech-language *Amerikán Národní Kalendář* almanac would have the time or inclination to significantly revise the received

Header of "Světoborný nález Majka Gruntoráda"
(Amerikán Národní Kalendář, 1932).

*Illustration by Leo Morey for "The Perfect Planet"
(Amazing Stories, May 1932).*

manuscript; conversely, *Amazing Stories* editors would traditionally strongly edit the content of their received texts, often recommending that authors make fundamental changes to their tales. For this reason, it is reasonable to conclude that the Czech-language version more closely approximates the original as written by Breuer.

The two versions chiefly differ in their closing sections. The "Světoborný nález Majka Gruntoráda" ends tragically when Matěj returns to the spaceship to inhale more of the gas, but he finds his rival there cavorting with his beloved Kačenka:

"[Majek] could see into the sphere all too well. From a distance, he was able to observe how Thompson and Kačenka approached to control console – the one whose secrets he, Matěj, had very strong respect for, and which he therefore kept at a safe distance. He was unable to suppress an instinctive warning cry: […] 'Be careful. Be very careful, or it will…' But it was too late. Kačenka raised her hand beckoning to Matěj to be silent. […] Thompson repeatedly grabbed her under the armpits and physically held her back. She half fell over the control console. As she grabbed the table to keep her balance, Kačenka inadvertently moved several levers on the console. […] A gust raced around the vessel as if it were a cyclone, sweeping Matěj to the ground and then throwing him back several steps. A vortex of sand appeared at the location of the sphere. Majek thought he saw a green stripe emerging from where the sphere had stood; with unbelievable bullet-like speed it lashed out sideways and upwards, where the manifestation, seemingly a mere fog-like smudge, disappeared, dissolving into the blue sky… The sphere was gone. All that remained was a deep gorge indented into the powdery sand…

Matěj ran down into the dent and exclaimed: 'Kačenka!'"[226]

Conversely, in "The Perfect Planet" the protagonist and his adversary reach an agreement in matters of love right inside the spaceship, where they randomly meet and then agree to work together:

"'That means,' Thompson said, stepping over to shut off the valve from which the gas was still escaping, 'that we'll have to use it regularly; and as soon as possible have it analyzed so that we could make some more. We'll both use the gas, and if Kitty prefers you, you're welcome and have my congratulations. Then we'll set up and manufacture the gas, not only for our own continued use, but for others. We'll supply it to begin with, until others get started. Before long, the whole world can have it. Then indeed old Mother Earth will be the Perfect Planet.'"[227]

In a sense, both versions typify the era and the periodical in which they were published. Star-crossed love that ends in tragedy serves as a perfect reflection of the literary output of contemporary-era Czech-American almanacs which were filled with stories that lacked high literary ambitions. Conversely, the idea of utilizing the aforementioned super gas for the betterment of all humanity reflected a spirit of optimism in the future that was typified in the science fiction pulp magazines of the time.

One other point of interest is worth noting here: Breuer's idea is strongly reminiscent of a widely celebrated story published two decades later, which became one of the most widely anthologized science fiction stories, namely "Flowers for Algernon" (1959) by the otherwise lesser known author Daniel Keyes,[228] who remains famous almost exclusively for this single story. In "Flowers for Algernon," too, the chief protagonist

Cover illustration by Robert Fuqua
for "The Raid from Mars"
(Amazing Stories, March 1939).

is a mentally disabled man, who becomes a genius, and – as his experimental treatment is only partially successful – slowly reverts to his original state. Keyes' tale also has a similar love story aspect as "The Perfect Planet." Of course, science fiction authors mutually inspiring each other is nothing new or surprising. However, if "Flowers for Algernon" came about in part as a result of Breuer's story, then this would undoubtedly represent yet another key contribution by Breuer to the annals of modern science fiction history.

The rise to success and subsequent fall from grace of Majek Gruntorád – the Czech-American nobody from Nebraska – almost augurs the fate of this character's creator. By the end of 1932, Miles J. Breuer (as well as his alter ego Miloslav J. Breuer) had all but disappeared from the literary scene. In December 1933, after more than a year's silence, Breuer published the mediocre story "The Strength of the Weak." The next effort was not until 1935, which saw the release of three published works. After that, up to his death ten years later, Miles J. Breuer only published seven more English-language, and two more Czech-language tales.

Despite the fact that Breuer's name continued to entice pulp magazine readers throughout the 1930s, his newer stories have failed to stand the test of time. Indeed, writing in his opus *Science-Fiction: The Gernsback Years*, ex-

Promotional issue of Unusual Stories advertised Miles J. Breuer's story which never appeared.

pert on early American science fiction Everett F. Bleiler[229] derided the quality of Breuer's later works as being "below Breuer's usual level," "a weak story," "routine,"[230] and so on. He was far from the only one. In a 2021 Facebook post Breuer's subsequent March 1939 effort, "The Raid from Mars" was described as "wafer thin" by contemporary author and historian Darrell Schweitzer.[231] Moreover, Breuer's final work "The Sheriff of Thorium Gulch" published in 1942, was described by editor Michael R. Page as the weakest of all his literary efforts.

Despite this apparent slide in quality, much interest continued during the second half of the 1930s on the part of magazine editors for Miles J. Breuer to contribute new stories. Ultimately, the majority of Breuer's final works were once again published in *Amazing Stories*; additional stories were issued in the unremarkable and short-lived *Comet Stories of Super Time and Space*[232] and *Future Fiction*,[233] and one in the unsuccessful semiprozine *Marvel Tales*.[234] And it was in the latter, which aimed at more ambitious science fiction, that perhaps Breuer's only truly notable work during this period was published, namely the 1935 satire "Mars Colonizes." In the story, some highly friendly aliens from the planet Mars move to Earth – but then the Martians set about buying up properties and businesses and gradually take over almost the entire planet's economy. This naturally causes great upset among the Earth's inhabitants, who then decide to rid the world of these "friendly" visitors.

Breuer's new stories were, by all accounts, set to be issued in numerous publications. For example, the new semiprozine *Unusual Stories*[235] advertized an upcoming Breuer story – alas, this apparently never materialized. Moreover, Breuer apparently was ready to offer a chapter for a serial novel in the fanzine *Science Fiction Digest*,[236] where almost every important science fiction author of the day had contributed.[237] Alas, this also never came to fruition, despite Breuer teasing a story that involved the "gaseous beings of Neptune."[238]

Notably, the years of Breuer's peak literary output coincide with the peak activities of the Breuer family's medical practice. In 1928, the surgery and laboratory in which both father Charles H. Breuer and sons Miles and Roland worked, moved from the Security Mutual Bldg. – the first skyscraper in Lincoln – to a newly built high-rise, namely the Federal Trust Bldg. That meant Miles J. Breuer becoming burdened with even more work, ultimately ending up serving as a pathologist to all three of the city's hospitals, and also serving in a medical chamber of commerce. Moreover, Breuer's time was also taken up with writing academic papers, of which the *Index of Physiotherapeutic Technic* was published in book form in 1925. The work "catalogs a variety of methods for physical therapy, using both tried and true traditional methods (i. e. the human touch) and new advances in understanding and technology that facilitate patient recovery."[239] It was evidently "one of the first such books on the topic of physical therapy."[240] From the outbreak of the war, Breuer's main specialization was tuberculosis, about which he published academic articles in publications such as the *Annals of Internal Medicine* and *American Review of Tuberculosis*. But he also wrote about other fields of medicine, including hygiene. Moreover, Breuer also contributed regular medical-themed articles to Czech-American publications – contributing dozens of such pieces in the likes of *Bratrský Věstník*, *Hospodář*, *Ženské Listy*, and *Pokrok Západu*.

In the 1920s the Breuer's medical practice was widely advetised in local press.

Gradually, however, Miles was left to run things by himself. In early 1929, father Charles set off for a six month round-the-world trip; a year later embarked on a months-long trip to Europe and the Middle East. Miles' brother Roland was also often absent from Nebraska, first on a one-year scholarship in San Francisco, and then later working in San Jose. This was followed by work in a sanatorium in Norton, Kansas, with Roland then staying in the state for an additional year heading his own surgery there. Ultimately both father Charles and brother Roland moved to California, which was the home of Roland's wife. In 1932, the surgery, now run singularly by Miles J. Breuer, relocated to the Stuart Bldg., yet another new high-rise in Lincoln constructed in 1927.

Raising three children also undoubtedly took a significant bite out of Miles J. Breuer's time during the 1920s. Both daughters ultimately followed their father's examples and became medical practitioners. Additionally, during the 1930s, Rosalie, the eldest daughter, also served as the chairwoman of Komenský club. This organization, which operated for decades, served as an umbrella institution for Czech students at University of Nebraska at Lincoln. Without question, the toughest blow for Miles J. Breuer came in 1939, with the tragic loss of his only son, Stanley. At the age of eighteen, the promising journalist died while hiking in Colorado.

But there was more, yet: "Breuer was extremely active in the local medical community and in other civic organizations, holding memberships and leadership roles in several medical associations, the Optimist's Club, the American Legion, the Elks, the Masons, the Chamber of Commerce, and the local schools,"[241] wrote Michael R. Page. But perhaps the greatest amount of time

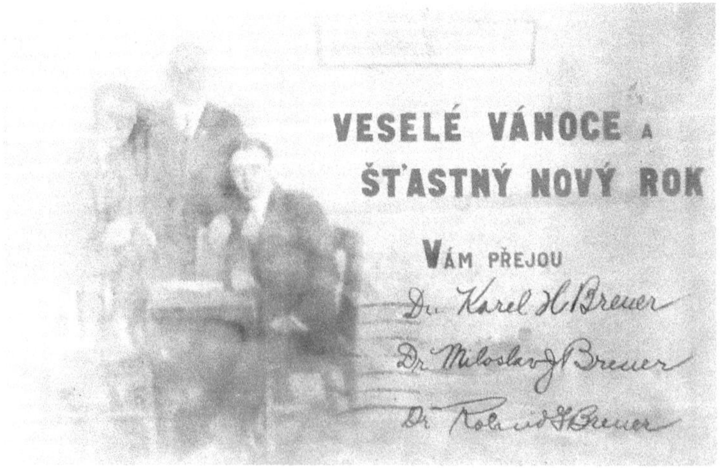

Christmas card of Karel, Miloslav, and Roland Breuer.

was taken up by Breuer's scouting activities. From 1920, Breuer served as the leader of a scout troop, organizing numerous activities for youngsters. Indeed, Breuer helped to impart one of his own passions to the scouts, namely mountain hiking. Naturally, Breuer also took an interest in all things modern, for example, founding a photographic club, the Lincoln Camera Society. Serving as its vice-president, Breuer wrote about photography in specialist publications[242] and also organized exhibitions of his travel photographs.[243] Later, he also began to shoot amateur cine films, for example documenting the training of local Sokol gymnasts in Omaha.[244] Breuer also regularly gave lectures on medicine, photography, and the current situation in Czechoslovakia – both in English and in Czech. And his interest in the social sciences, sociology and political science, were likewise reflected in his work as a member of the editorial board of the aforementioned academic magazine *Social Science*, where he also contributed reviews and articles. Which means that writing science fiction tales was relatively low on the list of Breuer's priorities. "As involved as Breuer was, it is a wonder that he had time for science fiction at all,"[245] noted Page.

Three generations of the Breuer family include Dr. Charles H. Breuer, 69 years of age, formerly a prominent Lincoln surgeon, now retired and living in Gilroy, Cal.; Dr. Miles J. Breuer, who has been a practicing physician in Lincoln for fifteen years, and Stanley Marcel Breuer, 7, son of Dr. Miles Breuer, and grandson of Dr. Charles Breuer. Dr. C. H. Breuer recently returned from a trip around the world.

Promotional photo showing Miles J. Breuer testing his medical equipment.

From Literature to "Juvenile Stuff"

As the 1930s progressed, Miles J. Breuer's enthusiasm for the budding new literary genre began to wane, and even transformed into outright scepticism. The author's growing ambivalence towards contemporary science fiction was, as an example, even expressed in his 1931 novelette "The Legion of the Fittest." The story's introduction features the 23rd century protagonist expressing himself pejoratively about visions of the future written three hundred years earlier: "I have before me a book published in 1931, [...] which sets forth very well the fantastic ideas of that time as to just what the world would be like today. That was just about the time at which scientific attempts at prophesying the future had their beginning; but these attempts during the first half of the twentieth century, still had about them more of imaginative fancy than of scientific accuracy."[246] Evidently, Breuer was fully aware of how a singular focus on scientific and technological advances, which many of his contemporaries viewed as being able to solve all of humanity's problems in the future, was more naïve than realistic. Accordingly, his protagonist exclaims: "we have made no staggering advances in science during the past two hundred years."[247]

And yet, Breuer's protagonist speaks fondly of his own 23rd century time period: "we have no poverty, illness, no unemployment. We have no courts nor wars nor strikes."[248] And so Breuer, despite his growing reticence, still had plenty of interest in musing about societies of the future, being "one of the writers who actively refined [*Amazing Stories* founder and editor Hugo] Gernsback's initial definition to insist on literary values of style, character, and psychologically nuanced themes – not dull stories of scientific pedagogy."[249] To this end, Breuer sought to write "stories that Gernsback distinguished as scientifiction, as opposed to the science-fantasy romances of [American writers Edgar Rice] Burroughs and [Abraham] Merritt [...] and the super-scientific space operas that would later emerge and come to dominate the magazine."[250] Breuer was clearly aware that it was the action-adventure style of Burroughs' John Carter Barsoom series set on Mars, first introduced in 1917, that strongly inspired the early science fiction movement of the 1930s. Indeed, such "gosh-wow adventures were attracting a younger and less discerning readership. Gernsback was all for encouraging the young readers, but not at the expense of bastardizing science fiction, but this is what was happening,"[251] notes historian Mike Ashley, commenting on the changing content of pulp magazines of the day. At odds with both Breuer's and Gernsback's concept of science fiction, the readers of the time in fact positively "responded to the 'super science' and [*Amazing Stories*] was soon selling around 150,000 copies a month."[252]

In January 1931 Breuer again expressed his affinity for science fiction via a letter sent to the new editor of *Amazing Stories*, T. O'Conor Sloane: "I am very much interested in your publication, and it gives me genuine pleasure every time you get out some good things."[253] Alas, as a contributing author, and one who perhaps most adhered to the so-called Wellsian paradigm, he did not hold back from expressing reservations about the very medium in which he published: "I've never been an editor and don't

Illustration by Frank R. Paul for "The Fitzgerald Contraction" (Science Wonder Stories, January 1930).

know how it feels; but I rather imagine that in these days of quantity production and high pressure living and superficial achievement, an editor of a science-fiction magazine must be up against it sometimes if he really prefers literature to twaddle. I judge that by the stuff I read in the general run of science-fiction magazines. As far as my own reading goes, ninety percent of present-day science-fiction as a whole is on about the same plane as the general run of Wild West and low-brow detective tales. I can imagine the editor raising his hands to heaven and supplicating Providence to send him something with the least bit of literary flavor in it."[254] Such efforts failed to spur a change in trends, and it wasn't until the advent of a new generation of science fiction authors emerging – names such as Isaac Asimov and Frederik Pohl – at the turn of the 1930s and 40s that such concepts were truly embraced.

Back between 1930 and 1932 Breuer had sixteen of his short stories published in pulp magazines (of which only four were published elsewhere than *Amazing Stories* or *Amazing Stories Quarterly*). Although being so close to Gernsback, surprisingly, only two stories, namely "The Fitzgerald Contraction" and its sequel, "The Time Valve" were published in his new pulp

Comparisons in Science Fiction
By Miles J. Breuer, M. D.

The principal reason that you no longer see my name in the science fiction magazines is because of the deterioration of the quality of the work that is published in these magazines. I have a professional standing to maintain, and I do not wish my name associated with the juvenile type of stuff that is now appearing under the caption of Science Fiction.

Ten years ago, when this type of fiction began to be first widely published, there was more originality in the stories and some literary style, and some ability in the construction of plots. However, in a few years the thing became commercialized, and a lot of professional hack writers took it up. Bulk magazines had to be filled, and these fellows who write in the yard kept them filled with a bunch of insufferable trash. During the past four or five years, it is only now and then that you find a story among these things that is worthy of being dignified by either the name of science fiction or the name of short stories. The present day stuff is not even adolescent; it is juvenile and less. It seems to be supplied chiefly to people who consume it in unconscious faith, something after the manner of a drug addict; people who never remember what they have read and are merely hungry for more and more.

Personally, I have lost interest. I find that it is impossible to get a story accepted that conforms somewhere near to ordinary literary standards. I am neither interested in reading or writing stuff that does not even have the appeal of Anderson's fairy tales.

Further I wish to say that I am still interested in writing some kind of fiction of good quality, and should be interested in any opportunity that offers itself for publication of this class of writing. At the same time I do not hesitate to say that I am not interested in writing for the pulp magazines which, at the present time, publish adolescent material under the misnomer of Science Fiction.

(1937)

magazine *Wonder Stories,* which wanted "to deal with science fiction 'realistically' and avoid the 'world-sweeping epic'."[255] Despite the fact that it was in this magazine that writers were producing the very best idea-driven science fiction in 1932 and 1933, Breuer's works never appeared in the pages of *Wonder Stories* again. Indeed, after 1932, Breuer's works would also only appear very rarely in other pulp magazines.

Breuer explained his disillusionment with the direction of contemporary science fiction again in a short 1937 text, published in the fanzine *Tesseract,* writing: "I am not interested in writing for the pulp magazines which, at the present time, publish adolescent material under the misnomer of Science Fiction."[256] But he was also careful to add that he was "still interested in writing some kind of fiction of good quality."[257] A year later, he proposed a new collaboration with fellow author Jack Williamson, with whom he had maintained a correspondence. But the plan to pen a series of works set on the Moon, which takes place in the same time period of the writing pair's previous novel *The Birth of a New Republic*, ultimately came to nothing. "[I] gave it up," recalled Williamson years later, "when I found that Breuer wanted to resume our work on the old basis, with me doing all the actual writing. He said that I had already done the job on the story that he would like to do."[258] In his final letter to Williamson written presumably in 1938, Breuer complained that "he was too busy 'with various and sundry things' to find time to work on any complete draft of the story."[259] It is likely that from this point on, Breuer most probably never again actively returned to creative writing as during the final five years of his life only two as yet unpublished short stories, most probably written earlier, saw the print for the first time. The other published stories in this period were mere reprints.

Breuer evidently remained inflexible in his conception of science fiction, never conceding that "science fiction needed to go through the juvenile growing pains before it could mature,"[260] as science fiction historian Mike Ashley expressed three-quarters of a century later. By the end of the 1930s, Breuer had largely dissociated himself from developments in science fiction literature. And yet, despite this, he clearly still had an interest in this genre, remaining an avid reader of such works, and remaining in very public contact with both science fiction authors and his fans. Indeed, Breuer provided some assistance in the writing of the first academic book on science fiction, *Pilgrims Through Space and Time: Trends and Patterns in Scientific and Utopian Fiction*[261] by literary historian J. O. Bailey.[262] Evidently, Breuer's role in this endeavour was far from minimal, as noted by Walter Gillings, in a review of the work in his *Fantasy Review*.[263] Specifically, Gillings writes that although the book deals predominantly with science fiction classics such as H. G. Wells, it also includes "the strange phenomenon of fandom," adding that "such devotees as Langley Searles[264] and [Forrest J.] Ackerman,[265] as well as the late lamented [H. P.] Lovecraft and Dr. [Miles J.] Breuer, have assisted [J. O. Bailey] in bringing the record as up to date as it is."[266] Alas, Miles J. Breuer never lived to see the publication of this pioneering chronicle of science fiction made with his assistance. Wartime restrictions meant that publication was delayed by several years, by which time Breuer had passed away.

Final Years

The decline of Breuer's literary output during the latter half of the 1930s was not merely the result of his growing disdain for the direction of the science fiction genre, but was also the result of declining health. Nebraska newspapers of the time speak of Breuer's frequent hospital visits, with this news quickly spreading to his friends in the science fiction community. The December 1933 issue of *Science Fiction Digest* noted that: "with this writing comes the sad word that Miles J. Breuer is confined to a sanatorium, with a nervous breakdown from overwork."[267] Two years later, in 1935, the Czech-language magazine *Hospodář* noted that Breuer had "at the start of March [...] undertaken a very difficult and serious operation, for which he had been prepared for some time, namely the removal of a malfunctioning kidney."[268] Breuer ultimately spent a month in hospital, and reports of the serious nature of the procedure are also confirmed by the fact that "prior to the operation [Breuer] revealed that he had absolutely no fear of death – but that he would prefer not to leave behind such a large number of unread books."[269] The serious state of Breuer's health was also confirmed by his lawyer, who years later wrote the following to Jack Williamson: "his health in 1938 was such that he was put to the limit of his vitality in his practice."[270] The Czech-language article "Padesátiletý člověk – co s ním?" (What to Do with a Fifty-year-old?), published several weeks before Breuer turned fifty, underscore his health concerns, whereby "the middle age years, from forty-five to fifty-five, are the most dangerous in the life of the modern man."[271]

By the mid-1930s, Breuer's personal life also began to fall apart. After almost twenty-five years, he ended his marriage – probably an unhappy one as it was supposedly forced upon him by his parents.[272] Subsequently, Breuer married his assistant Violet, but the couple divorced soon after in early 1944. The evidence points to a likely third marriage shortly prior to his death.[273] Here, too, Breuer used his writing to express himself, writing, evidently in his defence, a 1939 article, titled "What a Modern Husband Needs."[274]

Some time at the start of the 1940s, Breuer had yet another nervous breakdown, leading to an extended stay at a medical sanatorium.[275] Subsequently, he headed out to see his brother and father in California, but, alas, his health did not improve as a result. Indeed, a September 1941 Czech-language newspaper *Národní Pokrok* reports that: "He has been seriously ill for the past thirteen months. This led to extended hospital stays in California and Omaha, and now he has sufficiently recovered that he intends to resume his medical prac-

Dr. Miloslav J. Breuer

•

9615 Brighton Way

BEVERLY HILLS,   CALIF.

tice at the earliest possibility."[276] Ultimately, Breuer decided to permanently leave Nebraska and settle on the Pacific coast.

During the Second World War, Breuer considered working as a doctor in Brazil. However, upon receiving his California medical licence, he instead set up a private practice in Beverly Hills, most probably in late 1943 or 1944. During this period, Breuer's interest in science fiction remained, as he maintained an acquaintance with the likes of Forrest J. Ackerman. It is reasonable to assume that he would have been a member, or at least occasional participant, at events organised by the Los Angeles Science Fantasy Society.[277]

Miles J. Breuer passed away just a few months later, on 14 October 1945, aged 56. A brief Czech-language report on his death noted that "although he had been sick, his health had markedly improved in recent years, which meant his sudden passing came as a surprise to Breuer's friends."[278] As a veteran of the First World War, Breuer was buried at Los Angeles National Cemetery in Westwood, right under the windows of the Czech Consulate General in Los Angeles. Miles' father, Charles H. Breuer, 80 years old, died a year later,[279] while mother Barbara Breuer passed away in 1952, aged 87.[280]

With the passing of Miles J. Breuer, the community of American science fiction writers and fans lost one of its first stars. Without question, the author was a major and talented pioneer of the genre, and one who approached his works with an uncommon seriousness of purpose. "He was mainly concerned with putting a meaning into everything he wrote,"[281] noted Jack Williamson shortly after Breuer's death, incisively adding: "I believe he was actually capable of much better writing than appeared in his published work."[282] Indeed, Breuer was, in his eyes, a man with fantastic ideas, who, sadly often failed to properly process these into stories. As a result, Breuer was, according to science fiction expert Burnett Toskey,[283] an "inconsistent writer [...] capable of

Miles J. Breuer's burial place at Los Angeles National Cemetery.

very fine stories, but over half the time he wrote unmitigated tripe."[284] But, when Breuer succeeded, then, according to science fiction author Robert A. Heinlein, his works were "miles ahead of the stuff [...] of the period."[285] Although Breuer would no doubt have frowned at Toskey's assessment, he would conversely likely have agreed with Jack Williamson and Robert A. Heinlein. And he would certainly also have been happy that despite the comparatively small volume of his science fiction story output, he is nonetheless considered by many to have left a major footprint in the history of science fiction.

Miloslav J. Breuer
in the Context of
Czech-American Literature

There is a long history of Czech-language writing in the United States. The first Czech-language publication in the United States was produced in 1855; five years later saw the publication of the first Czech-language periodical, *Slowan Amerikánský* (American Slav). However, it wasn't until the mid1880s that Czech publishing gained any sort of permanent foothold in the United States. Arguably, Czech-American culture, art and literature reached an intellectual peak right after the First World War. This phenomenon naturally also concerned Czech-language periodicals – by 1925, at least nine such dailies, 33 weeklies, 6 bi-weeklies, 31 monthlies and more than 30 much-beloved almanacs were being published in the United States, totalling something in the order of 4,000–5,000 individual Czech-language publications per year.[286]

And it was from the ranks of the editors of such periodicals, along with their colleagues, that attempts at submissions of fiction were mostly found, with such stories typically written to cater for a specific Czech-language publication. Literature, aka "'entertaining' works, were viewed as a supplemental addition to periodicals. An emphasis was placed on readability, and authors tended to not have any lofty literary goals in this respect."[287] At the same time, only very few such authors of short stories had standalone books published. All of which meant that some stories were very much deemed by Czech-Americans to belong to the category of entertainment. In the book *Padesát let českého tisku v Americe* (Fifty Years of the Czech Press in America) published in 1911, at the same time as Breuer's first Czech-language story was issued, Czech-American banker and historian Tomáš Čapek[288] writes: "With only a few insignificant exceptions all [entertainment-type] works were firmly ensconced in magazines, anthologies […] and in almanacs. Thus, only a tiny number of former standalone works exist"[289]

Alas, hitherto no anthology or history of Czech-American prose has yet been published. One slight exception that covers only a fraction of published works is a study by Czech literary historian Vladimír Papoušek[290] *Česká literatura v Chicagu: Literární tvorba Čechoameričanů v letech 1880–1939* (Czech Literature in Chicago: Czech-American Literary Works, 1880–1939).[291] Examining the development of Czech-American literature and its content, Papoušek writes: "Prose were primarily written to be an almanac-type story, built on well-worn tropes of doomed love, ancestral feuds, fateful defeats, guilt and punishment. […] Another common type was the

Jan Havlasa *F. Jaromír Pšenka* *Clara Vostrovsky Winlow*

'travel' story – i.e. a story that takes place during travels through distant lands, in this case primarily through the Midwestern and Western wilderness of North America."[292] The character of such literary works evolved during the turn of the 20th century, when the "social story began to dominate, capturing the lives of the urban middle and upper strata of society."[293]

Despite expanding over several decades, Czech-American literature never achieved any great literary successes. And thus of the bibliographies containing hundreds of names of authors of prosaic works, we find that most penned only a handful, or even a single work. In principle, only three names fall outside this rule, both in terms of the quantity and quality of their works, namely, Pavel Albieri,[294] Jan Havlasa,[295] and F. Jaromír Pšenka.[296] This trio had several things in common: all were born in the Czech lands and arrived in the United States as adults. Moreover, all had already worked in either journalism or creative writing in their country of birth, with their American output a mere continuation of such efforts. The subject matter of a notable part of their respective outputs then became America, or more precisely 'Czech' America. Add to that, all three authors published both in Czech-American publications and books, and also continued to publish back home. In this sense, all were essentially Czech authors working in the United States.

And it is this very fact – that Czech-American literature was overwhelmingly written by those who had not been born in the United States, and was for its entire existence "in one way or another dependant on the arrival of new blood from the homeland,"[297] – that sets Miloslav J. Breuer apart from his literary brethren in the United States. While authors who wrote in the Czech language were predominantly immigrants, second-generation authors born in America wrote prose exclusively in English. Such was the case, for example, with Breuer's slightly older contemporary, Clara Vostrovsky Winlow,[298] who authored more than a dozen books for young readers, published during the

Světoborný nález Majka Gruntoráda.

Pro kalendář Amerikán napsal Dr. Miloslav J. Breuer.

Matěj Gruntorád rozmrzele kopl do chomáče stříbrošedé
šalvěje.

"Bylo to hloupé ode mne," bručel pro sebe, "rozzlobiti se na Ka
Mohl jsem pozorovat, že mne má stále ráda. Kdo to může míti ho
zlé, když jde raději s hochem, který má příjemné způsoby, krásně s
a dělá vše, aby se jí zalíbil? Dnešní dobou nelze už ovládati dě
křikem. Proč vždycky dělám tu nepravou věc?"

PADĚLANÉ ŽITÍ.

Pro kalendář "Amerikán" napsal dr. Miloslav J. Breuer, Lincoln, Nebraska.

Bylo půl dvanácté v noci. Ve filmovém divadle "Lyric" v městečku Plzni v Nebrasce se zavíralo. Poslední párek návštěvníků se již před čtvrt hodinou odebral do Ploužkovy lékárny na občerstvení, zmrzlinu, limonádu, nebo něco silnějšího. Lumír Jelínek, mla-

Lumír vyšel po schodech třetí poschodí budovy divadla odemkl pečlivé uzamknuté dvé Zadíval se ve velké místnosti, ujímající celé poschodí, na sku

U RADIOGRAFA.

Povídka od Miloslava J. Breuera.

U RADIOGRAFA.

Povídka od Miloslava J. Breuera.

Když jsem byl ještě mladým začátečníkem v Chica-
a měl jsem úřadovnu na Ashland Boulevard, byl jsem
en večer na zábavě v síni Libuše. Dal jsem se náho-
i do řeči s mladým mužem, který seděl naproti mne u
lku. Měl kotvový odznak v dírce u kabátu a choval se
o důstojník. Tuším že mne oslovil nejdříve.

"Všimnul jsem si, že vám říkají doktore," pravil;
zumíte X-paprskům?"

"To jest můj zvláštní obor," odvětil jsem.

"Řekněte mi, bylo by možno viděti diamant pomocí
paprsků?" Hleděl s napjetím na mne, jakoby byl úplně
omněl na lidi kolem nás a na tanec a hudbu v pozadí.

"To záleží na tom, v čem leží — totiž skrze co na něj

Jak utekla chimaera.

Pro kalendář Amerikán napsal Dr. Miloslav J. Breuer

Pan Izaiáš Zátek soudil, že se mu skytá vzácná příležitost. Hleděl zvě-
čavě na svazek papírů, jejž jsem držel v ruce. Až na to své neohrabané
Zátek zcela moderním tvorem; šat jeho přiléhal ve
eček zářil rozžehlou bílí neposkvrněné bělostí, slaměnák
v sezoně, způsobná cigareta — skutečně musel se člověk
ho čisté oholené tváře mezi poznal, že náleží k vyvole-

VYLÉČENÁ RAKOVINA.

Pro Duch Času napsal Dr. Miloslav J. Breuer, Lincoln, Nebr.

'Tak ty opravdu myslíš, že já bych
ti měl být nějakým způsobem pro-
spěšným!" zvolal můj strýc, a vypnul
rasa. Já jsem byl celý zoufalý nad
o kterém jsme právě jed
jsem si příliš nevšímal je-
ní. Jako každý mladý lé-
jsem, že vyhledával neb
dobré pověstí záleží jen na
ém případě.
te si na chvilku sedl," pra-
povím vám o tom." Usa-
ili pohodlně a dal si nohy
tíl; a aby měl pro ně na
musel odšoupnouti hroma-
lékařských časopisů. Jeho
l byl do nebe volající hrůzou!
jsem mu to, od té doby co
stal jeho společníkem, ale
Byl to kus lakového starodáv-
raburdi, asi sedm stop vyso-
ného ořechového dřeva, které
ylo čištěno od svého zrození;
ylo několik polic na knihy,
a řada přihrádek naplněných
depisy a papíry, na něž
y se jistě po čtvrt století ne-

Člověk bez hladu.

Povídka od dra. Miloslava J. Breuera

Po svém návratu ze studií v Praze a Vídni, rozhodl
sem se započíti' praxi v českém Chicagu, i zařídil jsem
si ordinovnu na západní 26. ulici. Brzy potom jsem oběd-
du první procovatelní návštěvy, v osobě slíčné mladé da-
my, bývalé dobrého mého přítele, doktora Volného. Sr-
dečně jsem ji uvítal, neboť jsem již dávno nevídel ani ji,
ani jejího manžela. Zdála se býti velice znepokojená. Dlouho nehovokovala.

"Pane doktore," pravila mi, "přicházím k vám jako
k příteli a jako k lékaři, a prosím vas o radu. Zdá se mi,
že můj manžel musí býti nějak nemocen."

"A nač se stěžuje?" ptám se.

Osudný paprsek.

Pro kalendář Amerikán napsal dr. Miloslav J. Breuer, Lincoln, Neb.

I.—Pokus.

Dr. Miloslav Breuer

Cestující jednatel firmy, který vše, co v následujících řádkách bude popsáno zavinil, přišel do naší nemocnice právě když jsem prozatímně obstarával její řízení za nepřítomnosti správce, dra Penrose. Obchodní zástupce onen byl vzorem uhlazené zdvořilosti a mluvil s vědátorskou zdrželivostí. Leč z jeho vylíčení vlastností a účinků nového uspávajícího prostředku, jenž mi nabídl a z výstřižků a otisků z odborných časopisů lékařských, jež mi předložil, dospěl jsem k přesvědčení, že tuto příležitost nesmím v zájmu nemocnice a pacientů nechat ujíti. Byl bych se rád poradil s doktorem Penrosem, tento se měl vrátiti teprve za dva dny; a lučební jednatel mi pravil, že je mu nutno opustiti Lincoln ještě téhož večera. Osvojil

Headers of various Miloslav J. Breuer's short stories published in Czech-American publications.

first quarter of the 20th century, translated two children's books from Czech into English, but never published anything in Czech.

Bilingual Miles, aka Miloslav J. Breuer, can reasonably be described as a major – perhaps even the most successful – Czech-American author of the first half of the 20th century, a time when Czech immigrants were making their greatest mark in the United States. In any event, he expressed strong opposition to views along the line that "second and third-generation immigrants no longer yielded new figures capable of expressing themselves in Czech with confidence [and] their acceptance of the Czech written word was more or less passive,"[299] as Vladimír Papoušek observed. Evidently, Breuer's colleagues were well aware of the author's uniqueness in this respect – for example, the anonymous author of his short obituary in *Bratrský Věstník* made sure to note that "he approached the Czech language in the manner that he continued to refine his skills, so as to be able to also write medical- and lifestyle-themed articles, which required an especially good grasp of lesser-used Czech words. In this sense, his diligence paid off, attaining a notable command of the language."[300]

However, Breuer's Czech-language published stories are nonetheless still riddled with archaic terms, Americanisms, or little-known neologisms. One such example of a never used neologism is the word "vzduchonos" (akin calling an airplane, an *air-carrier*) for an airplane of the future.[301] Another example is Breuer's term "kára" for the vehicles in the future – Breuer was most probably influenced by English word 'car' and thus misunderstood the meaning of phonetically similar Czech word 'kára', which – alas – in Czech means an obsolete and old 'cart.'

It should also be noted that Breuer's published texts would have been polished by the respective editors of the Czech-American periodicals, with such editors very often native born Czechs, who had spent parts of their lives in the homeland. Indeed, five recently unearthed Breuer manuscripts of Czech-language stories[302] indicate a grasp of Czech far worse that what was ultimately published. The manuscripts are replete with errors in terms of tense and inflection, use garbled Czech expressions, and character dialogue frequently has little in common with the contemporary Czech used in his native country. Accordingly, it is unsurprising that reading Breuer's works in English is a far more rewarding experience, with the words demonstrating a command of language that is sorely lacking in his Czech-language texts.

In terms of Czech literature in America, Breuer's lifelong writing in both the Czech and English languages is absolutely unique. The reason for this, unusually, is that, in fact, neither language could be regarded as his mother tongue. Being born in Chicago to Czech parents, Breuer (unlike many

Czech-American children) never attended a Czech school – instead, he mastered the language at first with help from his parents, and subsequently through self-teaching. Being raised in Nebraska, state with the highest percentage of people of Czech origin, also helped as especially in this state even "the second (first American-born) generation [...] was very proficient in Czech."[303]

But nor was English truly Breuer's native tongue either – for despite being born in the United States, he only learned the language at grade school in Omaha, and not at home, attending classes "at the Webster School with his sister Libuše [Libbie]. He generally did not speak English, because at home they spoke only Czech, with fellow pupils often making fun of them at playtime as a result. [Once] he was sent to the headmistress, responding to her rebukes with a combative pledge that he would learn English better than even she could speak."[304] The anonymous author of quoted text then notes – with a tinge of pride – that Breuer's subsequent stories "attest to the fact the Breuer really did keep his word, even surpassing the skills of most '100 percent' Americans, who only spoke one single native language."[305] Despite this, it still remains unclear whether Breuer began his creative writing career in the Czech or English language; nor the manner in which he transposed or translated his stories from his prime language of choice into the other.

Breuer also distinguished himself from other noted Czech-American writers of his day in that both his creative and journalistic writings were a hobby rather than a career. Perhaps this is why contemporary Czech-American press reports frequently refer to him as a doctor or scientist, only rarely invoking the word 'author' – which tended to fuel the tendency not to see Breuer as being a true fiction writer at all. The longest hitherto unearthed notice about Breuer's literary activities in Czech comes from the article published in Omaha-based periodical *Národní Pokrok*. The anonymous author primarily speaks of Breuer's English-language writing, but also mentions prose penned in Czech: "Miloslav J. Breuer of Lincoln takes the top position in terms of Nebraskan Czechs producing literature in the English language, [also] writing health-related advice for various medical magazines alongside his literary efforts. We recently obtained a copy of the noted American anthology *Amazing Stories*, in which is found the highly absorbing Breuer's tale 'The Appendix and the Spectacles'. The story evidences an expert knowledge of the field of medicine, but also contains a chunk of fantasy. The narrative is gripping and also, unusually, will engross all types of readers who enjoy a thrilling story. From the same anthology we learn that Dr. Miroslav [sic] J. Breuer has already written a whole series of similar stories, including "The Riot at Sunderas" [i.e. Sanderac] and "The Puzzle Duel." The young Czech doctor

also wrote several stories in the Czech language, of which one was issued via the *Amerikán Národní Kalendář* almanac several years ago. We wish him every future success in this field of endeavour!"[306]

The *Amerikán Národní Kalendář* almanac was the most read and most respected Czech-language publication in early 20th century Czech America. Launched in 1878, *Amerikán Národní Kalendář* offered the very best of Czech immigrant literature. During its roughly three-quarter century existence, the almanac published prosaic works by more than 80 authors.[307] Breuer himself had six stories published in it over the years (two in the 1910s and 1920s, and one in 1930s and 1940s). Of these, only one was not a science fiction

Czech-American artist Emanuel Václav Nádherný created the cover for Amerikán Národní Kalendář, the leading Czech-American almanac; it was used for more than half a century.

tale, and three were subsequently published in English in American pulp magazines. Despite this, the Czech-American literary community of the day paid Breuer little attention. This is likely due to the subject matter of Breuer's stories. Indeed, Czech-American literature at the turn of the 19th and 20th century had no other author penning even a single story that could be deemed to be of a science fiction nature. Because both Czech and Czech-American literary experts and journalists often "highlighted the fact that the Czech-American community was swamped with trashy literature,"[308] and because science fiction was viewed as belonging to such a lowly category at that time, then it is perhaps understandable why Miloslav J. Breuer's works were so frequently overlooked by his contemporaries.

Also of note is that, even during the peak of his success as an English-language author at the turn of the 1920s and 1930s, Breuer did not turn his back on the Czech language. During this time he also authored dozens of Czech-language popular articles on the subject of medicine, of which some examined the scientific aspects of this field. One such example is the article

"Možnosti a nemožnosti paprsků X" (What X-Rays Can and Can't Potentially Do),[309] or a booklet *Electricity for the Sick Man,*[310] the text of which was originally published in Czech.[311] Moreover, we know of at least three stories from the latter part of Breuer's life that were written in the Czech language. These include the aforementioned "Světoborný nález Majka Gruntoráda" from 1932, which was also concurrently published in a revised English-language version. Three years later, this was followed by "Háček v předpovědi," a reworked version of his 1910 story "The Flaw in the Premise." Breuer's body of literary works in Czech then closes in the autumn of 1942 with the story "Padělané žití" (Counterfeit Living).[312] This love story of an inventor of a groundbreaking new type of film that conveys all the sensations to the viewer is largely viewed as Breuer's weakest Czech-language work with a fantastical theme.

Soon after Breuer passed away in 1945 his literary works were forgotten by the Czech-American public as well as historians of Czech America. Bibliographer Ester Jerabek in her groundbreaking bibliography[313] at least mentions his stories, though only those six published in *Amerikán Národní Kalendář*. And after fifty years Miroslav Rechcígl, Jr., the most important historian and biographer of Czech-America, who wrote Breuer's very short bio for his 3-volume *Encyclopedia of Bohemian and Czech-American Biography*, was unaware of his Czech-language writing and only mentions his English-language works published in pulp magazines.[314] Otherwise Breuer is only occasionally mentioned as one of the founders of Čechie club,[315] never as a writer. And his family's homeland, the Czech Republic, was unaware about his existence until very recently. Perhaps surprisingly, despite visiting the birthplace of his parents at least once, Breuer never published any of his literary works in the contemporary press of then Czechoslovakia.

Discovering Miles and Miloslav

Miles J. Breuer died before rising to become any sort of living legend of American (and thus global) science fiction. His literary career, including as a science fiction author, peaked between the late 1920s and early 1930s – a decade earlier than science fiction really became so popular that it gave birth to its first stars, such as Isaac Asimov. However, as science fiction historian Michael R. Page observed, "the editorial blurb on a late guest editorial in *Startling Stories* in May 1940 designates him as a 'famous scientifiction writer,' showing that the memory of his impact on the field was still on the minds of the new generation."[316] But this did not last long – for Breuer passed away before the advent of the first post-war science fiction conventions, and was thus soon largely forgotten.

An attempt was made by Jack Williamson to shine a fresh spotlight on Breuer, when in 1949 the fellow science fiction author wrote to the administrator of Breuer's estate in Lincoln, that he would like to try to find a publisher to issue "a memorial volume containing [*Paradise and Iron*] and several of [Breuer's] short stories, perhaps an essay on him and his contributions to science fiction,"[317] albeit without success. Ultimately, Williamson also failed to publish as a standalone book their co-written novel *The Birth of a New Republic*, having been spurred to make such an attempt via a glowing letter from his good friend, the author Robert A. Heinlein.[318]

Breuer's short stories were thus never published in a single dedicated book. One reason is that prior to the 1950s, genre books were almost unheard of beyond the limited realms of science fiction fandom. Furthermore, no Breuer story was ever published in the highly influential pioneering science fiction anthologies which were collated at the turn of the 1940s and 50s by editor Donald A. Wollheim.[319] These anthologies found success far beyond the shores of the United States. And even though in

Reprint of The Birth of a New Republic was only published by a small publishing house in 1981.

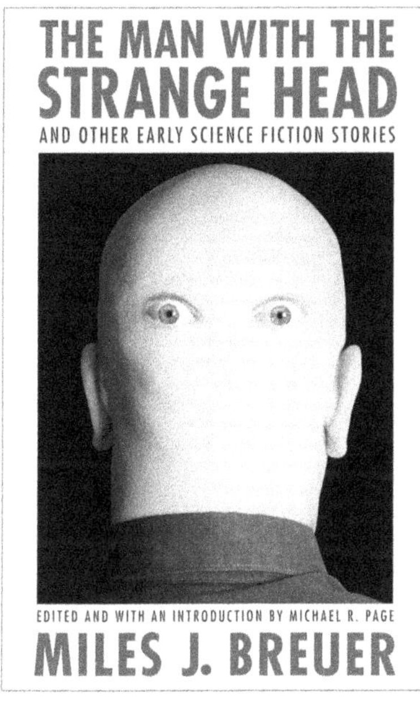
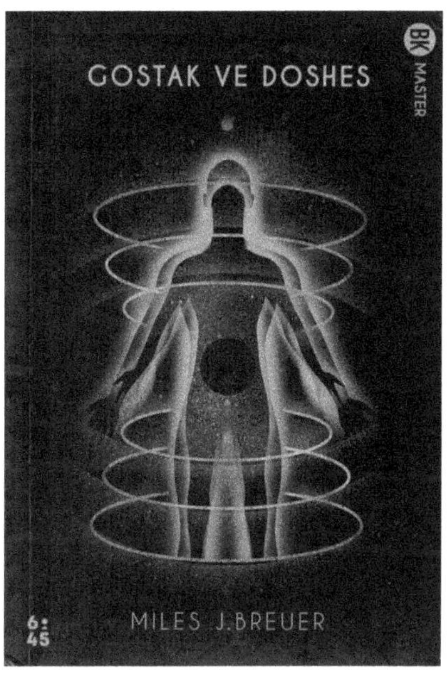

*Selections of Miles J. Breuer's short stories were published in English (2008),
and Turkish (2021).*

the subsequent decades Breuer's works regularly appeared in collections assembled by another early science fiction editor of the time, namely Groff Conklin,[320] Breuer himself remained a largely forgotten figure. None of the occasional reprints of his short stories led to any lasting resurgence of interest in the author. Meanwhile, old pulp magazines became fragile and gradually gathered dust in the hands of collectors, meaning that even locating and being able to freely read certain older stories became increasingly difficult over time.

But during the modern era, as pulp magazines have been properly archived and digitized, Breuer's stories have been re-evaluated by numerous science fiction editors around the globe. As a result, over the past decade or so, more than a dozen such stories have been translated into various languages and published. In 2021, the novel *The Birth of a New Republic* was translated into the Russian language, while Breuer's stories were published in Turkey in the same year under the title *Gostak ve Doshes* (The Gostak and the Doshes) – the first such collection of his works published in a foreign language.

In 2008, Nebraska-based science fiction historian Michael R. Page shone a fresh spotlight on Miles J. Breuer, publishing the first collection of his stories via the University of Nebraska Press, titled *The Man with the Strange Head and Other Early Science Fiction Stories*.[321] The book also included the first ever biography and bibliography of Breuer and his works. Page also discovered the correct date of the author's death – which had been the subject of some debate. While Nebraskan newspapers and also several Czech-language American periodicals carried obituaries shortly after the author's death at the end of 1945,[322] the wider American science fiction community only heard the news later, as evidenced by a brief mention of Breuer's passing in the fanzine *Fantasy Review* in 1947.[323] And yet, even as late as the early 2000s, some key science fiction encyclopaedias[324] erroneously listed Breuer's death as occurring in 1947.

In his book Michael R. Page specifically shone a spotlight on Miles J. Breuer's works from the era of science fiction pulp magazines. Page calculated that from the time of the publication of his story in *Amazing Stories* in 1927, Breuer "went on to publish thirty-six stories, two novels, three poems, two editorials, and numerous letters."[325] What was not included, however, in this tabulation was anything about Breuer's early literary career, and the initial publications of many of his later, better-known, science fiction stories. Moreover, Czech-language-writing of Miloslav J. Breuer and the respective wealth of works issued in Czech is also not mentioned. One reason may be that Page sourced an only semi-accurate biographical notice on the author's final English-language article from 1942, which states that Breuer "writes for publications in two languages: Czech and English. He conducts a health column in the largest Czech agricultural monthly in this country [*Hospodář*], and writes popular medical articles for many Czech periodicals." Crucially, no mention of any Czech-language fiction. The notice continued: "He has written a great deal of science fiction for magazines in English and is on the editorial board of *Social Science*."[326]

During the past five years, it has been possible to unearth numerous hitherto forgotten Breuer literary works. This has meant at least an additional 27 short stories[327] and 43 poems need to be added to his bibliography, as well as two articles on science fiction (both in English only) as well as four translations (two short stories and two poems) by diverse Czech authors to English.[328]

To date, only a relatively small proportion of Czech-American cultural and social magazines and other publications – both of the popular and academic or professional/trade varieties – have been digitized. Indeed, for many such publications, the question of even locating surviving copies has been a challenge in itself. All of this raises the likelihood that additional unknown Breuer stories will still come to light in the future. Which means, that drawing a line under a definitive bibliography of Miles J. Breuer, and giving these works their

Recent Czech-language books on Miles (Miloslav) J. Breuer.

rightful place among the pantheon of science fiction, is also not yet on the horizon.

In any event, the 2023 publication of the first Czech-language monograph on Breuer by the author of this text,[329] and the publication, eighteen months later, of a collection of all of Breuer's hitherto unearthed Czech-language prose published in the contemporary Czech-American press, titled *Osudný paprsek a další povídky raného česko-amerického spisovatele* (The Fatal Ray and Other Stories by Early Czech-American Writer, 2025)[330] represent just the beginning of a more complex study of the works of Miloslav J. Breuer. Accordingly, Breuer's place as a key figure in both Czech-American literature and Czech science fiction literature – and evidently the only one to regularly write in both English and Czech – will also have to wait.[331]

Los Angeles, January 2025

Notes

1   By the 1930s this term had already been largely supplemented with simply "science fiction".

2   In this text, the author deliberately mostly uses anglicised versions of names, as were being used at the time in the United States. The former Czech versions of such names are added in brackets, or are used as the dominant form when doing so is necessary for the understanding of the text.

3   Karel Bräuer (1842-?).

4   Most family-related information comes via a highly detailed Czech-language autobiography of Charles H. Breuer, which was serialised in the bi-weekly magazine *Hospodář* (Breuer K. 1940), as well as in a short Czech article (Anon. 1898), referencing other information from the period Czech-American press.

5   Breuer K. 1940:63.

6   August Geringer (1842–1930): the most successful publisher of Czech-language newspapers, magazines and books in the United States. From 1875, Geringer published the periodical *Svornost* in Chicago, which became the most influential Czech daily in America; that same year, he began publishing the weekly *Amerikán*, and in 1877 the first annual *Amerikán Národní Kalendář* (The American: a National Almanac) was published. He also published numerous Czech-language regional newspapers and magazines in the United States, as well as dozens of Czech-language books. Geringer's publishing house closed down in 1957. More on Geringer via Anon. 1926, Secká 2005, Jaklová 2010, Procházková – Kříž 2016 and others.

7   *Svornost*: the number-one Czech daily of its time in the United States, published by Geringer's publishing house in Chicago from 1875 to 1957.

8   Breuer K. 1940:163. Alas, Breuer made no mention of the authors of the translated texts in his memoirs, the first one in English is "The Missing Million." Literal translations of the others: "Mother and Son," "Number 99," and "Anarchist's Daughter."

9   Sokol (translated as "Falcon"): a Czech native gymnastic and cultural association founded in 1867 on the principles of the similar German "Turnverein." Popular among Czech compatriots all over the United States from the 1870s, with many branches surviving to this day. Played a significant role, pre-1918 Czechoslovak independence, in building Czech national identity, and in the battle against the subjugation of Czech aspirations within the Austro-Hungarian Empire.

10 Barbora Breuer, née Hullová (1864–1952).

11 Breuer K. 1940:276.

12 Breuer K. 1940:333.

13 *Chicagské Listy*: a competitor to the publications of August Geringer. Founded in 1882, changing owners and periodicity several times in the ensuing years, and finally shutting down in 1893.

14 Miles' younger sister Libbie Breuer (Libuše Anna Breuer), married name Scholten (1890–1978), also became a doctor, spending most of her life in California. Until the turn of the 1920s and 30s, promoted Czech literature and culture in Texas (for example, was an active member of the local Čechie club at the

University of Texas at Austin) and later in Nebraska (Komenský club at Omaha University); also worked at the Faculty of Slavonic Languages at the University of Nebraska. Translated into English numerous short stories and poems representing the crème of Czech literature from the turn of the 19th and 20th centuries (including works from authors Eliška Krásnohorská, Julius Zeyer, Karel Jaromír Erben, Vítězslav Hálek and Jan Neruda). Conversely, translated into Czech a number of Native American stories by US author Mary Catherine Judd, and also wrote several of her own works, published in numerous magazines.

15   Jan Rosický (1845–1910): one of the most noted Czech-American journalists; also published numerous noted Czech-American periodicals, for example the daily *Pokrok Západu* (American Progress), the magazine *Kwěty Americké* (American Blossoms) and the agricultural monthly/biweekly *Hospodář*. Also founded the Czech printing house, the National Printing Company in Omaha, Nebraska.

16   *Hospodář*: one of the most significant and longest-running Czech-American magazines. Founded in 1891 in Omaha, Nebraska as a publication intended primarily for farmers; but also covered numerous other subjects, including literature. Published mainly as a monthly and shut down in 2012.

17   *Pokrok Západu* (Western Progress): a noted weekly founded in Omaha in 1871, featured both news- and literature-related sections. Publication ceased in 1920.

18   Breuer K. 1940:389.

19   Breuer K. 1940:390.

20   Breuer K. 1940:445 writes that he started at the university in autumn 1893, although this may have in fact been a year earlier.

21   Roland Breuer (1894–1954) was a talented pianist ever since childhood, performing at numerous Czech cultural events in Nebraska and Texas. He also translated several Czech-language poems into English. Similarly to father Charles and brother Miles, he studied medicine and worked as a doctor, briefly in Nebraska, and then most of his life in California.

22   *Nový Domov*: a Catholic magazine, published weekly or bi-weekly, 1895–1970.

23   Senn Edwin Breuer (1899–1921).

24   Breuer K. 1940:494.

25   The text primarily uses the English name Miles J. Breuer, despite the author signing his Czech texts as "Miloslav J. Breuer." The Czech version of the name is used here only for the purposes of understanding the specific passage or within quotes.

26   *Amerikán* (Chicago, IL), 20 March 1895, No. 28, pg. 11, quote via Marholeva 2020:236.

27   Anon. 1939:114.

28   Breuer M. 1900:3.

29   Breuer M. 1901:3.

30   *David City News* (David City, NE), 10(1), 8 November 1900, pg. 4; *Butler County Press* (David City, NE), 27(100), 2 November 1900, pg. 3.

31   Anon. 1939:114.

32   Breuer K. 1940:540.

33   Anon. 1901:4.
34   Nor did he resist American patients; articles and advertisements were also published in English-language publications, for example via Anon. 1902:8, even including two photographs.
35   Anon. 1901:4.
36   Ibid.
37   Breuer K. 1940:540.
38   Anon. 1939:114.
39   Evidently, John (Jan) Hulla Jr., likely a relative of Barbara Breuer.
40   *Wilberské Listy* (Wilber, NE), 4(19), 11 October 1905, pg. 4.
41   *Wilberské Listy* (Wilber, NE), 4(50), 16 May 1906, pg. 4.
42   Anon 1939:114.
43   In a mere few years he moved and opened his practice, and/or pharmacy in a number of other cities in Texas, namely Taylor, Austin, Cameron, Waco, and Houston.
44   *Obzor* (Hallettsville, TX), 20(48), 29 June 1911, pg. 1.
45   *The University of Texas Magazine* began publishing in 1885. First published via a university literary association, then later – at the time of Breuer's studies – by a student association. In 1916 merged with university magazine *Longhorn*, which remains in publication till today.
46   After Miles J. Breuer departed for Galveston, younger sister Libbie Breuer, in the summer of 1912, herself embarked on work in the field of editing.
47   All three of these stories were reissued only via the Czech-American monthly *Bratrský Věstník*, with which Breuer later had a close working relationship.
48   Conklin – Fabricant 1963:14.
49   In their notes after a quote from a letter penned by Julia Breuer, the editors add: "And the same goes for us, too. Nothing with this title appears in any bibliography of Dr. Breuer's short stories, and consequently we are unable to provide it with an American magazine credit. If anyone knows of its previous appearance in the English language, the editors would appreciate being informed about it." Conklin – Fabricant 1963:14.
50   *10 Story Book* was published in Chicago from 1901 to 1940. The monthly magazine originally contained largely mediocre and sub-standard fare, the best of which were selected via a $1,000 prize-winning competition. The syndicated contents of the magazine were then offered to dailies across the United States. After 1919 it turned into a snappy and spicy girlie magazine known more for their photos than literary qualities.
51   Today, thanks to newspaper digitalization efforts, more than a dozen such reprints have been identified. And beyond doubt, as these efforts continue, more editions will be found.
52   The only identified comment in this respect relates to a mediocre offering titled "The Valley of Kazib," about which the unknown author notes: "It is like impressionistic art, either Supergood or Dambad. This is Dambad." *The Haverfordian* (Haverford, PA), 31(9), February 1910, pg. 229.
53   *San Antonio Express* (San Antonio, TX), 46, 4 May 1911, pg. 2
54   Čapek 1920:101.
55   Anon. 1939:115.

56   Míček 1932:177.

57   Edward Micek (Eduard Míček, 1891–1962): a noted representative of the Czech compatriot movement in Texas, also a professor of Slavic philology at the University of Texas. Published books in Czechoslovakia on US education system, as well as textbooks on Czech-language and culture in Texas.

58   These were a true elite of "Czech" Texas. Čechie's vice-president was Charles Chernosky, a future notable lawyer, county judge and president of the influential Slavonic Benevolent Order of the State of Texas; other members included Louis Mikeska, a future chemist and university teacher; Edward Krenek, a future farmer and teacher; and Josef Kopecky, a future doctor and university professor. More about them via Hudson – Maresh 1934.

59   Míček 1949:1.

60   More about the founding and history of Čechie via Hudson – Maresh 1934: 194–197 and Míček 1929, 1932, 1949.

61   *Obzor* (Hallettsville, TX), 19(7), 16 September 1909, pg. 1

62   More, for example, via Anon. 1911.

63   Breuer M. 1911:61.

64   Breuer M. 1911:60.

65   František Herites (1851–1929): in his day a noted Czech writer and editor, repeatedly visited the United States and was a popular figure among the Czech--American community there.

66   Alois Dostál (1858–1934): today a largely forgotten Czech Catholic priest and writer of short stories, novels and theatrical plays.

67   Vítězslav Hálek (1835–1874): noted Czech poet, writer and journalist, best known for his collection of lyrical poems *Večerní písně* (Evening Songs, 1859).

68   Svatopluk Čech (1846–1908): noted Czech writer, journalist, and poet, best known for his two satirical novels about ordinary Czech, Mr. Brouček, namely *Nový epochální výlet pana Broučka, tentokráte do XV. století* (The New Epochal Excursion of Mr. Brouček, this time to the 15th Century, 1888). Book--length poem *Písně otroka* (Songs of a Slave, 1895) is set in Africa, but it is an allegory of the subjugated Czech nation, it was meant to act as an encouragement to the oppressed, as a call to fight.

69   Breuerová 1917:41. At the start of 1909, Libbie Breuer published two dozen poems and short stories on the pages of the student magazine, as well as works translated from Czech into English.

70   *Obzor*: a Texas quarterly published between 1891–1914.

71   *Obzor* (Hallettsville, TX), 20(50), 13 July 1911, pg. 5 + 20(51), 20 July 1911, pg. 5.

72   *Bratrský Věstník*: monthly publication of Západní Česko-Bratrská Jednota (Western Bohemian Fraternal Association), important Czech-American insurance company, was published in Czech since 1898 first in Omaha, Nebraska, later on in Cedar Rapids, Iowa (though for many years the editor in chief resided in Omaha). During its final five decades it was published only as the English-language *Fraternal Herald* but still continued to promote Czech-American history and traditions. It ended its run in 2020.

73   F. Jaromír Pšenka (1875–1939): writer and journalist; editor of many of the most noted Czech-language periodicals published in Chicago by publisher Au-

gust Geringer, namely the almanac *Amerikán Národní Kalendář*. The most noted Czech author in America during the first half of the 20th century; his most celebrated Czech-American-themed work is a novel named after its protagonist, namely *Washington Závora* (1910).

74   A roughly 100,000 increase within a mere decade; according to census data, in 1910, only 531,193 Czech native speakers lived in the United States – per Čapek 1926:621.

75   Numbers according to Čapek 1911:53–56.

76   Breuer K. 1940:723.

77   *The Lincoln Star* (Lincoln, NE), 16, 18 August 1918, pg. 8. – Supplement *The Lincoln Sunday Star*.

78   Julia (Julie) Breuer, née Strejc (1891–1962).

79   Kopecky 2020: unpaginated.

80   Rosalie Eva Breuer, married name Neligh (1917–2003): during the 1930s served as the chairwoman of Komenský club at Omaha University. Studied medicine; after graduating, began working in neighbouring Iowa; spent her final years in Colorado.

81   Stanley Breuer (1921–1939): tragically died during his first year at university while on a mountain-climbing trip.

82   Mildred Renee Breuer, married name Dale (1926–1983); also studied medicine in Nebraska; pediatrician, from the 1950s ran a medical practice in Los Angeles.

83   Stanley Serpan (Stanislav Šerpán) (1887–1940): arrived in America in 1900. From 1905, a secretary and close collaborator to publisher Jan Rosický (note 15), also writing in his weekly *Osvěta Americká* (American Enlightenment) as well as for numerous other Czech-American periodicals. After his death in 1910, Serpan took over Rosický's post, also becoming the head of the business section of the monthly *Hospodář*, operating a bookstore with imported Czech publications and published numerous titles. At the same time, worked as a notary and continued working for a transportation company also founded by Rosický. From 1912 up to his death, Serpan ran the *Bratrský Věstník* monthly (which was, albeit published in Cedar Rapids, Iowa). From 1920, also served as a Czechoslovak consul based in Omaha, Nebraska; from 1925, up to his resignation in 1931, served as honorary consul. More on Serpan in a hitherto unpublished work by Olša, Jr. (rkp).

84   The only Czech language story which has been referenced in overviews of Breuer's science fiction bibliographies (such as isfdb.org) thanks to the English-language anthology *Great Science Fiction About Doctors*, which is supplemented with quotes from letters by his former wife: "It was first published in the Czech language in *Bratrsky Věstník* [in Czech] *in about 1916*" (Conklin – Fabricant 1963:14).

85   The first two were published under the same name, i.e.: "The Stone Cat" (1927) and "The Hungry Guinea-Pig" (1930), with "Případ učené hlavy" published as "The Inferiority Complex" (1930).

86   One other similar story was published in 1924, namely "Vyléčená rakovina" (Cured Cancer) via the Chicago-based magazine *Duch Času* (Spirit of the Times).

87   Not science fiction, or even a fantasy tale, it was nonetheless published in 1928 as "The Puzzle Duel" in Gernsback's *Amazing Stories Quarterly*.

88   Czech-language American periodicals published a number of Breuer's letters from France, for example Breuer M. 1918a, Breuer M. 1918b. Page 2008:XIV also notes that the archives of the Nebraska State Historical Society hold a small collection of Breuer's wartime photographs.

89   More on the hospital via Beachly 1919.

90   "Dva franky za hodinu" was published right after the war's end in the renowned *Amerikán Národní Kalendář* almanac for the year 1920; a decade later it was published in English under the title "An Instructor in French" within the pages of *Bratrský Věstník*.

91   *Weird Tales*: an American pulp magazine, which, from 1923–54, published works spanning the entire range of fantastic fiction – from science fiction, to fantasy, to horror. Among its most famous published authors are H. P. Lovecraft and Robert E. Howard.

92   Michael Ashley – private email January 2025.

93   Greer 1921:4.

94   One similar work titled "A Medical Utopia" (Reed 1916) had already been published in this, evidently authored by the noted Californian doctor from Santa Monica, Edward N. Reed (1877?–1948). The publication of this story may have been the result of an impulsive act by Breuer to submit his fiction to an academic magazine.

95   "Osudný paprsek" is the only one of Breuer's Czech-language works to have been illustrated. Of a total of four illustrations, only the most interesting, presenting the town of Lincoln in the future, is signed "B. Butler," which could mean that its author was the American illustrator Bud Butler (Alban B. Butler Jr.). Why *Amerikán Národní Kalendář* almanac would turn to an American illustrator remains unclear, as is the question of whether this could be a reprint from an American publication where the story was first issued; if so, such a publication has yet to be identified.

96   *Social Science*: magazine published by Pi Gamma Mu (ПГМ), the oldest honour society in the social sciences in the United States since 1926, now known as *International Social Science Review*.

97   Breuer M. 1926a:153–154.

98   Anon. 1939:114.

99   Breuer M. 1926a:172.

100   Breuer M. 1926a:178.

101   Breuer M. 1926a:174.

102   Breuer M. 1926a:172.

103   Breuer M. 1926a:174.

104   Ibid.

105   Alas, Breuer never used the word "robot" in his writings, despite, as an avid reader of Czech literature, almost certainly being familiar with the play *R. U. R. Rossum's Universal Robots*, in which the Czech author Karel Čapek used the word (invented by his brother Josef Čapek) for the first time. More on the devising of the word "robot" via Veis 2021.

106   Breuer M. 1926:278. The Czech text from 1924 and the English text from 1926

are essentially identical; thus, the quotes stem from the English published version.

107   Ibid.
108   Breuer M. 1926:279.
109   Breuer M. 1926:278.
110   Breuer M. 1926:282.
111   Breuer M. 1926:290.
112   Ibid.
113   Breuer M. 1926:291.
114   Ibid.
115   Ibid.
116   Breuer M. 1926:292.
117   Breuer M. 1926:295
118   Ibid.
119   Braun 2019.
120   Breuer M. 1926:289.
121   Ibid.
122   Breuer M. 1926:277.
123   Breuer M. 1930:304.
124   Since 2021, autonomous vehicles produced by Waymo are licensed to operate as taxis in Phoenix, AZ; since 2023, in San Francisco, CA; since 2024, in Los Angeles, CA, and Austin, TX.
125   Breuer M. 1930:304.
126   Breuer M. 1930:324.
127   Breuer M. 1926:290.
128   Braun 2019.
129   Breuer M. 1931:139.
130   Breuer M. 1931:134.
131   Breuer M. 1931:143.
132   Breuer M. 1931:147.
133   Charles IV. (1316–1378): Bohemian King and Roman Emperor. Viewed by modern Czechs as one of key figures of Czech history; adherents view the period of his reign as the period of the greatest development of the Czech lands during the Middle Ages.
134   Jan Žižka (ca. 1360–1424): successful Czech general who was a contemporary and follower of the protestant reformist Jan Hus. Widely viewed as the most celebrated Czech military commander, though also the military leader of the Hussite movement which economically destroyed the Czech lands
135   Breuer M. 1931:136.
136   Breuer M. 1931:144.
137   Ibid.
138   Breuer M. 1931:145.
139   Breuer M. 1931:147.
140   Breuer M. 1931:146.
141   Breuer M. 1931:135.
142   Breuer M. 1931:144.
143   Breuer M. 1931:139.

144 Breuer M. 1931:149.

145 "The Fatal Ray" was also published in *The American Journal of Clinical Medicine*.

146 Gernsback 1926b:3.

147 *Science and Invention*: US monthly popular-science magazine published from 1913–31. Originally published as *The Electrical Experimenter*. For most of its existence its editor was Hugo Gernsback.

148 Howard Phillips Lovecraft (1890–1937): US author of science fiction, fantasy and horror, best known for his creation of the Cthulhu Mythos fictionalized mythology.

149 Gernsback 1926a:773.

150 Ashley 2004:103.

151 David H. Keller (1880–1966): US author, physician and psychiatrist; one of the most influential science fiction writers of the early pulp era. Published most of his output in magazines edited by Hugo Gernsback.

152 Ashley 2004:86.

153 Michael Ashley (b. 1948): British editor and researcher best known for his works on the history of science fiction magazines (originally in four volumes from 1974–78, with a fully updated and expanded version published since 2000).

154 Alpheus Hyatt Verrill (1871–1954): US naturalist, explorer and author of numerous youth and adventure science fiction mainly in the 1920s.

155 Edmond Hamilton (1904–1977): US author, influential early science fiction writer best known for his space operas.

156 More in the chapter "Mentor Breuer and His Apprentice Williamson".

157 S. P. Meek (1894–1972): US army officer and early science fiction writer active in pulp magazines in the 1930s.

158 Harl Vincent (pen-name of Harold Vincent Schoepflin, 1893–1968): popular US author, who published in pulp science fiction magazines from the beginning of the 20th century through to middle of the Second World War.

159 Walter Gillings (1912–1979): influential British science fiction editor, publisher of early fanzine *Scientifiction* (1937–1938), the first UK science fiction magazine *Tales of Wonder* (1937–1942), and various other periodicals and series.

160 Quote via Swartz 2017:9.

161 Breuer took an interest in the future of medicine, both as a writer and also as a practitioner himself – as is evident, for example, in his article "The Doctor Peeps into the Future" (Breuer 1930b).

162 T. O'Conor Sloane (1851–1940): US inventor, writer and editor. Editor of *Scientific American* from 1886–96. Later a close collaborator of Hugo Gernsback; after his forced departure from *Amazing Stories* in 1929, headed the magazine until 1938.

163 Another twenty names were listed after Keller and Breuer.

164 Sloane 1929:103.

165 Ibid.

166 *Science Wonder Stories*: US pulp science fiction magazine, published by Hugo Gernsback from 1929–30; subsequently, until 1936, went under the shortened name *Wonder Stories*. Initially a sister publication *Science Wonder Quarterly* was also published.

167   *Air Wonder Stories:* US pulp magazine edited by Hugo Gernsback published from 1929–30.

168   The subsequent sequel, "The Time Valve" sees our Lunar travellers visiting present-day Chicago.

169   Robert Silverberg (b. 1935): one of the most significant and prolific US science fiction authors. His most significant works include the series *Majipoor* (1980–2001) and *Gilgamesh* (1984–9), as well as the novels *Thorns* (1967) and *Dying Inside* (1972).

170   A comment in a debate on the FictionMags website, dated 2 May 2008.

171   Ashley 2004:158.

172   *Astounding Stories of Super–Science*: US pulp magazine, which began publication in 1930; changed its name several times over the ensuing three decades, and since 1960 going under the name *Analog*.

173   William Clayton (1884–1946): London-born US pulp magazine publisher.

174   The Czech and English versions of the story are essentially identical.

175   Breuer 1930d:346.

176   Breuer 1930d:347.

177   Breuer 1930d:346.

178   Breuer 1930d:347.

179   Breuer 1926:294.

180   Breuer 1926:295.

181   It is worth noting that in any version of these Breuer stories the word 'robot' never appears, though – by this time – the word 'robot' was already common in the pages of *Amazing Stories*, as attested to by the fact that it was used by the anonymous author of the *Paradise and Iron* lead paragraph. We will never learn why Breuer never used the word 'robot' as it is likely that he would have been aware of Karel Čapek's (1890–1938) famous play, *R. U. R. Rossum's Universal Robots* (1921).

182   Breuer 1930d:401.

183   Ibid.

184   Breuer 1930c:1147.

185   Page 2008:XXV.

186   Clare Winger Harris (1891–1968): US writer active in various pulp magazines since the early 1920s and 1930s, often dubbed as the first female science fiction writer. Frequently, her main characters are strong women.

187   Ashley 2004:90.

188   Williamson 1983:14.

189   Gernsback 1926b:3.

190   Jack Barnette: US author of two stories for pulp science fiction magazines, little is known about him other than that he lived in Baltimore.

191   *Amazing Stories* (New York, NY), 4(6), September 1929, pg. 570.

192   *Amazing Stories* (New York, NY), 4(8), November 1929, pg. 759–760.

193   *Amazing Stories* (New York, NY), 4(11), February 1930, pg. 1093.

194   Page 2008:XXII.

195   Breuer 1929.

196 Breuer 1929:291.
197 Williamson 1928.
198 Page 2008:XVII.
199 Ibid.
203 G. Peyton Wertenbaker (1907–1968): US writer, one of the 'pioneers of science fiction,' published in Hugo Gernsback's pulp magazines since the early 1920s to early 1930s.
201 Breuer M. 1930e:86.
202 Ibid.
203 Breuer M. 1930e:86–87.
204 *Amazing Stories* (New York, NY), 3(4), July 1928, pg. 370.
205 Ibid.
206 *Cosmos*: the first science fiction fanzine, soon renamed to *Cosmology*, with 17 issues published from 1930–32.
207 Williamson 2005:61.
208 Williamson 1981:5–6.
209 Ibid.
210 Sheridan 1949–50:7.
211 Ackerman 1933.
212 The former name may perhaps have been fitting for the magazine, but was likely deemed too long for a standalone book.
213 Williamson 1981:7.
214 Ibid.
215 Ibid.
216 Williamson 1981:6.
217 Leo Morrey (1889–1965): US illustrator of Peruvian origin, one of the most visible authors of science fiction pulp magazines covers in the 1930s, active in the genre until the early 1960s.
218 H. M. Wesso (pen-name of Hans Waldemar Wessolowski, 1894–1948): US illustrator of German origin, prolific author of b/w interior illustrations of the 1930s science fiction pulp magazines.
219 Lowndes 2004:321.
220 Robert A. Heinlein (1907–1988): one of the most noted science fiction authors of the 1940s–70s. Authored more than forty novels, including *Starship Troopers* (1959), *Stranger in a Strange Land* (1961) and *The Moon Is a Harsh Mistress* (1966).
221 Williamson 1981:7.
222 Ferber 2021.
223 Abraham Merritt (1884–1943): US editor and noted author of adventure literature that bordered science fiction and fantasy; wrote his first genre story in 1917.
224 Williamson 1981:9.
225 Breuer 1932a:141.
226 Breuer 1932b:147.
227 Breuer 1932a:143.
228 Daniel Keyes (1927–2014): US science fiction writer and editor, best known

for short story "Flowers for Algernon" (1959), expanded into a novel of the same title (1966), and filmed for the screen as *Charly* (1968).

229 Everett F. Bleiler (1920–2010): noted US editor, bibliographer and historian of science fiction; his most significant work on early science fiction is *Science-Fiction: The Gernsback Years: A Complete Coverage of the Genre Magazines Amazing, Astounding, Wonder, and Others from 1926 Through 1936* (2008).

230 Bleiler 1998:35.

231 Darrell Schweitzer (b. 1952): US writer, editor and critic of science fiction and fantasy.

232 *Comet Stories of Super Time and Space*: pulp science fiction magazine, with five issues published from 1940–41.

233 *Future Fiction*: pulp science fiction magazine; 17 issues published from 1939–43. Later revived from 1950–60.

234 *Marvel Tales*: science fiction semiprozine, five issues with limited distribution were published from 1934–35.

235 *Unusual Stories*: sister magazine to *Marvel Tales*, with only three issues published 1934–35.

236 *Science Fiction Digest*: noted early fanzine founded in 1932; from 1934–37 published as *Fantasy Magazine*.

237 Ultimately the collaborative novel was co-authored by 17 authors including many current or future science fiction top names such as David H. Keller, Otis Adelbert Kline, John W. Campbell, Raymond A. Palmer, Abraham Merritt, Edward E. Smith, P. Schuyler Miller, and Edmond Hamilton.

238 Quote via the website cosmos-serial.com

239 Page 2008:XVI.

240 Ibid.

241 Page 2008:XIV.

242 The article "Amatérská fotografie ve Spojených státech" (Amateur Photography in the United States) (Breuer 1930a) seems to be Breuer's only text published in interwar Czechoslovakia.

243 *Národní Pokrok* (Omaha, NE), 14(36), 29 March 1935, pg. 7.

244 *Bratrský Věstník* (Cedar Rapids, IA), 32(8), August 1929, pg. 339.

245 Page 2008:XV.

246 Breuer M. 1931:134.

247 Breuer M. 1931:135.

248 Ibid.

249 Page 2008:XVI.

250 Ibid.

251 Ashley 2005:62.

252 Ibid.

253 *Amazing Stories* (New York, NY), 5(10), January 1930, pg. 952.

254 Ibid.

255 Ashley 2008:64.

256 Breuer M. 1937:5.

257 Ibid.

258 Williamson 1981:9.

259 Ibid.
260 Ashley 2008:63.
261 The book was initially set for publication at the start of the 1940s, but was delayed until 1947 as a result of the outbreak of the Second World War.
262 J. O. Bailey (1903–1979): American literary scholar who authored the first academic book on science fiction. His studies did not cover the emerging science fiction fandom, nor pulp magazines and fanzines, and thus only a small amount of the book's subject matter examines these areas.
263 *Fantasy Review*: noted British science fiction semiprozine published from 1947–1950.
264 A. Langley Searles (1920–2009): American publisher of the influential non-fiction fanzine *Fantasy Commentator* which focused mainly on early science fiction.
265 Forrest J. Ackerman (1916–2008): arguably the most famous 'science fiction fan' of all times, the creator of the term 'sci-fi', and an avid collector and editor. Famed as the editor of science fiction, horror and fantasy film magazine *Famous Monsters of Filmland*, published from 1958–1983.
266 Gillings 1947:9.
267 Quote via First Fandom Experience.org. See also Page 2008:XXXIII.
268 *Hospodář* (Omaha, NE), 45(8), 20 April 1935, pg. 61.
269 Ibid.
270 Williamson 1981:9.
271 Breuer M. 1938b.
272 Kopecky 2020:unpaginated.
273 Breuer's third wife's name might by Ruby: Christine Dale – private email January 2025.
274 Breuer M. 1939b.
275 Page 2008:XXXIII.
276 *Národní Pokrok* (Omaha, NE), 21(10), 19 September 1941, pg. 8.
277 The Los Angeles Science Fantasy Society (LASFS): founded 27 October 1934, the world's oldest continuously active science fiction and fantasy club.
278 Hájek 1945:4.
279 *Čechoslovák and Westské Noviny* (West, TX), 36(1), 3 January 1947, pg. 8.
280 *Bratrský Věstník* (Cedar Rapids, IA), 55(4), April 1952, pg. 127.
281 Sheridan 1949–50:7.
282 Ibid.
283 Burnett Toskey (b. 1929): noted science fiction fan, and the editor of the celebrated *Cry of the Nameless* fanzine.
284 Toskey 1956:14.
285 Patterson 2014:17.
286 For the Czech press in the United States, see, for example, Čapek 1911 (covering period until 1910), Formanová – Gruntorád – Přibáň 1999 (period after 1945), Jaklová 2010.
287 Papoušek 2001a:24.
288 Tomáš Čapek (Thomas Capek, 1861–1950): US banker of Czech origin, author of numerous books on Czech-American history. His monograph *Naše Amerika* (Our America, 1926) is a substantive and well-researched book on history of

the Czechs in the United States. Less thorough is his earlier English-language monograph *The Čechs (Bohemians) in America: A Study of Their National, Cultural, Political, Social, Economic and Religious Life* (1920).

289 Čapek 1911:67.

290 Vladimír Papoušek (b. 1957): Czech literary scientist and the author of dozens of books on Czech literature; head of the Czech Studies Institute at the South Bohemian University in České Budějovice.

291 Several additional shorter texts were also issued by different authors, for example Sturm 1978, and Machann 1979. The objectively poor quality of Czech literature in America was itself covered by numerous contemporary publications. Numerous works can also be found on Czech journalists in America.

292 Papoušek 2001a:18.

293 Papoušek 2001a:19.

294 Pavel Albieri (real name Jan Mucek, 1861–1901): Czech author and journalist; penned numerous literary works, with some of these taking place in the United States. Also authored several travelogues covering his travels across America.

295 Jan Havlasa (real name Jan Klecanda, 1883–1964): a prolific and successful author of travelogues, novels and short story collections. Penned more than fifty books, published in large print runs in interwar Czechoslovakia. Lived in the United States prior to the First World War, after the war appointed Czechoslovak Envoy to Brazil. Worked for the League of Nations, and was again named Czechoslovak Envoy during the Second World War, this time to Chile. Spent the final decades of his life in Los Angeles once again – in both cases publishing his writing in the local Czech-language presses. During the 1950s, published several books in the United States. Despite being better known for his novels and short stories set in Japan and Polynesia, Havlasa authored more than a dozen books set in North America, in particular in California and Arizona. Numerous Czech-language works have been authored about the author's life and works; but in the United States, he is practically unknown today.

296 See note 73.

297 Papoušek 2001a:26.

298 Clara Vostrovsky Winlow (1871–1963): US author born of Czech parents, whose debut youth-oriented novel was titled *Barbora: A Little Bohemian Cousin* (1911). Subsequently wrote more than a dozen similar works; also worked as a translator from Czech and Russian into English. Viz Olša, Jr. 2022.

299 Papoušek 2001a:26.

300 Anon. 1945a:446.

301 "Mister Shephard creates air-carriers. In your day, these were referred to as airplanes." (Breuer 1922:103).

302 This author managed to obtain manuscripts from the archive of Breuer's relatives of four subsequently published and well-known works, namely, "Osudný paprsek", "Případ učené hlavy", "Vyléčená rakovina" and "Háček v předpovědi" (original manuscript title: "Háček v návěsti"), as well as the hitherto unknown non-genre story "Klukovské hlouposti" (Boyhood Follies).

303 Šašková-Pierce 1993:213.

304 Anon. 1939:114.

305 Ibid.

306 *Národní Pokrok* (Omaha, NE), 8(15), 9 November 1928, pg. 7.

307 Machann 1979:33.

308 Papoušek 2001a:97.

309 Breuer M. 1938a.

310 Breuer M. 1925a.

311 "Translated and revised from the Chicago Daily Svornost of June 23, 1923." (Breuer M. 1925a:16).

312 Translated into English by Carleton Bulkin as "A Contrivance of Life" and published in Spanish English-language science fiction magazine *Helice* in 2023.

313 Jerabek 1976.

314 Rechcígl 2016:979.

315 For example in Machann – Mendl 1991:130.

316 Page 2008:XXIII.

317 Letter by Jack Williamson to J. L. McMaster dated 2 April 1949. Quote after Page 2008:XXIII.

318 Patterson 2014:17.

319 Donald A. Wollheim (1914–1990): one of the most active US fans in the early science fiction era; subsequently an author himself, but primarily an editor and publisher, who enjoyed a position of great influence on the development of the genre for more than half a century.

320 Groff Conklin (1904–1968): noted US editor, whose genre anthologies, starting with *The Best of Science Fiction* (1946), were the first of their kind directed at the wider public.

321 Page 2008.

322 Among others Hájek 1945:4.

323 *Fantasy Review* (London), 1(2), 1947, pg. 5.

324 Tuck 1974:66, Gunn 1988:65, Clute – Nicholls 1993:157 etc.

325 Page 2008:XIII.

326 Breuer M. 1942:273.

327 It is certain that other Breuer stories remain to be re-discovered. For example, in a letter to *Amazing Stories*, dated July 1928, Breuer notes that he was also the author of the (today lost) short story "A Little Here Below." Moreover, Breuer's descendants own the manuscripts of the following unknown English-language short stories: "The Blood of a Child," and "The Typhoid Murders," which may or may not have been published in the past.

328 Hitherto 114 literary works by Miles J. Breuer have been published and catalogued.
Exclusively in English: 2 novels, 46 short stories, 45 poems.
Exclusively in Czech: 6 short stories, 1 poem.
In both languages: 11 short stories.
In total, 11 of the short stories listed above have been issued in at least two significantly reworked versions.

329 Jaroslav Olša, Jr.: *Miloslav (Miles) J. Breuer: Česko-americký spisovatel u zrodu moderní science* fiction (Miles /Miloslav/ J. Breuer: Czech-American Writer at the Birth of Modern Science Fiction). Prague: Nová vlna, 2023.

330 Hlous – Olša, Jr. – Rampas – Rampasová 2025.

331 A rediscovery of Miloslav J. Breuer by the world of Czech literature was the subject of a short presentation by Jaroslav Olša, Jr on the occasion of the science fiction convention Minicon in Prague in autumn 2019 and a subsequent article in the Czech science fiction magazine *XB-1* (Olša, jr. 2020), which accompanied the first Czech-language translation of perhaps Breuer's most famous story, "The Gostak and the Doshes" (Breuer 2020). This was followed by an exhibition about Breuer's life and works (along with an accompanying booklet – Olša, Jr. 2020), at the Front Gallery of the Consulate General of the Czech Republic in Los Angeles (October 2021 to March 2022); at Loscon 48 (Los Angeles, November 2022); at the American Centre in Prague (February-March 2023), and in Ostrava (autumn 2023); and as part of the North American Science Fiction Convention Pemmi-Con (Winnipeg, July 2023). In addition, several presentations were given on the subject, for example for the Los Angeles Science Fantasy Society (2021), at Loscon 48 (November 2021) and for the Společnost pro vědy a umění (the Czechoslovak Society of Arts and Sciences) in New York (February 2024).

Fiction and Poetry
by Miles / Miloslav[1] J. Breuer:
Preliminary Bibliography

This bibliography contains all (as yet discovered) published fiction and poetry written by Miloslav / Miles J. Breuer. It is arranged chronologically by first edition regardless of the language in which it was first published. If a short story has been substantially revised or expanded, it is listed as a new bibliographic entry (the note indicates the previous or subsequent edition). On the other hand, if the story has been published in both Czech and English and it is practically the same text only in a different language, it is listed as a single bibliographic entry.

In the case of publications reprinted after 1945, the author has relied primarily on commonly available publications on science fiction (encyclopedias, bibliographies), or The Internet Speculative Fiction Database (isfdb.org), where data on reprints of Breuer's original works have not been further verified. On the other hand, for newly discovered early publications (whether published in Czech or English), the author tried to verify the edition according to the original edition; if this was not possible and the bibliographic reference is based only on secondary source, it is mentioned in the footnote.

Although this bibliography also includes unknown works written by Breuer in English, the biggest bibliographical gaps are in the list of his works published in Czech-language periodicals in the United States. In the first two decades of the twentieth century, the peak period of the Czech press in the United States, no fewer than nine daily newspapers, forty-three weeklies, six fortnightly newspapers, and thirty-one monthly magazines were published in Czech in this country, and there were also thirty very popular calendars, almanacs, and other yearbooks. Because fiction and poetry was published not only in a few literary or, more often, widely distributed cultural and entertainment magazines, but also in specialized journals, which often had their own literary columns, it is difficult, if not impossible, to trace all of Miloslav J. Breuer's literary works. Although a larger number of Czech titles from the United States have been digitized in recent years, both in the Czech Republic and in the United States, this is still only a fraction of the total production. Thus, not even important periodicals are available to historians in digital formats. Additionally, a significant number of journals are not available at all, because the

---

1 With no exception all English-language texts were published under the name Miles, all Czech-language text as Miloslav.

surviving volumes of Czech-American periodicals are severely incomplete in both Czech and American libraries.

It is therefore certain that many of Miloslav J. Breuer's hitherto unknown short stories are yet to be discovered, and it is almost certain that many of the stories which, according to this bibliography, were first published in Amazing Stories will also have an early Czech (and perhaps even English) versions. At the same time, it cannot be ruled out that thanks to the additional stories discovered published in Czech, it will be possible to resolve the dispute whether Breuer was also the author of the six "medical" science fiction stories set in the near future, published in *Amazing Stories* under the pen-name W. Alexander, which we do not present here.

Bibliographic information on translations are based on information available in bibliographies from various countries and – with a few exceptions – have not been verified.

Fiction

1908
"The Night and the Demon Fear." *The University of Texas Magazine* (Austin, TX), 23(6), March 1908, pg. 277–282.

"The Power of Darkness."[2] *The University of Texas Magazine* (Austin, TX), 23(8), May 1908, pg. 415–420.

1909
"The Dumb Man." *The University of Texas Magazine* (Austin, TX), 24(4), January 1909, pg. 208–211.

"The Adventures of the Bronze Mahadeva." *10 Story Book* (Chicago, IL), 8(11), April 1909.[3]
   Repr. *Daily Star-Journal* (Warrensburg, MO), 13 March 1909, pg. 2.
   Repr. *Mexico Evening Ledger* (Mexico, MO), 22(96), 17 March 1909, pg. 3.
   Repr. *The Millerton Progress* (Millerton, OK), 4(14), 18 March 1909, pg. 5.
   Repr. *Beloit Daily Gazette–Times* (Beloit, KS), 2, 19 March 1909, pg. 2.
   Repr. *The Checotah Times* (Checotah, OK), 8(?), 19 March 1909, pg. 6.
   Repr. *The Huttig News* (Huttig, AR), 2(47), 20 March 1909, pg. 3.
   Repr. *The Fairbury Blade* (Fairbury, IL), 38/49), 14 May 1909, pg. 8.
   Repr. *The Reveille–New Era* (Hill City, KS), 4, 22 April 1909, pg. 4.

2 Rewritten as "The Unknown Hand at Gergy" (1931).
3 Not seen – mentioned in *Brenham Evening Press* (Brenham, TX), 15(253), 19 March 1909, pg. 1. All the following reprints were syndicated by the publisher of *10 Story Book*.

Repr. *Battle Creek Enquirer* (Battle Creek, MI), 17(110), 24 April 1909, pg. 3.

Repr. *The Pomona Republican* (Pomona, KS), 12, 29 April 1909, pg. 4.

Repr. *McKean Country Miner* (Smethport, PA), 46(23), 17 June 1909, pg. 7.

Repr. *The Daily Register* (Red Bank, NJ), 32, 6 October 1909, pg. 6. – author uncredited.

Repr. *The Jessamine Journal* (Nicholasville, KY), 36(41), 8 October 1909, pg. 4.

Repr. *The Huttig News* (Huttig, AR), 3(41), 5 February 1910, pg. 3.

Repr. *The Celina Democrat* (Celina, OH), 16(15), 28 July 1911, pg. 8.

Repr. *The Post–Crescent* (Appleton, WI), 5 June 1912, pg. 4.

Repr. *The Merrill Daily Herald* (Merrill, WI), 3 February 1913.

Repr. *Farmer City Journal* (Farmer City, IL), 47, 5 October 1917, pg. 7.

Repr. *Daily Review Atlas* (Monmouth, IL), 66(177), 30 July 1921, pg. 6.

"The Stone Cat."[4] *The University of Texas Magazine* (Austin, TX), 24, Commencement Number, 1909, pg. 391–402.

  – (Czech)[5] as "Kamenná kočka." *Bratrský Věstník* (Cedar Rapids, IA), 19(9), September 1916, pg. 273–274. + 19(10), October 1916, pg. 297–298, 301.

  Repr. In: *Osudný paprsek a další povídky raného česko-amerického spisovatele*. Ed. František Hlous – Jaroslav Olša, Jr. – Zdeněk Rampas – Michaela Rampasová. Praha: Nová vlna 2024, pg. 6–15.

"The Face in the Air." *The University of Texas Magazine* (Austin, TX), 25(2), November 1909, pg. 112–122.

"An Appology for Grinds." *The University of Texas Magazine* (Austin, TX), 25(3), December 1909, pg. 134–139.

1910

"The Valley of Kazib." *The University of Texas Magazine* (Austin, TX), 25(4), January 1910, pg. 212–217.

"The Flaw in the Premise."[6] *The University of Texas Magazine* (Austin, TX), 25(5), February 1910, pg. 272–277.

"The Man Without an Appetite."[7] *The University of Texas Magazine* (Austin, TX), 25(6), March 1910, pg. 354–362.

"The Power of What Is Beyond." *The University of Texas Magazine* (Austin, TX), 25(7), April 1910, pg. 371–382.

---

4   Rewritten under the same title and published in 1927.
5   Czech edition is slightly edited and localized for the Czech-American reader.
6   Rewritten text published in Czech as "Háček v předpovědi" (1935).
7   Rewritten text published in Czech as "Člověk bez hladu" (1916).

"The Ghost of the Big Hussar." *The University of Texas Magazine* (Austin, TX), 25(8), May 1910, pg. 447–458.

"The Will and the Way." *The University of Texas Magazine* (Austin, TX), 26(2), November 1910, pg. 55–64.
- (Czech)[8] as "Vůle a cesta." *Bratrský Věstník* (Cedar Rapids, IA), 23(3), March 1920, pg. 75–77.
  Repr. In: *Osudný paprsek a další povídky raného česko-amerického spisovatele*. Ed. František Hlous – Jaroslav Olša, Jr. – Zdeněk Rampas – Michaela Rampasová. Praha: Nová vlna 2025, pg. 25–32.

1911

"An Age of the Seven." *The University of Texas Magazine* (Austin, TX), 26(4), January 1911, pg. 135–142.

"The Rift In The Hedge." *The University of Texas Magazine* (Austin, TX), 26(7), April 1911, pg. 310–317.

"The Yellow Dwarf." *The University of Texas Magazine* (Austin, TX), 26(8), May 1911, pg. 358–366.

"Sestřička. Arabeska z texaského života" (Little Sister. Arabesque from the Texan Life). *Obzor* (Hallettsville, TX), 20(50), 13 July 1911, pg. 5 + 20(51), 20 July 1911, pg. 5.
  Repr. In: *Osudný paprsek a další povídky raného česko-amerického spisovatele*. Ed. František Hlous – Jaroslav Olša, Jr. – Zdeněk Rampas – Michaela Rampasová. Praha: Nová vlna 2025, pg. 172–181.

1912

"He That Seeketh." *The University of Texas Magazine* (Austin, TX), 27(5), February 1912, pg. 183–189.

"The Three Princesses. A Fairy Tale for Grown Folks." *The University of Texas Magazine* (Austin, TX), 27(6), March 1912, pg. 229–239.

1916

"Člověk bez hladu."[9] *Bratrský Věstník* (Cedar Rapids, IA), 19(7), July 1916, pg. 213–215 + 19(8), August 1916, pg. 235–236.
  Repr. In: Olša, Jr., J.: *Miloslav (Miles) J. Breuer: Česko-americký spisovatel u zrodu moderní science fiction*. Praha: Nová vlna 2023, pg. 85–93.
  Repr. In: *Osudný paprsek a další povídky raného česko-amerického spisovatele*.

---

8 Czech edition is slightly edited and localized for the Czech-American reader.
9 Czech edition is rewritten version of the 1910 English text.

Ed. František Hlous – Jaroslav Olša, Jr. – Zdeněk Rampas – Michaela
Rampasová. Praha: Nová vlna 2025, pg. 16–24.

   – (English) "The Man Without an Appetite."[10] In: *Great Science Fiction About
   Doctors*. Ed. Noah D. Fabricant – Groff Conklin. New York: Collier Books
   1963, pg. 15–28.

   – Trans. (Spanish) as "El hombre sin apetito." Tr. by B. Samarbete. *Nueva
   Dimensión* (Barcelona, Spain), 1971, 21, pg. 73–82.

1917

"Hladové morče"[11] (The Hungry Guinea-Pig). *Bratrský Věstník* (Cedar Rapids, IA),
   20(7), July 1917, pg. 194–195 + 20(8), srpen 1917, pg. 240–241.
   Repr. In: *Osudný paprsek a další povídky raného česko-amerického spisovatele*.
   Ed. František Hlous – Jaroslav Olša, Jr. – Zdeněk Rampas – Michaela
   Rampasová. Praha: Nová vlna 2025, pg. 33–41.

"U radiografa" (Visiting a Radiographer). *Bratrský Věstník* (Cedar Rapids, IA),
   20(9), September 1917, pg. 273–274 + 20(10), říjen 1917, pg. 298–299.
   Repr. In: *Osudný paprsek a další povídky raného česko-amerického spisovatele*.
   Ed. František Hlous – Jaroslav Olša, Jr. – Zdeněk Rampas – Michaela
   Rampasová. Praha: Nová vlna 2025, pg. 144–150.

"Jak utekla chimaera" (How Chimera Escaped). In: *Amerikán Národní Kalendář
   na rok 1918*. Chicago, IL: Aug. Geringer 1917, pg. 199–206. – Roč. (Vol.) 41.
   Repr. In: *Osudný paprsek a další povídky raného česko-amerického spisovatele*.
   Ed. František Hlous – Jaroslav Olša, Jr. – Zdeněk Rampas – Michaela
   Rampasová. Praha: Nová vlna 2025, pg. 42–51.

1918

"Zrak pana Plachého" (Mr. Plachý´s Sight). *Bratrský Věstník* (Cedar Rapids, IA),
   21(4), April 1918, pg. 121–124.
   Repr. In: *Osudný paprsek a další povídky raného česko-amerického spisovatele*.
   Ed. František Hlous – Jaroslav Olša, Jr. – Zdeněk Rampas – Michaela
   Rampasová. Praha: Nová vlna 2025, pg. 151–162.

"The Death Clandestine."[12] *Bratrský Věstník* (Cedar Rapids, IA), 21(11), November
   1918, pg. 364–365 + 21(12), December 1918, pg. 395–397.

---

10 1963 English edition copies 1916 Czech edition. It is not a reprint of 1910 English
    text.
11 Rewritten text published in English as "The Hungry Guinea-Pig" (1930).
12 Shortened and rewritten text published as "The Puzzle Duel" (1928).

1919

"The American Ghost." *Bratrský Věstník* (Cedar Rapids, IA), 22(6), June 1919,
     pg. 181–182 + 22(8), August 1919, pg. 240–241.

"Sherlock Holmes Gets Busy." *The American Journal of Clinical Medicine*
     (Chicago, IL), 26(10), October 1919, pg. 705–711.

"Dva franky za hodinu" (Two Franks per Hour). In: *Amerikán Národní Kalendář
     na rok 1920*. Chicago, IL: Aug. Geringer, 1919, pg. 201–207. – Roč. (Vol.) 43.
     Repr. In: *Osudný paprsek a další povídky raného česko-amerického spisovatele*.
          Ed. František Hlous – Jaroslav Olša, Jr. – Zdeněk Rampas – Michaela
          Rampasová. Praha: Nová vlna 2025, pg. 163–170.
     – Rev. (English)[13] as "An Instructor in French." *Bratrský Věstník* (Cedar
          Rapids, IA), 32(10), October 1929, pg. 418–420.

1922

"Osudný paprsek" (The Fatal Ray). In: *Amerikán Národní kalendář na rok 1923*.
     Chicago, IL: Aug. Geringer 1922, pg. 97–116. – Roč. (Vol.) 46.
     Repr. In: *Osudný paprsek a další povídky raného česko-amerického spisovatele*.
          Ed. František Hlous – Jaroslav Olša, Jr. – Zdeněk Rampas – Michaela
          Rampasová. Praha: Nová vlna 2025, pg. 52–76.
     – (English) as "The Fatal Ray."[14] *The American Journal of Clinical Medicine*
          (Chicago, IL), 29(5), May 1922, pg. 348–352 + 29(6), June 1922,
          pg. 428–430 + 29(7), July 1922, pg. 480–485.
     Repr. *Social Science* (Winfield, KS), 1(2), 1926, pg. 149–176.

1923

"Případ učené hlavy"[15] (The Boffin's Story). *Bratrský Věstník* (Cedar Rapids, IA),
     26(3), March 1923, pg. 77–78.
     Repr. In: *Osudný paprsek a další povídky raného česko-amerického spisovatele*.
          Ed. František Hlous – Jaroslav Olša, Jr. – Zdeněk Rampas – Michaela
          Rampasová. Praha: Nová vlna 2025, pg. 77–81.

1924

"Vyšší tvor" (The Superior Being). *Bratrský Věstník* (Cedar Rapids, IA), 27(9),
     September 1924, pg. 271–272 + 27(10), October 1924, pg. 298–301 + 29(11),
     November 1924, pg. 333–334.
     Repr. In: Olša, Jr., J.: *Miloslav (Miles) J. Breuer: Česko-americký spisovatel
          u zrodu moderní science fiction*. Praha: Nová vlna 2023, pg. 94–112.
     Repr. In: *Osudný paprsek a další povídky raného česko-amerického spisovatele*.

---

13 English edition is slightly edited version of the Czech original.

14 Rewritten and expanded version published as "Rays and Men" (1929).

15 Rewritten and expanded version published in English as "The Inferiority
     Complex" (1930).

Ed. František Hlous – Jaroslav Olša, Jr. – Zdeněk Rampas – Michaela
Rampasová. Praha: Nová vlna 2025, pg. 82–100.
- (English) as "The Superior Race."[16] *Social Science* (Winfield, KS), 1(3),
1926, pg. 271–295.

"Vyléčená rakovina" (Cancer Cured). *Duch Času* (Chicago, IL), 47(8), 30
November 1924, pg. 124–125.
Repr. In: *Osudný paprsek a další povídky raného česko-amerického spisovatele*.
Ed. František Hlous – Jaroslav Olša, Jr. – Zdeněk Rampas – Michaela
Rampasová. Praha: Nová vlna 2025, pg. 182–186.

1926

"Muž se zvláštní hlavou" (The Man with the Strange Head). In: *Amerikán Národní
Kalendář na rok 1927*. Chicago, IL: Aug. Geringer 1926, pg. 191–198. –
Roč. (Vol.) 50.
Repr. In: *Osudný paprsek a další povídky raného česko-amerického spisovatele*.
Ed. František Hlous – Jaroslav Olša, Jr. – Zdeněk Rampas – Michaela
Rampasová. Praha: Nová vlna 2025, pg. 101–110.
- (English) as "The Man with the Strange Head." *Amazing Stories* (New York,
NY), 1(10), January 1927, pg. 940–943, 970.
Repr. In: *Big Book of Science Fiction*. Ed. Groff Conklin. New York, NY:
Crown Publishers 1950, pg. 133–139.
Repr. In: *The Classic Book of Science Fiction*. Ed. Groff Conklin. New York,
NY: Bonanza Books 1978.
Repr. In: *Amazing Science Fiction Anthology: The Wonder Years 1926–1935*.
Ed. Martin H. Greenberg. Lake Geneva, WI: TSR 1987, pg. 209–222.
Repr. In: Breuer, M. J.: *The Man with the Strange Head and Other Early Science
Fiction Stories*. Ed. Michael R. Page. Lincoln, NE: University of Nebraska
Press 2008, pg. 1–11.
Repr. In: *The Best of Amazing Stories: The 1927 Anthology*. Ed. Steve Davidson
– Jean Marie Stine. No place given: Experimenter Publishing Company 2015,
pg. 62–71.

1927

"The Stone Cat."[17] *Amazing Stories* (New York, NY), 2(6), September 1927,
pg. 553–555, 608.

- Trans. (Italian) as "Il gatto di pietra." Tr. by Roberta Rambelli. In: *Gli anni di
Gernsback. Storia della Fantascienza 2*. Ed. Luigi Cozzi. Bologna: Perseo
Libri 1990, pg. 415–421.

---

16 Rewritten and expanded version published as a novel *Paradise and Iron* (1930).
17 Rewritten version of the story published under the same title in 1909.

"The Riot at Sanderac." *Amazing Stories* (New York, NY), 2(9), December 1927, pg. 878–881.

1928

"The Puzzle Duel."[18] *Amazing Stories Quarterly* (New York, NY), 1(1), Winter 1928, pg. 133–136.

"The Appendix and the Spectacles." *Amazing Stories* (New York, NY), 3(9), December 1928, pg. 774–779.
> Repr. In: *The Science Fiction Galaxy*. Ed. Groff Conklin. New York, NY: Perma Books 1950, pg. 160–174.
> Repr. In: *The Mathematical Magpie: Being More Stories, Mainly Transcendental, plus Subsets of Essays, Rhymes, Music, Anecdotes, Epigrams, and other Prime Oddments and Diversions, Rational or Irrational, All Derived from the Infinite Domain of Mathematics*. Ed. Clifton Fadiman. New York, NY: Simon & Schuster 1962.
> Repr. In: *The Mathematical Magpie: Being More Stories, Mainly Transcendental, plus Subsets of Essays, Rhymes, Music, Anecdotes, Epigrams, and other Prime Oddments and Diversions, Rational or Irrational, All Derived from the Infinite Domain of Mathematics*. Ed. Clifton Fadiman. No place given: Copernicus 1997.
> Repr. In: Breuer, M. J.: *The Man with the Strange Head and Other Early Science Fiction Stories*. Ed. Michael R. Page. Lincoln, NE: University of Nebraska Press 2008, pg. 12–24.
> Repr. In: *The Best of Amazing Stories: The 1928 Anthology*. Ed. Steve Davidson – Jean Marie Stine. Experimenter Publishing Company 2016, pg. 92–107.

> – Trans. (Polish) as "Wyrostek robaczkowy i pince-nez." Tr. by Artur Nowakowski. *Hynh+* (Łódź), 2021, 3, pg. 78–89.

1929

"The Captured Cross-Section." *Amazing Stories* (New York, NY), 3(11), February 1929, pg. 968–974.
> Repr. In: *Avon Fantasy Reader #12*. Ed. Donald A. Wollheim. New York, NY: Avon Books 1950, pg. 67–79.
> Repr. In: *Fantasia Mathematica: Being a Set of Stories, Together with a Group of Oddments and Diversions, All Drawn from the Universe of Mathematics*. Ed. Clifton Fadiman. New York, NY: Simon & Schuster 1958, pg. 140–154.
> Repr. In: *Other Dimensions: Ten Stories of Science Fiction*. Ed. Robert Silverberg. New York, NY: Hawthorn Books 1973, pg. 95–113.
> Repr. In: *The Best of Amazing Stories: The 1929 Anthology*. Ed. Steve Davidson – Jean Marie Stine. No place given: Experimenter Publishing Company 2017, pg. 52–71.

---

18 Shorter and rewritten version of "The Death Clandestine" (1918).

– Trans. (Japanese) as "Yojigen hoteishiki". Tr. by Minamiyama Hiroshi.
SF Magajin, 1964, 1(51).
    Repr. In: *Sekai SF zenshu* 31 Ed. Fukushima Masami – Noda Masahiro – Ito
    Norio. Tokyo: Hayakawa Shobo 1971.
– Trans. (Spanish) as "Puerta a la cuarta dimensión." Tr. uncredited.
In: *Cacumen* (Madrid, Spain), 6, Julio 1983.
    Repr. In: *Puerta a la cuarta dimension y otros cuentos de mente*. Ed. Jaime
    Poniachik. No place given (Spain): Zugarto 1992, pg. 149–168.

"Buried Treasure." *Amazing Stories* (New York, NY), 4(1), April 1929, pg. 38–47.

"Rays and Men."[19] *Amazing Stories Quarterly* (New York, NY), 2(3), July 1929,
pg. 360–379

"The Book of Worlds." *Amazing Stories* (New York, NY), 4(4), July 1929,
pg. 294–299.
    Repr. In: *Avon Science Fiction Reader No. 2*. Ed. Donald A. Wollheim. New
    York, NY: Avon Books 1951, pg. 115–123.
    Repr. *Fantastic Stories* (Flushing, NY), 18(4), April 1969, pg. 46–55.
    Repr. In: *New Horizons: Yesterday's Portraits of Tomorrow*. Ed. August Derleth.
    Sauk City, WI: Arkham House 1999, pg. 213–224.
    Repr. In: *Beyond Time*. Ed. Mike Ashley. London: British Library 2019,
    pg. 97–113.

– Trans. (German) as "Das Buch der Welten." Tr. by Wolfgang Hohlbein –
Dieter Winkler. In: *Titan – 17*. Ed. Ronald M. Hahn – Wolfgang Jeschke.
München (Germany): Heyne Verlag 1981.

"The Girl from Mars"[20] (with Jack Williamson). New York, NY: Stellar Publishing
Corporation 1929. 24 pg. – Science Fiction Series #1.
    Repr. (excerpt) In: Williamson, J.: *The Early Williamson*. New York, NY:
    Doubleday 1975, pg. 16–34.
    Repr. (excerpt) In: Williamson, J.: *The Early Williamson*. London, UK: Sphere
    1978, pg. 39–62.
    Repr. In: Williamson, J.: *The Prince of Space / The Girl From Mars*. New York,
    NY: Gryphon Books 1998.
    Repr. (excerpt) In: *The Collected Stories of Jack Williamson. Vol. 1: The Metal
    Man and Others*. Royal Oak (MI): Haffner Press 1999, pg. 15–32.

---

19 Expanded and rewritten version of "The Fatal Ray" (1924), and "Osudný paprsek"
(1924).

20 Written most probably as "The Egg from the Lost Planet" – as quoted in
Ackerman, Forrest J.: "My Science Fiction Collection." *The Fantasy Fan*, 1(4),
December 1933.

– Trans. (Spanish) as "La muchacha de Marte." Tr. uncredited. *Los Cuentos Fantásticos* (Mexico), 1952, 38, pg. 37–47.

Repr. *Los Cuentos Fantásticos* (Spain), 2011, 38, pg. 37–47.

– Trans. (Spanish) as "La muchacha de Marte." Tr. by Amparo García Burgos. In: Williamson, J.: *Lo mejor de Jack Williamson*. Barcelona (Spain): Martínez Roca 1979, pg. 37–56.

– Trans. (Russian) as "Девушка с Марса" (Devushka s Marsa). Tr. by И. Фудим (I. Fudim), А. Заушникова (A. Zaushnikova). In: Уильямсон, Д.: *Девушка с Марса*. Ed. Андрей Бурцев (Andrey Burtsev). Irkutsk: Starstown, 2020, pg. 285–312.

"A Baby on Neptune" (with Clare Winger Harris). *Amazing Stories* (New York, NY), 4(9), December 1929, pg. 791–799.

Repr. as "Child of Neptune" In: *Tales of Wonder and Super-Science* (Kingswood, Surrey, UK), 14, 1941, pg. 54-?.

Repr. In: Harris, C. W.: *Away from the Here and Now: Stories in Pseudo-Science*. Philadelphia, PA: Dorrance 1947, pg. 146–182.

Repr. In: *Flight into Space: Great Science-Fiction Stories of Interplanetary Travel*. Ed. Donald A. Wollheim. New York, NY: Fredrick Fell 1950, pg. 203–230.

Repr. In: *Flight into Space: Great Science-Fiction Stories of Interplanetary Travel*. Ed. Donald A. Wollheim. No place given: Cherry Tree / Fantasy Books 1951.

Repr. as "The Dead World." In: *The Dead World*. Ed. Unknown. No place given (Australia): Malian Press 1953, pg. 3–14. – American Science Fiction Magazine #15.

Repr. In: *Gosh! Wow! (Sense of Wonder) Science Fiction*. Ed. Forrest J. Ackerman. Nevada City, CA: Sirius Science Fiction 1982, pg. 82–98.

Repr. In: Harris, C. W.: *Away from the Here and Now*. No place given: Ramble House 2011.

Repr. In: *The Best of Amazing Stories: The 1929 Anthology*. Ed. Steve Davidson – Jean Marie Stine. Experimenter Publishing Company 2017, pg. 20–51.

Repr. In: Harris, Clare Winger: *The Artificial Man and Other Stories*. No place given: Belt Publishing 2019.

Repr. In: *Born of the Sun*. Ed. Mike Ashley. London: British Library 2020, pg. 289–318.

– Trans. (Spanish) as "El pequeńo sobre el planeta Neptuno." In: *La Novela Fantástica 1*. (no place given) (Argentina): Héctor César Zappalorti 1937, pg. 61–77.

– Trans. (Italian) as "Il piccolo Nettuniano." Tr. by Nicola Fantini. In: *Il senso del meraviglioso*. Ed. Sandro Pergameno. Milano: Editrice Nord 1989, pg. 33–58. – Grandi Opere Nord 17.

– Trans. (Italian) as "Un bambino, su Nettuno." Tr. by Mariangela Sala.
In: *Gli anni di Gernsback. Storia della Fantascienza 2*. Ed. Luigi Cozzi.
Bologna: Perseo Libri, pg. 1133–1156.

1930

"The Hungry Guinea-Pig."[21] *Amazing Stories* (New York, NY), 4(10), January
1930, pg. 926–935.
Repr. In: *Science Fiction Adventures in Mutation*. Ed. Groff Conklin. New York,
NY: Vanguard Press 1955, pg. 33–54.
Repr. *Amazing Stories* (New York, NY), 35(10), October 1961, pg. 112–134.
Repr. *Science Fiction Classics Annual* (no place given), 1970, pg. 66–88.
Repr. *The Ascent of Wonder: The Evolution of Hard SF*. Ed. David Hartwell –
Kathryn Cramer. New York, NY: Tor 1994, pg. 499–513.

– Tr. (Italian) as "La Cavia Affamata." Tr. by Roberta Rambelli In: *I Mutanti.*
Le migliore opera della fantascienca di tutti i tempi sui poteri mentali e le
mutazioni genetiche. Ed. Sandro Pergameno. Milano: Editrice Nord 1983,
pg. 391–412. – Grandi Opere Nord 9.

"The Fitzgerald Contraction." *Science Wonder Stories* (New York, NY), January
1930, pg. 678–695, 744.
Repr. *Startling Stories* (New York, NY), 7(1), January 1942, pg. 94–105.
Repr. *Startling Stories*, 7(1), 2011, pg. 94–105. – facsimile

"The Gostak and the Doshes." *Amazing Stories* (New York, NY), 4(12), March
1930, pg. 1142–1149, 1185.
Repr. In: *Avon Fantasy Reader No. 10*. Ed. Donald A. Wollheim. New York,
NY: Avon Novels 1949, pg. 92–106.
Repr. In: *Science-Fiction Adventures in Dimension*. Ed. Groff Conklin. New
York, NY: Vanguard Press 1953, pg. 216–234.
Repr. In: *Science Fiction Adventures in Dimension*. Ed. Groff Conklin. London,
UK: Grayson and Grayson 1955.
Repr. In: *Great Science Fiction by Scientists*. Ed. Groff Conklin. New York, NY:
Collier Books 1962, pg. 61–82.
Repr. In: *Science Fiction Adventures in Dimension*. Ed. Groff Conklin. New
York, NY: Berkley Medallion 1965.
Repr. *Science Fiction Classics*, 2, Fall 1967, pg. 96–109.
Repr. In: *The Arbor House Treasury of Science Fiction Masterpieces*. Ed.
Robert Silverberg – Martin H. Greenberg. New York, NY: Arbor House
1983, pg. 169–181.
Repr. In: *Amazing Stories: 60 Years of the Best Science Fiction*. Ed. Isaac
Asimov – Martin H. Greenberg. New York, NY: TSR 1985, pg. 29–42.

---

21 Rewritten version of the original Czech text "Hladové morče" (1917).

Repr. In: *Great Tales of Science Fiction*. Eds. Robert Silverberg – Martin H. Greenberg. No place given: Galahad Books, 1988, pg. 169–181.

Repr. In: Breuer, M. J.: *The Man with the Strange Head and Other Early Science Fiction Stories*. Ed. Michael R. Page. Lincoln, NE: University of Nebraska Press 2008, pg. 25–43.

Repr. In: *Sense of Wonder: A Century of Science Fiction*. Ed. Leigh Ronald Grossman. Cabin John, MD: Wildside 2011.

    – Trans. (Italian) as "Il gostak e i dosh". Tr. by Paola Francioli – Elena Lante. In: *Racconti di fantascienza scritti dagli scienziati*. Ed. Groff Conklin. Milano: Rizzoli 1965, pg. 88–119.

    – Trans. (Russian) as "Куздра и бокры" (Kuzdra i bokry). Tr. by Нинель Евдокимова (Ninel′ Evdokimova). In: *Карточный домик* (Kartochnyi domik). Ed. Uncredited. Москва (Moskva): Мир (Mir) 1969. - Зарубежная фантастика (Zarubezhnaya fantastika).

    – Trans. (Czech) as "Gostak a doše." Tr. by Richard Podaný. *XB–1* (Praha), 11, 2020, pg. 13–19.

    – Trans. (Turkish) as "Gostak ve Doshes." Tr. by Atakan Karaduman. In: Breuer, M. J.: *Gostak ve Doshes*. İstanbul: Altıkırkbeş Yayın 2021, pg. 114–138.

"The Driving Power."[22] *Amazing Stories*, (New York, NY), 5(4), July 1930, pg. 306–311, 323.

    – Repr. as "Lady of the Atoms." *Tales of Wonder and Super-Science* (Kingswood, Surrey, UK), Autumn 1941, No. 15, pg. 47–52.

"The Time Valve." *Wonder Stories* (New York, NY), 2(2), July 1930, pg. 102–115.

"Paradise and Iron."[23] *Amazing Stories Quarterly* (New York, NY), 3(3), Summer 1930, pg. 292–363, 401.

Repr. In: Breuer, M. J.: *The Man with the Strange Head and Other Early Science Fiction Stories*. Ed. Michael R. Page. Lincoln, NE: University of Nebraska Press 2008, pg. 44–256.

    – Trans. (Italian) as *Il paradiso e il ferro*. Tr. by Roberta Rambelli. Bologna: Perseo Libri 1992, 216 pg. – Biblioteca di Nova SF 12.

"A Problem in Communication." *Astounding Stories of Super-Science* (New York, NY), September 1930, pg. 293–309.

Repr. In: Breuer, M. J.: *The Man with the Strange Head and Other Early Science*

---

22 Original title "The Driving Force" – according to the manuscript in hands of Miles J. Breuer's descendants.

23 Expanded version of a short story "The Superior Race" (1926), and "Vyšší tvor" (1924).

Fiction Stories. Ed. Michael R. Page. Lincoln, NE: University of Nebraska Press 2008, pg. 257–284.

"The Inferiority Complex."[24] *Amazing Stories* (New York, NY), 5(6), September 1930, pg. 535–539, 566.

1931

"The Birth of a New Republic" (with Jack Williamson). *Amazing Stories Quarterly* (New York, NY), 4(1), Winter 1931, pg. 4–73, 89.
   Repr. New Orleans, LA: PDA Press 1981. 80 pg.
   Repr. In: Williamson J.: *The Collected Stories of Jack Williamson. Vol. 1: The Metal Man and Others*. Royal Oak, MI: Haffner Press 1999, pg. 239–426.

   – Trans. (Italian) as *Nascita di una nuova repubblica*. Tr. by Roberta Rambelli. Bologna: Perseo Libri 1991, 222 pg. – Biblioteca di Nova SF 9.
   – Trans. (Russian) as "Рождение новой республики" (Rozhdenie novoy respubliki). Tr. uncredited. In: Уильямсон, Д.: *Камень с Зеленой Звезды*. (Kamen' s zelyonoy zvezdy) Санкт-Петербург (Sankt Peterburg): Северо-Запад (Severo-Zapad) 2018, pg. 197–356.
   – Trans. (Russian) as *Рождение новой республики* (Rozhdenie novoy respubliki). Tr. Uncredited. Moskva: T8 RUGRAM 2020. 320 pg.

"On Board the Martian Liner." *Amazing Stories* (New York, NY), 5(12), March 1931, pg. 1080–1089, 1139.
   Repr. In: Breuer, M. J.: *The Man with the Strange Head and Other Early Science Fiction Stories*. Ed. Michael R. Page. Lincoln, NE: University of Nebraska Press 2008, pg. 285–311.

"The Unknown Hand at Gergy."[25] *Bratrský Věstník* (Cedar Rapids, IA), 34(5), May, pg. 209–211.

"The Legion of the Fittest". *Social Science* (Winfield, KS), 1931, 6(2), pg. 134–155.

"The Time Flight." *Amazing Stories* (New York, NY), 6(3), June 1931, pg. 274–281.

"The Demons of Rhadi-Mu." *Amazing Stories Quarterly* (New York, NY), 4(4), Fall 1931, pg. 506–520.

1932

"Mechanocracy." *Amazing Stories* (New York, NY), 7(1), April 1932, pg. 6–15.
   Repr. In: Breuer, M. J.: *The Man with the Strange Head and Other Early Science*

---

24 Expanded and rewritten version of "Případ učené hlavy" (1923).
25 Rewritten version of "The Power of Darkness" (1908).

Fiction Stories. Ed. Michael R. Page. Lincoln, NE: University of Nebraska Press 2008, pg. 312–338.

   – Trans. (Turkish) as "Mekanokrasi." Tr. by Atakan Karaduman. In: Breuer, M. J.: *Gostak ve Doshes*. İstanbul: Altıkırkbeş Yayın 2021, pg. 9–44.

"The Einstein See-Saw." *Astounding Stories* (New York, NY), 10(1), April 1932, pg. 74–89.
   Repr. In: *Avon Fantasy Reader #15*. Ed. Donald A. Wollheim. New York, NY: Avon Novels 1951, pg. 77–93.
   Repr. In: *Anthology of Sci-Fi V21: The Pulp Writers*. Ed. Uncredited. No place given: Spastic Cat Press 2013.

"Světoborný nález Majka Gruntoráda"[26] (Majek Gruntorád's Epochal Discovery). In: *Amerikán Národní Kalendář na rok 1933*. Chicago, IL: Aug. Geringer 1932, pg. 135–148. – Roč. (Vol.) 56.
   Repr. *Interkom* (Praha), 2021, 7–8, pg. 18–24.
   Repr. In: Olša, Jr., J.: *Miloslav (Miles) J. Breuer: Česko-americký spisovatel u moderní science fiction*. Praha: Nová vlna 2023, pg. 113–130.
   Repr. In: *Osudný paprsek a další povídky raného česko-amerického spisovatele*. Ed. František Hlous – Jaroslav Olša, Jr. – Zdeněk Rampas – Michaela Rampasová. Praha: Nová vlna 2025, pg. 111–128.

"The Perfect Planet."[27] *Amazing Stories*, 7(2), May 1932, pg. 136–143.
   Repr. as "The Breath of Utopia." *Tales of Wonder and Super-Science #16* (Kingswood, Surrey, UK), 1942, pg. 31–40.

"The Finger of the Past." *Amazing Stories* (New York, NY), 7(8), November 1932, pg. 703–708, 733.
   Repr. In: Breuer, M. J.: *The Man with the Strange Head and Other Early Science Fiction Stories*. Ed. Michael R. Page. Lincoln, NE: University of Nebraska Press 2008, pg. 339–349.
   Repr. In: *The Garden of Fear and Other Stories of the Bizarre and Fantastic*. Ed. uncredited (William L. Crawford). Whitefish, MT: Kessinger 2010, pg. 39–64.

   – Trans. (Turkish) as "Geçmişin Parmağı." Tr. by Atakan Karaduman. In: Breuer, M. J.: *Gostak ve Doshes*. İstanbul: Altıkırkbeş Yayın 2021, pg. 45–59.

---

26 English version "The Perfect Planet" has various parts of the story rewritten.
27 Czech version "Světoborný nález Majka Gruntoráda" has various parts of the story different.

1933

"The Strength of the Weak" *Amazing Stories* (New York, NY), 8(8), December
  1933, pg. 33–43.

1935

"Háček v předpovědi."[28] *Bratrský Věstník* (Cedar Rapids, IA), 38(1), leden 1935,
  pg. 8–10.
  Repr. In: *Osudný paprsek a další povídky raného česko-amerického spisovatele*.
    Ed. František Hlous – Jaroslav Olša, Jr. – Zdeněk Rampas – Michaela
    Rampasová. Praha: Nová vlna 2025, pg. 129–135.

"Millions for Defense." *Amazing Stories* (New York, NY), 9(11), March 1935,
  pg. 77–87
  Repr. In: Breuer, M. J.: *The Man with the Strange Head and Other Early Science
    Fiction Stories*. Ed. Michael R. Page. Lincoln, NE: University of Nebraska
    Press 2008, pg. 350–365.

  – Trans. (Turkish) as "Savunma İçin Milyonlar." Tr. by Atakan Karaduman.
    In: Breuer, M. J.: *Gostak ve Doshes*. İstanbul: Altıkırkbeş Yayın 2021,
    pg. 60–79.

"Mars Colonizes." *Marvel Tales* (Everett, PA), 1(5), Summer 1935, pg. 237–250.
  Repr. In: *The Garden of Fear and Other Stories*. Ed. uncredited [William L.
    Crawford]. Los Angeles, CA: Crawford Publication 1949, pg. 39–64.
  Repr. In: Breuer, M. J.: *The Man with the Strange Head and Other Early Science
    Fiction Stories*. Ed. Michael R. Page. Lincoln, NE: University of Nebraska
    Press 2008, pg. 366–393.
  Repr. In: *The Complete Marvel Tales*. Ed. William L. Crawford. No place given:
    Lance Thingmaker 2012, pg. 5237–5250. – facsimile of the complete set
    of Marvel Tales

  – Trans. (Spanish) as "Marte coloniza." Translator uncredited. *Los Cuentos
    Fantásticos* (Mexico), 1949, 16, pg. 26–45.
  Repr. *Los Cuentos Fantásticos* (Spain), 2015, 16, pg. 26–45. – facsimile.
  – Trans. (Turkish) as "Mars Kolonileşiyor." Tr. by Atakan Karaduman.
    In: Breuer, M. J.: Gostak ve Doshes. İstanbul: Altıkırkbeş Yayın 2021,
    pg. 80–113.

"The Chemistry Murder Case." *Amazing Stories* (New York, NY), 10(6), October
  1935, pg. 73–83.

---

28 Czech text is rewritten version of the English text published as "The Flaw in the
  Premise" (1910).

1936

"Mr. Dimmitt Seeks Redress." *Amazing Stories,* (New York, NY), 10(11), August
   1936, pg. 91–101.
   Repr. *Amazing Stories* (Flushing, NY), 40(8), October 1966, pg. 97–110.

1937

"The Company or the Weather." *Amazing Stories* (New York, NY), 11(3), June
   1937, pg. 51–52.

   – Trans. (Polish) as "Kłopoty z pogodą." Tr. by Witold Bartkiewicz. *Hynh+*
      (Łódź), 2020, 3/4 (lato/jesień), pg. 190–192.

1938

"Mr. Bowen's Wife Reduces." *Amazing Stories* (New York, NY), 12(1), February
   1938, pg. 118–124.
   Repr. *Amazing Science Fiction* (Flushing, NY), 44(3), September 1970,
      pg. 108–114.

1939

"The Raid from Mars." *Amazing Stories* (New York, NY), 13(3), March 1939,
   pg. 8–21.
   Repr. *Space Adventures,* 1970, Winter, pg. 56–69.
   Repr. *Strange Adventures* #2, April 2006.

"The Disappearing Papers." *Future Fiction* (New York, NY), 1(1), November 1939,
   pg. 74–76.

1940

"The Oversight." *Comet Stories of Super Time and Space* (Springfield, MA), 1(1),
   December 1940, pg. 40–52.
   Repr. In: Breuer, M. J.: *The Man with the Strange Head and Other Early Science
      Fiction Stories.* Ed. Michael R. Page. Lincoln, NE: University of Nebraska
      Press 2008, pg. 394–414.

1942

"The Sheriff of Thorium Gulch." *Amazing Stories* (New York, NY), 16(8), August
   1942, pg. 44–64.
   Repr. *Amazing Stories Quarterly* (New York, NY), 3(2), 1943, pg. 44–64.

"Padělané žití" (Counterfeit Living[29]). In: *Amerikán Národní Kalendář na rok 1943.*
   Chicago, IL: Aug. Geringer 1942, pg. 51–55. – Roč. (Vol.) 66.
   Repr. In: *Osudný paprsek a další povídky raného česko-amerického spisovatele.*

---

29 Translated as "The Contrivance of Life."

Ed. František Hlous – Jaroslav Olša, Jr. – Zdeněk Rampas – Michaela
Rampasová. Praha: Nová vlna 2025, pg. 136–142.

– Trans. (English) as "The Contrivance of Life." Tr. by Carleton Bulkin. *Hélice*
(Spain), 9(1), 2023, pg. 129–134.

Poetry

1900

"A Queer Thing." *David City News* (David City, NE), 10(3), 22 November 1900,
pg. 3.

1901

"Legend of the Stars." *The Banner-Press* (David City, NE), 28(22), 5 February
1901, pg. 3.

1903

"Algebra." *The Crete Vidette-Herald* (Crete, NE), 32(49), 2 April 1903, pg. 5.

1907

"An Autumn Sunset." *The University of Texas Magazine* (Austin, TX), 23(3),
December 1907, pg. 134.

1908

"The Land Where the Stray Notes Go." *The University of Texas Magazine* (Austin,
TX), 23(5), February 1908, pg. 267. – signed M. J. B.

"The Dance of the Elves." *The University of Texas Magazine* (Austin, TX), 23(6),
March 1908, pg. 282. – signed M. J. B.

"People Are Saying." *The University of Texas Magazine* (Austin, TX), 23(6), March
1908, pg. 315.

"Fear." *The University of Texas Magazine* (Austin, TX), 23(7), April 1908, pg. 353.

"The Promise of the Autumn." *The University of Texas Magazine* (Austin, TX),
24(1), October 1908, pg. frontispiece.

"Labor." *The University of Texas Magazine* (Austin, TX), 24(1), October 1908,
pg. 48

"From the Capitol Dome." *The University of Texas Magazine* (Austin, TX), 24(2), November 1908, pg. 60.

"A Picture." *The University of Texas Magazine* (Austin, TX), 24(2), November 1908, pg. 86.

1909

"The Thief." *The University of Texas Magazine* (Austin, TX), 24(4), January 1909, pg. 167–168.

"The Ghost." *The University of Texas Magazine* (Austin, TX), 24(4), January 1909, pg. 190.

"From My Window." *The University of Texas Magazine* (Austin, TX), 24(5), February 1909, pg. 270.

"To Science." *The University of Texas Magazine* (Austin, TX), 24(5), February 1909, pg. 270.

"To the Varsity From an Absent One." *The University of Texas Magazine* (Austin, TX), 24, Commencement Number, 1909, pg. 390.

"The Train." *The University of Texas Magazine* (Austin, TX), 24, Commencement Number, 1909, pg. 403.

"The Far Horizon." *The University of Texas Magazine* (Austin, TX), 25(1), October 1909, pg. 37–38.

"Heaven." *The University of Texas Magazine* (Austin, TX), 25(3), December 1909, pg. frontispiece.
Repr. *Komenský* (Lincoln, NE), 2(?), 1910, pg. 12.

"Gems." *The University of Texas Magazine* (Austin, TX), 25(3), December 1909, pg. 151.

"There´s One That Talked to Me of Wealth." *The University of Texas Magazine* (Austin, TX), 25(3), December 1909, pg. 157.

1910

"Martyr." *The University of Texas Magazine* (Austin, TX), 25(4), January 1910, pg. 233.

(untitled). *The University of Texas Magazine* (Austin, TX), 25(5), February 1910, pg. 301.

"Unknown Shores." *The University of Texas Magazine* (Austin, TX), 25(6), March 1910, pg. 337.

"My Valley." *The University of Texas Magazine* (Austin, TX), 25(6), March 1910, pg. 349.

"Science." *The University of Texas Magazine* (Austin, TX), 25(7), April 1910, pg. 411.
    Repr. In: *The Cactus. The Year Book of the University of Texas (Austin, TX), Vol. 19, 1912. Unpaginated*

"Dolorosae." *The University of Texas Magazine* (Austin, TX), 25(7), April 1910, pg. 416.

"The Flit of Light." *The University of Texas Magazine* (Austin, TX), 25(8), May 1910, pg. 466–467.

"Traeumerei." In: *The Cactus. The Year Book of the University of Texas* (Austin, TX), Vol. 17, 1910, pg. 263. – as Miles J. Breurer.

1911

"Whispered." *The University of Texas Magazine* (Austin, TX), 26(5), February 1911, pg. 211.
    Repr. In: *The Cactus. The Year Book of the University of Texas* (Austin, TX), Vol. 18, 1911, pg. 321.

"In His Image." *The University of Texas Magazine* (Austin, TX), 26(7), April 1911, pg. 299–300.

"Oh Lady on the Auto Seat." In: *The Cactus. The Year Book of the University of Texas* (Austin, TX), Vol. 18, 1911, pg. 304.

"The Scientist." In: *The Cactus. The Year Book of the University of Texas* (Austin, TX), Vol. 18, 1911, pg. 303.

"When You Were in College." In: *The Cactus. The Year Book of the University of Texas* (Austin, TX), Vol. 18, 1911, pg. 322.

1912

"Sit Lux." *The University of Texas Magazine* (Austin, TX), 27(9), June 1912, pg. 344.

"On A Stroll." *The University of Texas Magazine* (Austin, TX), 28(1), October 1912, pg. 32.

"On the Sea-Wall." *The University of Texas Magazine* (Austin, TX), 28(2), November 1912, pg. 75.

1913

"Afloat Alone." *The University of Texas Magazine* (Austin, TX), 28(9), June 1913, pg. 388.

"The Harbor to Me." *The University of Texas Magazine* (Austin, TX), 28(9), June 1913, pg. 416.

"Ex Visibus Freshmanorum." In: *The Cactus. The Year Book of the University of Texas* (Austin, TX), Vol. 20, 1913. Unpaginated

1918

"Sonnet to Prof. Masaryk." *Bratrský Věstník* (Cedar Rapids, IA), 21(6), June 1918, pg. 189.

1927

"The Specter." *Weird Tales* (Chicago, IL), March 1927, pg. 360.

1930

"Vis Scientiae." *Amazing Stories* (New York, NY), 5(2), May 1930, pg. 139. Repr. *Amazing Stories* (New York, NY), 41(3), August 1967, pg. 115.

"Sonnet to Science." *Amazing Stories* (New York, NY), 5(9), December 1930, pg. 856.

1943

"Proč bondy?" (Why War Bonds?). *Národní Pokrok* (Omaha, NE), 22(37), 26 March 1943, pg. 7.
Repr. In: *Osudný paprsek a další povídky raného česko-amerického spisovatele*. Ed. František Hlous – Jaroslav Olša, Jr. – Zdeněk Rampas – Michaela Rampasová. Praha: Nová vlna 2025, pg. 188.

Translations from Czech into English

1908

Hálek, Vítězslav: "The Watch of the Dead" (orig. Mrtvých stráž). *Osvěta Americká* (Omaha, NE), 16(18), 25 November 1908, pg. 10.
> Repr. *The University of Texas Magazine* (Austin, TX), 24(3), December 1908, pg. 149–150. – autor neuveden.

1911

Herites, František: "A Leaf From An Old Book" (orig. "List v staré knize"). *The University of Texas Magazine* (Austin, TX), 26(4), February 1911, pg. 193–200.

1912

Dostál, Alois: "Fern Blossoms" (orig. title not known). *The University of Texas Magazine* (Austin, TX), 27(7), May 1912, pg. 287–297.

1915

Čech, Svatopluk: "Songs of a Slave. Song IX" (orig. "Písně otroka. IX"). *Komenský* (Omaha, NE), 7(7), July 1915, pg. 143.

Science fiction related articles

1929

"The Future of Scientifiction." *Amazing Stories Quarterly* (New York, NY), 2(3), Summer 1929, pg. 291.
> Repr. *Science Fiction Classics*, Summer 1968, pg. 4–5.

> – Trans. (Czech) as "Budoucnost scientifiction." In: Olša, Jr., J.: *Miloslav (Miles) J. Breuer: Česko-americký spisovatel u zrodu moderní science fiction*. Praha: Nová vlna 2023, pg. 131–133.

1937

"Comparisons in Science Fiction." *Tesseract* (San Francisco, CA), 2(2), February 1937, pg. 5.

> – Trans. (Czech) as "Srovnávání v science fiction." Repr. In: Olša, Jr., J.: *Miloslav (Miles) J. Breuer: Česko-americký spisovatel u zrodu moderní science fiction*. Praha: Nová vlna 2023, pg. 134.

1939

"Meet the Authors: Miles J. Breuer." *Amazing Stories* (New York, NY), 13(3), March 1939, pg. 125.

1940

"The New Frontier: A Guest Editorial." *Startling Stories* (New York, NY), 3(3),
    May 1940, pg. 111.

1942

"The Assembly-Line for Writers." *The Writer* (Boston, MA), 55(9), September
    1942, pg. 273–275.

Letters to pulp magazines and fanzines

Amazing Stories (New York, NY), 2(3), June 1927, pg. 390.
Amazing Stories (New York, NY), 3(4), July 1928, pg. 370.
Amazing Stories (New York, NY), 3(5), August 1928, pg. 468.
Amazing Stories (New York, NY), 3(10), January 1929, pg. 957.
Amazing Stories (New York, NY), 4(6), September 1929, pg. 569–570.
The Comet or *Cosmology* (Chicago, IL), between 1930–1933.[30]
Amazing Stories (New York, NY), 4(11), February 1930, pg. 1093.
Amazing Stories (New York, NY), 5(1), April 1930, pg. 86–87.
Amazing Stories (New York, NY), 5(2), May 1930, pg. 181, 183.
Amazing Stories (New York, NY), 5(7), October 1930, pg. 662.
Amazing Stories (New York, NY), 5(10), January 1931, pg. 952, 954.
Wonder Stories (New York, NY), 3(1), June 1931, pg. 139–140
Amazing Stories (New York, NY), 13(4), April 1939, pg. 126.

---

30   Not seen – *Science Fiction Bibliography*, Vol. 1. No. 1 (Austin, TX: Science
    Fiction Syndicate 1935), pg. 5 notes that the fanzine first named *The Comet*,
    later renamed *Cosmology* featured "*letters and articles by* (...) *Miles J. Breuer.*"

Bibliography

Ackerman, Forrest J. (1933): "My Science Fiction Collection." *The Fantasy Fan* (Elizabeth, NJ), 4, December.

Ackerman, Forrest J. (ed.) (1982): *The Gernsback Awards 1926*. Los Angeles: Triton Books.

Adamovič, Ivan (1995): *Slovník české literární fantastiky a science fiction* (Dictionary of Czech Fantastic and Science Fiction Literature). Praha: R3.

Adamovič, Ivan (2010): *Vládcové vesmíru. Kronika české science fiction od Svatopluka Čecha po Jana Weisse* (Rulers of the Universe: Chronicle of Czech Science Fiction from Svatopluk Čech to Jan Weiss). Praha: Albatros – Triton.

Adamovič, Ivan – Olša, jr., Jaroslav (1994): "Where Robot Born: History of Czech Science Fiction." In: Olša, jr., Jaroslav (ed.): *Vampire and other Science Stories from Czech Lands*. New Delhi: Star Publication.

Anon. (1898): "Dr. C. H. Breuer." *Hospodář* (Omaha, NE), 8(12), 15 August.

Anon. (1901): "Omaha Sanitarium. Český léčební ústav" (Omaha Sanitarium: Czech Medical Institution). *Pokrok Západu* (Omaha, NE), 31(16), 20 November.

Anon. (1902): "The Omaha Sanitarium." *The Omaha Daily Bee* (Omaha, NE), 12 January. – Supplement *The Illustrated Bee*.

Anon. (1908): "Nejsme dosud národně ztraceni" (We Are Not Lost Nationally, Yet). *Kansaské Rozhledy* (Wilson, KS), 4(44), 25 November.

Anon. (1911): "Český den ve Waco, Texas" (Czech Day in Waco, Texas). *Amerikán Národní Kalendář na rok 1912*. Chicago: Aug. Geringer. – Vol. 35.

Anon. (1916): "Českoamerická literatura" (Czech-American Literature). *Slavie* (Chicago, IL), 55(10[3728]), 21 January.

Anon. [R. Jaromír Pšenka?] (1926): "Padesát let prvního českého denního časopisu mimo hranice vlasti, ‚Svornosti' v Chicagu, Ill" (Fifty Years of the First Czech Daily Outside of Homeland: 'Svornost' in Chicago, Ill.). In: Pšenka, R. Jaromír (ed.): *Zlatá kniha československého Chicaga* (Golden Book of Czechoslovak Chicago). Chicago: Aug. Geringer.

Anon. (1937): "Čtyřicet roků Západní Česko Bratrské Jednoty" (Forty Years of Western Bohemian Fraternal Society). *Amerikán Národní Kalendář na rok 1938*. Chicago: Aug. Geringer 1937. – Vol. 61.

Anon. (1938a): "Science Fiction Association – Executive Committee Report." *Novae Terrae* (London), 2(10), April.

Anon. (1938b): "Science-Fiction Association Report." *Novae Terrae* (London), 2(12), June.

Anon. (1939a): "Klub Čechie při Texaské státní universitě" (Čechie Club at State University of Texas). In: *Naše dějiny* (Our History). Granger: Národní Svaz Českých Katolíků v Texas.

Anon. [Stanislav Šerpán?] (1939b): "Zdravotní rádce Hospodáře. K 50. narozeninám Dra. Miloslava J. Breuera" (Medical Advisor of Hospodář: On the Occassion of the 50th Birthday of Doctor Miloslav J. Breuer). *Hospodář* (Omaha, NE), 49(1), 1 January.

Anon. (1945a): "Dr. Miloslav J. Breuer zemřel" (Doctor Miloslav J. Breuer Passed Away). *Bratrský Věstník – Fraternal Herald* (Cedar Rapids, IA), 48(12), December.

Anon. (1945b): "Dr. Miloslav J. Breuer zemřel" (Doctor Miloslav J. Breuer Passed Away). *Hospodář* (Omaha, NE), 55(22), 15 November.

Ashley, Michael (1977): *The History of the Science Fiction Magazines. Part One. 1926–1934*. London: New English Library.

Ashley, Michael (2004): "The Gernsback Days." In: Ashley, Michael – Lowndes, Robert A.: *The Gernsback Days: A Study of the Evolution of Modern Science Fiction from 1911 to 1936*. Holicong: Wildside Press.

Ashley, Mike (2008): "Science Fiction Magazines: The Crucibles of Change." In: Seed, David (ed.): *A Companion to Science Fiction*. Oxford: Blackwell.

Auerbach, Ella F. – Tyler, Albert F. (eds.) (1928): *History of Medicine in Nebraska*. Omaha: Magic City Printing.

Bailey, J. O. (1947): *Pilgrims Through Space and Time. Trends and Patterns in Scientific and Utopian Fiction*. New York: Argus.

Barkan, Elliott Robert (2007): *From All Points: America's Immigrant West*. Bloomington – Indianapolis: Indiana University Press.

Beachly, Belle (1919): "Base Hospital 49." *Nebraska History and Record of Pioneer Days* (Lincoln, NE), 2(2).

Benešová, Marie (1950): "Narozeniny klubu [Čechie] našich studentů" (Birth Anniversary of the Club [Čechie] of Our Students). *Čechoslovák and Westské Noviny* (West, TX), 34(45), 10. listopadu.

Bleiler, Everett F. – Bleiler, Richard J. (1998): *Science-Fiction. The Gernsback Years*. Kent: Kent State University Press.

Booker, M. Keith (2015): *Historical Dictionary of Science Fiction in Literature*. Lanham: Rowman and Littlefield.

Braun, Robert (2019): "Autonomous Vehicles: From Science Fiction to Sustainable

Future." In: Aguiar, Marian – Mathieson, Charlotte – Pearce, Lynne (eds.): *Mobilities, Literature, Culture*. New York and London: Palgrave Macmillan.

Breuer, Karel H. (1899): *Nemoce koňské* (Diseases of Horses). Omaha: Národní tiskárna.

Breuer, K. H. (1908): *Domácí léčení* (Home Treatment). Omaha: Národní tiskárna.

Breuer, Karel H. (1915): *Vzpomínky z cesty po Evropě* (Memories of Travels in Europe). Omaha: Národní tiskárna.

Breuer, Karel H. (1920): "Čeština na Univerzitě nebraské povolena" (Czech Language Teaching at University of Nebraska Approved). *Pokrok Západu* (Omaha, NE), 30(5), 3 March.

Breuer, Karel H. (1923a): "Zázračné léčení stroji" (Miraculous Healing Machines). *Hospodář* (Omaha, NE), 32(23), 5 January.

Breuer, Karel H. (1923b): *Zdravověda* (Health Science). Chicago: Aug. Geringer.

Breuer, Karel H. (1926): "Od proslulého českoamerického lékaře, autora ‚Zdravovědy'" (From the Renowned Czech-American Physician, Author of ‚Health Science'). In: Pšenka, R. Jaromír (ed.): *Zlatá kniha československého Chicaga* (Golden Book of Czechoslovak Chicago). Chicago: Aug. Geringer.

Breuer, K. H. (1940): "Život českoamer. lékaře" (Life of Czech-American Medical Doctor). *Hospodář* (Omaha, NE), 50(1), 1 January + 50(2), 15 January + 50(3), 1 February + 50(4), 15 February + 50(5), 1 March + 50(6), 15 March + 50(7), 1 April + 50(8), 15 April + 50(9), 1 May + 50(10), 15 May + 50(11), 1 June + 50(12), 15 June + 50(13), 1 July + 50(14), 15 July + 50(15), 1 August.

Breuer, Miles J. (1900): "A Queer Thing." *David City News* (David City, NE), 10(3), 22 November.

Breuer, Miles J. (1901): "Legend of the Stars." *The Banner-Press* (David City, NE), 28(22), 5 February.

Breuer, Miloslav J. (1911): "Proč máme zůstati Čechy?" (Why Should We Remain Czechs?). *Komenský* (Omaha, NE), 2(4).

Breuer, Miloslav (1918a): "Od našich hochů" (From Our Boys). *Pokrok Západu* (Omaha, NE), 48(7), 4 September.

Breuer, Miloslav (1918b): "Od našich hochů" (From Our Boys). *Pokrok Západu* (Omaha, NE), 48(11), 2 October.

Breuer, Miles J. (1918c): "Thomas Garrigue Masaryk." *The Belleville Telescope* (Belleville, KS), 47(42), 27 June.
Repr. *The Mahaska Leader* (Mahaska, KS), 13(48), 28 June.
Repr. *Bratrský Věstník* (Cedar Rapids, IA), 21(6), 1918, June.

Breuer, Miles J. (1921): "Planning Future Hospitals." *The Lincoln Star* (Lincoln, NE), 19, 20 August.

Breuer, Miloslav J. (1922): "Osudný paprsek" (The Fatal Ray). *Amerikán Národní Kalendář na rok 1923*. Chicago: Aug. Geringer. – Vol. 46.

Breuer, Miloslav J. (1924): "Vyšší tvor" (The Superior Being). *Bratrský Věstník* (Cedar Rapids, IA), 27(9), September + 27(10), October + 29(11), November.

Breuer, Miles J. (1925a): *Electricity for the Sick Man*. Lincoln: (no publisher) 1925.

Breuer, Miles J. (1925b): *Index of Physiotherapeutic Technic*. Omaha: American College of Radiology and Physiotherapy.

Breuer, Miles J. (1925c): "The Race Between Civilization and Catastrophe." *Social Science* (Winfield, KS), 1(1).

Breuer, Miles J. (1926): "The Superior Race." *Social Science* (Winfield, KS), 1(3).

Breuer, Miles J. (1928): "The Hobby That Builds Character." *The American Annual of Photography 1929*. Boston: American Photographic Publishing Company.

Breuer, Miles J. (1929): "The Future of Scientifiction." *Amazing Stories Quarterly* (New York, NY), 2(3), Summer.

Breuer, Miloslav J. (1930a): "Amatérská fotografie ve Spojených státech" (Amateur Photography in the United States). In: Paďouk, Rudolf (ed.): *Umělecká fotografie a její tvorba* (Artistic Photography). Olomouc: Nakladatelství R. Prombergra.

Breuer, Miles J. (1930b): "The Doctor Peeps Into the Future." *Bratrský Věstník* (Cedar Rapids, IA), 33(9), September.

Breuer, Miles J. (1930c): "Gostak and the Doshes." *Amazing Stories* (New York, NY), 4(12), March.

Breuer, Miles J. (1930d): "Paradise and Iron." *Amazing Stories Quarterly* (New York, NY), 3(3), Summer.

Breuer, Miles J. (1930e): "A Tribute to G. Peyton Wertenbaker from a Brother Author." *Amazing Stories* (New York, NY), 5(1), April.

Breuer, Miles J. (1931): "The Legion of the Fittest." *Social Science* (Winfield, KS), 6(2).

Breuer, Miles, J. (1937): "Comparisons in Science Fiction." *Tesseract* (San Francisco, CA), 2(2), February.

Breuer, Miloslav J. (1938a): "Možnosti a nemožnosti paprsků X" (The possibilities and impossibilities of X-rays). *Bratrský Věstník* (Cedar Rapids, IA), 41(5), May.

Breuer, Miloslav J. (1938b): "Padesátiletý člověk – co s ním?" (What to Do with a Fifty-year-old?). *Bratrský Věstník* (Cedar Rapids, IA), 41(11), November.

Breuer, Miles J. (1939a): "Meet the Authors: Miles J. Breuer." *Amazing Stories* (New York, NY), 13(3), March.

Breuer, Miles J. (1939b): "What a Modern Husband Needs." *Social Science* (Winfield, KS), 14(3).

Breuer, Miles J. (1940): "The New Frontier." *Startling Stories* (New York, NY), 3(3), May.

Breuer, Miles J. (1942): "The Assembly-Line for Writers." *The Writer*, 55(9), September.

Breuerová, Libuše A. (1917): "Dopis z Texasu" (Letter from Texas). *Komenský* (Omaha, NE), 9(1?).

Bubeníček, Rudolf (1939): *Dějiny Čechů v Chicagu* (History of the Czechs in Chicago). Chicago: [self published].

Bulkin, Carleton (2024): "Introduction." In: Procházková, Emilie: *The Martians: Transcribed from the Beyond*. Joshua Tree: Space Cowboy Books.

Callus, Ivan – Grech, Victor – Thake-Vassallo, Clare (2011): "',Not Only the World As It Is, but the World as It Will Be': Medicine in Science Fiction." *SFRA Review*, 297, Summer.

Čapek, Tomáš (1911): *Padesát let českého tisku v Americe* (Fifty Years of Czech Press in America). New York: František Brodský – Tomáš Čapek – Michael Pilnáček – František A. Sovák – Albert Winternitz.

Čapek, Thomas (1920): *The Čechs (Bohemians) in America: A Study of Their National, Cultural, Political, Social, Economic and Religious Life*. Boston – New York: Houghton Mifflin.

Čapek, Thomas – Vostrovský Čapek, Anna (1918): *Bohemian (Čech) Bibliography. A Finding List of Writings in English Relating to Bohemians and the Čechs*. New York – Chicago: Fleming H. Revell.

Čapek, Tomáš (1926): *Naše Amerika* (Our America). Praha: Národní rada československá.

Čapek, Tomáš (1935): *Moje Amerika. Vzpomínky a úvahy (1861–1934)* (My America. Memories and Considerations /1861–1934/). Praha: Fr. Borový.

Chada, Joseph (1981): *The Czechs in the United States*. New York: SVU Press.

Clute, John – Langford, David (2025): *The Encyclopedia of Science Fiction*. www.sf-encyclopedia.com

Clute, John – Nicholls, Peter (eds.) (1993): *The Encyclopedia of Science Fiction*. London: Orbit.

Conklin, Groff – Fabricant, Noah D. (eds.) (1963): *Great Science Fiction About Doctors*. New York: Collier Books.

Dojiva, Radomil – Olša, Jr., Jaroslav (2022): "Mini-Dictionary (Instead of Epilogue)." In: Dojiva, Radomil – Olša, Jr., Jaroslav – Rampas, Zdeněk –

Stračárová, Dana (eds.): *Bradbury's Shadow: Chronicle of Czech Science Fiction, vol. 3: Fandom Authors of the 1980s*. Prague: Nová vlna.

Dojiva, Radomil – Stračárová, Dana (2022): "Living Science Fiction." In: Dojiva, Radomil – Olša, Jr., Jaroslav – Rampas, Zdeněk – Stračárová, Dana (eds.): *Bradbury's Shadow: Chronicle of Czech Science Fiction, vol. 3: Fandom Authors of the 1980s*. Prague: Nová vlna.

Dubovický, Ivan (2018): *Češi v Americe a česko-americké vztahy v průběhu pěti staletí – Czechs in America and Czech-American Relations in a Course of Five Centuries*. Praha: Epocha.

Dubovický, Ivan – Kraft, David – Secká, Milena (2003): *Češi v Americe. České vystěhovalectví do Ameriky a česko-americké vztahy v průběhu pěti staletí* (Czechs in America: Czech Emigration to America and Czech-American Relations Over Five Centuries). Praha: Communicatio Humana – C. H. Expo – Pražská edice.

Eckertová, Eva (2004): *Kameny na prérii. Čeští vystěhovalci v Texasu* (Stones on the Prairie: Czech Emigrants in Texas). Praha: Lidové noviny.

Eckert, Eva (2006): *Stones on the Prairie: Acculturation in America*. Bloomington: Slavica Publishers.

Elliot, Jeffrey M. (1983): "Jack Williamson: In at the Creation." In: Elliot, J. M.: *Pulp Voices*. San Bernardino: The Borgo Press.

Emerson, Jim (2020): *Futures Past: A Visual History of Science Fiction: 1926: The Birth of Modern Science Fiction*. [no place]: www.sfhistory.net.

Emerson, Jim (2021): *Futures Past. A Visual History of Science Fiction: 1927: Dawn of the SF Blockbuster*. [no place]: www.sfhistory.net.

Ferber, Sandy (2021): "The Birth of a New Republic: Of Lunarian Bats and Atomic Vortexes." https://fantasyliterature.com/reviews/the-birth-of-a-new-republic/

Fischer-Nebmaier, Wladimir – Oberly, James W. – Steidl, Annemarie (eds.) (2017): *From a Multiethnic Empire to a Nation of Nations: Austro-Hungarian Migrants in the US, 1870–1940*. Innsbruck – Wien – Bozen: Studie Verlag.

Formanová, Lucie – Gruntorád, Jiří – Příbáň, Michal (1999): *Exilová periodika. Katalog periodik českého a slovenského exilu a krajanských tisků vydávaných po roce 1945* (Exile Periodicals: Catalogue of the Periodical Publications of Czech and Slovak Exulants and Compatriots Published After 1945). Praha: Libri prohibiti – Ježek.

Gavaler, Chris (2015): *On the Origin of Superheroes: From the Big Bang to Action Comics No. 1*. Iowa City: University of Iowa Press.

Gernsback, Hugo (1926a): "$500.00 Prize Story Contest." *Amazing Stories* (New York, NY), 1(8), December.

Gernsback, Hugo (1926b): "A New Sort of Magazine." *Amazing Stories* (New York, NY), 1(1), April.

Gillings, Walter (1947): "The Saga of Science Fiction." [review of Bailey, J. O.: Pilgrims Through Space and Times]. *Fantasy Review* (London), 1(5), October-November.

Greer, Lynnelle (1921): "Dr. Miles J. Breuer Tells of Dream in Which He Pictured Lincoln 154 Years from Now." *The Lincoln Star* (Lincoln, NE), 25 December. – Supplement *The Lincoln Sunday Star*.

Gunn, James (ed.) (1979): *The Road to Science Fiction 2: From Wells to Heinlein*. New York: New American Library.

Gunn, James (ed.) (1988): *The New Encyclopedia of Science Fiction*. New York: Viking.

Habenicht, Jan (1910): *Dějiny Čechův Amerických*. St. Louis: Hlas. Translated as *History of Czechs in America*. St. Paul: Czechoslovak Genealogical Society International 1996.

Hájek, Ant. (1945): "Naši studenti uctili památku prvého předsedy klubu [Čechie]" (Our Students Honoured the Memory of the First President of the Club [Čechie]). *Věstník* (West, TX), 33(47), 21 November.

Hájková, Dagmar (2011): ´Naše česká věc.´ *Češi v Americe za první světové války* (´Our Czech Cause´: Czechs in America during the First World War). Praha: Nakladatelství Lidové noviny.

Hlous, František – Olša, Jr., Jaroslav – Rampas, Zdeněk – Rampasová, Michaela (eds.) (2025): *Osudný paprsek a další povídky raného česko-amerického spisovatele* (The Fatal Ray and Other Stories of Early Czech-American Writer). Praha: Nová vlna.

Hribal, C. J. (ed.) (1991): *The Boundaries of Twilight: Czecho-Slovak Writing from the New World*. Minneapolis: New Rivers Press.

Hudson, Estelle – Maresh, Henry R. (1996 [1934]): *Czech Pioneers of the Southwest: The History of a People in the Development of a Nation*. Houston: Western Lithograph.

Jaklová, Alena (2010): *Čechoamerická periodika 19. a 20. století* (Czech-American Periodicals of the 19th and 20th Centuries). Praha: Academia.

Jerabek, Esther (1976): *Czechs and Slovaks in North America: A Bibliography*. New York: Czechoslovak Society of Arts and Sciences in America – Chicago: Czechoslovak National Council of America.

Kašpar, Oldřich (1986 [1992]): *Tam za mořem je Amerika. Dopisy a vzpomínky českých vystěhovalců do Ameriky v 19. století* (There's America Across the Sea: Letters and Memoirs of Czech Emigrants to America in the 19th Century). Pardubice: Kora.

Knight, Damon (ed.) (1975): *Science Fiction of the Thirties*. Indianapolis – New York: Botts-Merrill.

Konecny, Lawrence H. – Machann, Clinton (2004): *Perilous Voyages: Czech and English Immigrants to Texas in the 1870s*. College Station: Texas A+M University Press.

Kopecky, Sam (2020): *From Moravia to Texas. A Czech Immigrant Family's Pioneering Journey*. [no place given]: Trafford.

Korytová-Magstadt, Štěpánka (1993): *To Reap a Bountiful Harvest: Czech Immigration Beyond the Mississippi, 1850–1900*. Iowa City: Rudi Publishing.

Kraut, Alan M. (1982): *The Huddled Masses: The Immigrant in American Society, 1880–1921*. Wheeling: Harlan Davidson.

Kříž, Jaroslav (2022): *Česká Amerika: Chicago* (Czech America: Chicago). Praha: Epocha.

Kříž, Jaroslav – Křížová, Lenka (2017*): Střípky z českého Chicaga. Edice dokumentů k dějinám Čechů v americkém Chicagu v letech 1848–1918* (Snippets from Czech Chicago: An Edition of Documents on the History of Czechs in Chicago, USA, 1848–1918). Praha: Academia.

Kříž, Jaroslav – Procházková, Lenka (2016): "The American Dream in 'Czech' Chicago: August Geringer's Publishing Activities." *Comenius: Journal of Euro-American Civilization*, 1.

Kunovjánek, Vladimír (1989): *Děravý Josefův plášť. K některým otázkám etnického a národnostního vývoje USA* (Joseph's Leaky Cloak. On Some Issues in the Ethnic and National Development of the United States). Praha: Horizont.

Kussi, Peter (ed.) (1990): *Toward the Radical Center: A Karel Čapek Reader*. Highland Park: Catbird Press.

Laska, Vera (1978): *The Czechs in America 1633–1977: A Chronology and Fact Book*. Dobbs Ferry: Oceana Publications.

Lowndes, Robert A. (2004): "Yesterday's Worlds of Tomorrow." In: Ashley, Michael – Lowndes, Robert A.: *The Gernsback Days: A Study of the Evolution of Modern Science Fiction from 1911 to 1936*. Holicong: Wildside Press.

Machann, Clinton (1979): "Hugo Chotek and Czech-American Fiction." *Melus* (Los Angeles, CA), 6(2), Summer.

Machann, Clinton (1993): "Evidence of Assimilation in Pavel Albieri's Nevěsta za padesát dolarů (Bride for Fifty Dollars)." *Nebraska History* (Lincoln, NE), 74(3-4).

Machann, Clinton – Mendl, Jr., James W. (eds.) (1991*): Czech Voices: Stories from Texas in the Amerikán Národní Kalendář*. College Station: Texas A+M University Press.

Marholeva, Krasimira (2020): *Mezi starou a novou vlastí: integrace a sebeidentifikace českého společenství v USA v druhé polovině XIX. století* (Between Old and New Homeland: Integration and Self-identification of the Czech Community in the United States in the Second Half of the 19th Century). Diss. Fakulta humanitních studií, Univerzita Karlova.

McCaffrey, Larry (1991): "An Interview with Jack Williamson." *Science Fiction Studies*, 18(2), July.

Míček, Edward (1929): "Universitní klub ‚Čechie' a vyučování české řeči a literatuře na Texasské státní universitě" (Čechie University Club and Learning of the Czech Language and Literature at Texas State University). In: Míček E.: *Duch americké výchovy* (The Spirit of American Education). Praha: Sfinx.

Míček, Eduard (1932): "Čeština na amerických školách" (Czech Language at American Schools). In: Míček, E.: *Amerika se učí* (America Learns). Praha: Sfinx.

Míček, Eduard (1949): "Z malých počátků – From Small Beginnings." *Věstník* (West, TX), 37, 17 August.

Murphy, Robin R. (2020): "Autonomous Cars in Science Fiction." *Science Robotics* (Washington, DC), 5(39), February.

Musil, Ferdinand L. (1933): *Československá Amerika. Ze spolkového a národního života Čechů a Slováků ve Spoj. Státech a v Kanadě roku 1932* (Czechoslovak America: From the Life of Czechs and Slovaks in the United States and Canada in 1932). Chicago: Denní Hlasatel.

Neff, Ondřej (1981): *Něco je jinak. Komentáře k české literární fantastice* (Something Is Otherwise: Notes on Czech Fantastic Literature). Praha: Albatros.

Neff, Ondřej – [Kramer, Alexandr] (1986): *Všechno je jinak. Kapitoly o světové science fiction* (Everything Is Otherwise: Chapters on Science Fiction Around the World). Praha: Albatros.

Neff, Ondřej – Olša, jr., Jaroslav (eds.) (1995): *Encyklopedie literatury science fiction* (Encyclopedia of Science Fiction Literature). Praha: AFSF – H+H.

Nekola, Martin (2017): *České Chicago* (Czech Chicago). Praha: Nakladatelství Lidové noviny.

Nekola, Martin (2022): *Czechs in the Northwest: Idaho, Montana, Oregon, Washington*. Los Angeles: Consulate General of the Czech Republic in Los Angeles.

Nekola, Martin (2024): *Metropole české Ameriky* (Cities of Czech America). Praha: Universum.

Nesvadbík, Lumír – Polišenský, Josef (1996): *Češi a Amerika. Úvod do studia dějin vystěhovalectví. II* (Czechs and America: Introduction to the Study of the History of Emigration. II). Praha: Karolinum.

Niewiadowski, Andrzej – Smuszkiewicz, Antoni (1990): *Leksykon polskiej literatury fantastycznonaukowej*. (Lexicon of Polish Science Fiction Literature). Poznań: Wydawnictwo Poznańskie.

Norwood, Rick (2004): "The Gostak and the Doshes: Reminiscences of a Mathematics Undergraduate in the 1960s." *Math Horizons*, 11(4).

Olša, jr., Jaroslav (1995): "Česká science fiction v krajanských a exilových vydáních" (Czech Science Fiction in Publications of Compatriots and Exiles). In: Adamovič, I.: *Slovník české literární fantastiky a science fiction* (Encyclopedia of Czech Fantastic Literature and Science Fiction). Praha: R3.

Olša, jr. Jaroslav (2020a): *The Amazing Breuer: Early Czech-American Science Fiction Author Miloslav (Miles) J. Breuer (1889–1945)*. Praha: Nová vlna – Los Angeles: Consulate General of the Czech Republic in Los Angeles.

Olša, jr., Jaroslav (2020b): "Miloslav / Miles J. Breuer a české kořeny klasické americké science fiction" (Miloslav / Miles J. Breuer and Czech Roots of Classic American Science Fiction). *XB–1* (Praha), 11.
Repr. *Interkom* (Praha), 7-8, 2021.

Olša, jr., Jaroslav (2022): "První česko-kalifornská spisovatelka a překladatelka" (The First Czech-Californian Writer and Translator). *Plav* (Praha), 1.

Olša, Jr., Jaroslav (2023): *Miloslav (Miles) J. Breuer: Česko-americký spisovatel u zrodu moderní science fiction* (Miloslav /Miles/ J. Breuer: Czech-American Writer at the Birth of Modern Science Fiction). Praha: Nová vlna.

Olša, Jr., Jaroslav (2024): *V odlesku Hollywoodu: Čeští a českoslovenští konzulové v Los Angeles*. (In the Limelight of Hollywood: Czech and Czechoslovak Consuls in Los Angeles). Praha: Nová vlna.

Olša, Jr., Jaroslav (manuscript): *Czechoslovakia's Consulates in the US West, Southwest and Midwest (1920 to 1950)*. [in print].

Opatrný Josef (1993): "Problems in the History of Czech Immigration to America in the Second Half of the Nineteenth Century." *Nebraska History* (Lincoln, NE), 74(3-4).

Page, Michael R. (2008): "Miles J. Breuer. Science Fiction Pioneer of the Nebraska Plains." In: Breuer, Miles J.: *The Man with the Strange Head and Other Early Science Fiction Stories*. Lincoln – London: University of Nebraska Press.

Papoušek, Vladimír (2001): *Česká literatura v Chicagu. Literární tvorba Čechoameričanů v letech 1880–1939* (Czech Literature in Chicago. Literature of the Czech-Americans, 1880–1939). Olomouc: Votobia.

Papoušek, Vladimír (2005): "Objevování Ameriky. Česká literatura ve Spojených státech" (Discovering America: Czech Literature in the United States). *Dějiny a současnost* (Praha), 27(9).

Patterson, Jr., William H. (2014): *Robert A. Heinlein In Dialogue with His Century. Vol. 2. 1948–1988. The Man Who Learned Better.* New York: Tor Books.

Peprník, Jaroslav (2002): *Amerika očima české literatury od vzniku USA po rok 2000. I+II.* (America as Seen by Czech Literature since the Creation of the United States to 2000. I+II). Olomouc: Univerzita Palackého.

Peprník, Jaroslav (2012): *Češi a anglofonní svět: kontakty a percepce (lexikon osob od středověku po rok 1989). I+II.* (Czechs and the Anglophone World: Contacts and Perception /Personal Encyclopedia from the Medieval Times to 1989/). Olomouc. Univerzita Palackého.

Pohl, Frederik (2000 [1978]): *The Way the Future Was: A Memoir.* London: Granada.

Polišenský, Josef (1992): *Úvod do studia dějin vystěhovalectví do Ameriky. I* (Introduction to the Study of the History of Emigration to America. I). Praha: Univerzita Karlova.

Rechcígl, Miroslav (2000): *Postavy naší Ameriky. Poučné a zábavné čtení ze života zahraničních Čechů* (Personalities of Our America: Educational and Entertaining Reading from the Lives of Czechs Abroad). Praha: Pražská edice.

Rechcígl, Jr., Miroslav (2005): *Czechs and Slovaks in America.* [no place given]: Czechoslovak Society of Arts and Sciences. – East European Monographs, Boulder.

Rechcígl, Jr., Miroslav (2011): *Czech American Bibliography: A Comprehensive Listing with Focus on the US and with Appendices on Czechs in Canada and Latin America.* Bloomington: Author House.

Rechcígl, Jr., Miroslav (2015): *Czech It Out: Czech American Biography Sourcebook.* Bloomington: Author House.

Rechcígl, Jr., Miroslav (2016): *Encyclopedia of Bohemian and Czech-American Biography. I+II+III.* Bloomington: Author House.

Rechcígl, Jr., Miroslav (2017): *Beyond the Sea of Beer: History of Immigration of Bohemians and Czechs to the New World and Their Contribution.* Bloomington: Author House.

Reed, Edward N. (1916): "A Medical Utopia." *The American Journal of Clinical Medicine* (Chicago, IL), 23(1–11).

Rosická, Růžena (1928): *Dějiny Čechů v Nebrasce* (History of Czechs in Nebraska). Omaha: Český historický klub v Nebrasce.

Samuel, Julie (1952): "Barbora Breuerová." *Bratrský Věstník – Fraternal Herald* (Cedar Rapids, IA), 55(4), April.

Šašková-Pierce, Míla (1993): "Czech-language Maintenance in Nebraska." *Nebraska History* (Lincoln, NE), 74(3-4).

Šatava, Leoš (1996): "Vystěhovalectví do USA" (Immigration to the United States). In: Brouček, S. (ed.): *Češi v cizině 9.* (Czech in Abroad 9) Praha: Ústav pro etnografii a folkloristiku ČSAV.

Science Fiction Bibliography. Vol. 1, No. 1. Austin: The Science Fiction Syndicate.

Secká Milena (2005): "August Geringer – nakladatel, mecenáš a lidumil" (August Geringer – Publisher, Patron and Philanthropist). In: *Problematika historických a vzácných knižních fondů Čech, Moravy a Slezska – lidé okolo knih* (Historical and Rare Book Collections of Bohemia, Moravia and Silesia: People Around Books). Brno: Sdružení knihoven České republiky – Olomouc: Vědecká knihovna.

Sheridan, Thomas (1949-50): "Thomas Sheridan Tells the Romantic Life Story of Shy Jack Williamson, Who Might Have Been a Cowboy but Became Instead a Space-Time Ranger." *Science-Fantasy Review*, 4(17), Winter.

Silverberg, Robert (1953): "The First Issue." *SF* (Silver Spring, MD), 7.

Sloane, T. O'Conor (1929): "Amazing Stories." *Amazing Stories* (New York, NY), 4(2), May.

Smith, Curtis C. (ed.): *Twentieth-Century Science-Fiction Writers.* Chicago – London: St. James Press.

Smuszkiewicz, Antoni (1982): *Zaczarowana gra: Zarys dziejów polskiej fantastyki naukowej* (Enchanted Game: History of Polish Science Fiction). Poznań: Wydawnictwo Poznańskie.

Spaulding, E. Wilder (1968): *The Quiet Invaders: The Story of the Austrian Impact upon America.* Vienna: Österreichischer Bundesverlag für Unterricht, Wissenschaft und Kunst.

Strejček, Karel (1938): *Průvodce po čs. zahraničí* (Guide to Czechoslovakia Abroad). Praha: Komenský.

Sturm, Rudolf (1978): "Czech Literature in America." In: Aycock, Wendell M. – Zyla, Wolodymyr T. (eds.): *Ethnic Literatures Since 1776: The Many Voices of America. Part 1.* Lubbock: Texas Tech Press.

Swartz, Jon D. (2017): "Neglected Genre Authors: The Science Fiction of Miles J. Breuer, M.D." *The National Fantasy Fan* (Worcester, MA), 76(4), April.

Temple, William F. (1938): "The British Fan in His Natural Haunt. No. 1. Eric C. Williams." *Novae Terrae* (London), 2(10).

Toskey, Burnett R. (1956): "Amazing in Review. Part V, 1930." *Cry of the Nameless* (Seattle, WA), 88, February.

Truesdale, Dave (1976): "Jack Williamson: Interview." *Tangent*, 5.

Tuck, Donald H. (1974): *The Encyclopedia of Science Fiction and Fantasy, Volume 1: Who's Who, A-L.* Chicago: Advent.

Veis, Jaroslav (2021): "Robot, the Most Famous Czech Celebrates 100 Years." https://locusmag.com/2021/02/jaroslav-veis-guest-post-robot-the-most-famous-czech-celebrates–100-years/

Vlha, Marek (2015): *Mezi starou vlastí a Amerikou. Počátky české krajanské komunity v USA 19. století* (Between the Old Homeland and America: The Beginnings of the Czech Expatriate Community in the United States in the 19th Century). Brno: Matice moravská.

Vojan, J. E. S. (1915): "Santa Claus a česká Amerika" (Santa Claus and Czech America). *Jednou za Čas* (Chicago, IL), 1(5), December.

Vrbenská, Františka (2023): "Čechoameričan na úsvitu fantastiky" (Czech-American at the Birth of Science Fiction). *XB-1* (Praha), 2023, 11. [review of Olša, Jr. 2023]

Williamson, Jack (1928): "Scientifiction, Searchlight of Science." *Amazing Stories Quarterly* (New York, NY), 1(4), Fall.

Williamson, Jack (1981): "Introduction." In: Breuer, Miles J. – Williamson, Jack: *The Birth of a New Republic*. New Orleans: PDA Enterprises.

Williamson, Jack (1984): *Wonder's Child: My Life in Science Fiction*. New York: Bluejay Books.

Winter, Wilma (1921): "How's Your Health These Days? Tell Your Dreams to the Doctor and Let Him Decide." *Lincoln Star* (Lincoln, NE), 10 April.

Zemek, Bedřich (1947): *Češi a Slováci v Americe* (Czechs and Slovaks in America). Praha: Ministerstvo informací. – Československé epištoly, 5-6.

Ziberov, Dmitriy (1987): *Sovetskaya fantastika 20-40-kh godov* (Soviet Science Fiction of the 1920s–1940s). Moskva: Pravda.

Žižka, Arnošt Jan (1932): *Kulturní přínosy amerických Čechů* (Cultural Contributions of Czech Americans). Praha: [self-published]. – Special imprint from the magazine *Vychovatel*, Vol. 46+47.

Index

Breuer, Alois 12
Breuer, Barbara (Barbora) 15, 16, 83, 96, 98
Breuer, Charles Hugh (Karel Hugo) 12–21, 26, 29, 30, 75–77, 83, 96, 97
Breuer, Hynek 12
Breuer, Julia (Julie) 23, 30, 98, 100
Breuer (Bräuer), Karel (Sr.) 12, 96
Breuer, Libbie (Libuše) 27, 89, 96, 98, 99
Breuer, Matilda 12
Breuer, Mildred 30, 100

Breuer, Miles (Miloslav) J.
<u>Fiction in English</u>:
"Adventures of the Bronze Mahadeva, The" 23, 112
"Age of the Seven, An" 114
"American Ghost, The" 32, 116
"Appendix and the Spectacles, The" 51, 89, 118
"Appology for Grinds, An" 113
"Baby on Neptune, A" 59, 120
Birth of a New Republic, The 67–69, 81, 92, 93, 123
"Blood of a Child, The" 109
"Book of Worlds, The" 51, 119
"Buried Treasure" 52, 119
"Captured Cross-Section, The" 51, 118
"Chemistry Murder Case, The" 125
"Company of the Weather, The" 126
"Death Clandestine, The" 32, 115, 118
"Demons of Rhadi-Mu, The" 123
"Disappearing Papers, The" 126
"Driving Power, The" 122
"Dumb Man, The" 112
"Einstein See-Saw, The" 124
"Face in the Air, The" 113
"Fatal Ray, The" 34, 36, 38, 43, 44, 47, 52, 64, 103, 116, 119
"Finger of the Past, The" 124
"Fitzgerald Contraction, The" 54, 79, 121
"Flaw in the Premise, The" 22, 91, 113, 125
"Ghost of the Big Hussar, The" 27, 114
"Girl from Mars, The" 67, 119
"Gostak and the Doshes, The" 58, 93, 110, 121
"He That Seeketh" 114
"Hungry Guinea-Pig, The" 31, 100, 115, 121
"Inferiority Compex, The" 10, 31, 51, 100, 116, 123
"Instructor in French, An" 101, 116
"Legion of the Fittest, The" 43–47, 78, 123
"Man with the Strange Head, The" 11, 48, 49, 93, 117

Creighton Medical College 16
Crete, NE 19, 20
Cry of the Nameless (SF fanzine) 108
Cyrano de Bergerac 62
Czechoslovakia 77, 91, 99, 106, 108
Czech Republic 91

Dale, Christine 9, 107
Daniel, Jan 20
David City, NE 17, 18
David City News (periodical) 97
Des Moines, IA 32
Dostál, Alois 26, 99
Dubovický, Ivan 9
Duch Času (Czech-American periodical) 13, 100

Electrical Experimenter, The (periodical) 103
Emerson, Jim 9
Erben, Karel Jaromír 97

Fabricant, Noah D. 23
Famous Monsters of Filmland (periodical) 107
Fantasy Commentator (SF fanzine) 107
Fantasy Magazine (SF fanzine) 106
Fantasy Review (SF fanzine) 81, 94, 107, 109
Fort Riley, KS 32
France 11, 32, 33, 101
Franklin, Benjamin 69
Fraternal Herald (Czech-American periodical) 100
Fuqua, Robert 73
Future Fiction (SF magazine) 74, 106

Galveston, TX 28, 38, 98
Geringer, August 13, 17, 28, 96, 100
Germany 11
Gernsback, Hugo 11, 23, 31, 34, 48, 50, 52–54, 61, 64, 65, 67, 78, 101, 103–106
Gillings, Walter 52, 81, 103
Gilroy, CA 77

Haggard, H. Rider 18
Hálek, Vítězslav 27, 97, 99
Halletsville, TX 16, 26, 27
Hamilton, Edmond 51, 103, 106
Harris, Clare Winger 59, 104
Haverfordian, The (periodical) 98

Lovecraft, H. P. 48, 81, 101, 103
Lowndes, Robert W. 69

McMaster, J. L. 109
Malešov (Bohemia, now the Czech Republic) 12
Manchester (Britain) 46
Marseilles (France) 46
Marvel Tales (SF magazine) 74, 106
Masaryk, Tomáš Garrigue 27
Meek, S. P. 51, 103
Merritt, Abraham 11, 69, 78, 105, 106
Míček, Eduard (Micek, Edward) 25, 99
Mikeska, Louis 24, 99
Miller, P. Schuyler 106
Minicon 110
Minnesota 12
Morey, Leo 54, 60, 69, 71, 105
Muhlena, David 9

Nádherný, Emanuel Václav 89
Naples (Italy) 46
Národní Pokrok (Czech-American periodical) 82, 89, 106, 107, 109
Národní Tiskárna (National Printing Co.) 15, 97
Nebraska 11, 12, 15, 17, 18, 20, 29–32, 45, 66, 70, 76, 82, 83, 89, 93, 97, 98, 100
Nebraska State Historical Society 101
Neff, Ondřej 9
Nekola, Martin 9
Neligh, Dave 9
Neligh, Ian 9
Neruda, Jan 97
New Jersey 25
New Mexico 66
New Orleans, LA 45
New Prague, MN 12
New York, NY 12, 24, 25, 75, 111
North American Science Fiction Convention (NASFiC) 110
Norton, KS 76
Nový Domov (Czech-American periodical) 16, 97

Obzor (Czech-American periodical) 27, 98, 99
Oklahoma 12
Olša, Jr., Jaroslav 109, 110
Omaha, NE 15–17, 19, 30, 45–46, 77, 82, 89, 90, 97, 99, 100
Omaha Sanitarium 19
Omaha University 26, 33, 98, 100

Miles J. Breuer:
The Superior Race[1]

I.
A Very Strange Ship.

"If you love mysteries, there's one for you!" The aged clerk caught me by the arm. "That's John B. Kaspar. Thirty years I've worked here, and all that time I've had him on my mind. I know it is he." He pointed across the huge wareroom piled full of nautical supplies, at a whitehaired old man, still older than himself.

"Kaspar," I said; "I never even heard such a name."

"It has been forgotten for thirty years. He was a millionaire. He owned half a county where oil was discovered. And he was an inventor, famous for many improvements in automobile construction. Near forty years it is, that he disappeared, completely, with his money, his family, everything! He and I went to school together. It is five years since he was last in this place. He always buys raw rubber and camphor, immense supplies of them. About every five years, he comes. Once I tried to speak to him, and for an instant it seemed that he recognized me. Then, a frightened expression seemed to cross his face, and he gazed at me without recognition, and insisted that I mistook him for someone else. His disappearance was the greatest puzzle in history, and it has never been solved. Look; he seems to act as though he were in someone's power – I wish I were a young man!"

A sudden impulse seized me. Here was a rare opportunity for a little adventure, or for some sort of a pickle, as my father would have said. I had just graduated from the university, and was taking a little holiday, before setting out to look for my life's work. The waiting world would have to wait awhile for me to revolutionize it, while I basked in the bright Galveston sun, and idled away a few days. I was staying with my aged uncle, old enough really to have been my grandfather, who was the chief shipping clerk at the warehouse of the huge ship supply firm of Martin and Myrtle.

I resolved to follow the mysterious stranger, to learn, if I could, what was the mystery surrounding him. His purchases consisted of a considerable number of bales, which were being loaded on automobile trucks for the purpose of

---

1 This novelette was originally published in Czech as "Vyšší tvor" in three installments in *Bratrský Věstník* monthly (September to November, 1924), and later on in English as "The Superior Race" in *Social Science* quarterly (1926). This English text is practically identical to the earlier Czech text.

156

being taken to the dock. I swung myself on the back of one of the trucks, as it started away. That one impulse was all I needed to launch me on a strange and terrible adventure; after that, no turning back was possible.

The trucks drove up on a dock at which was anchored a solitary vessel. The latter was about a hundred feet long, and resembled a private yacht. The whole ship was enameled black, like an automobile. Everything on it was clean and glistening. No one appeared on its deck; the ship's derricks swung around, lifted the loads from the trucks, and lowered them into the hold. The white-haired old man stood and watched it absently, never noticing me, and when it was finished, went on board, and disappeared down a hatchway. Not a soul was in sight anywhere. The trucks turned around and drove away; I stood and gazed awhile, and then slipped up the gangplank on the ship's deck. As I did so, a great searchlight in the bows swung around toward me; it was not lighted, and I could see an exaggerated reflection of myself in its parabolic mirror. There was a stirring of machinery in the depths of the vessel beneath my feet, a rattle and a rumble; the anchor splashed up out of the water, the hawsers fell loose and were whirred around a windlass. The ship swung around and moved away from the dock.

Suddenly, out of the distance, an automobile dashed swiftly up on the dock, to the very water's edge, and two men leaped out. One was the aged chief clerk, pointing his finger at me. The other was a young giant of a longshoreman, who swung a big package over his head and hurled it over the widening interval of water between the ship and the dock, to my very feet. The old man was waving his hand and shouting: "That is for you!" Before I recovered from my amazement at the swift succession of surprises, the ship was speeding down the channel, between the jetties, toward the sea; and the city was just a thin gray streak. A journey on rather short notice, I thought. I picked up the package, and looked around. It was rapidly growing dark, and behind us was one of those glorious sunsets for which Galveston is famous.

I saw a stairway through a hatch, and descended, into a narrow passageway with several doors. At the further end, a lighted crack was visible under a door. I opened the door into the first cabin and looked in, finding the button which turned on the electric light. There was a bunk there, a chair, and a wash-stand; comfortable but not luxurious. Two or three more cabins were exactly the same; none showed signs of occupancy; and I returned to the first, where I opened my package. The first thing I found was a typewritten letter:

"My dear boy: I had to act quickly. I well knew what you intended doing – just what I would do if my old bones permitted. I have thought of it for many years. I could not let you go with bare hands; there might be danger. Here are some things you might need. I threw together what I could during the short time I had. Good luck to you. I shall hope for your safe return, and also that I may still be alive when you return, so that I may listen to your adventures." It was from my old uncle.

The package contained a pair of heavy marching shoes, a pith hat for tropic wear; a pocket electric flashlight and a supply of batteries, a compass, two automatic pistols, a .25 caliber, and a .45 caliber, with a belt, holsters, and a dozen boxes of shells, a field-glass, hand-ax, pocket camera and films, a camp cooking kit, a supply of dried emergency ration, and a knapsack in which everything could be carried.

Before I had looked the things over it was completely dark outside. I hung the pistols at my belt, and with the flashlight in my hand, went out on deck. Supplied as I was, I felt ready for anything. Galveston was only a feeble reflection in the sky behind us. The speed of the vessel must have been remarkable, from the way the spray flew from the bows. And, though I searched every accessible cranny and corner in the ship, each step giving me courage for the subsequent one, I found not a single living thing. Only the room with the light under the door, I left for the last. But, on the bridge there was no one, no one at the wheel. There was no forecastle; in its place was a storeroom filled with bales. The fore hatch led to the engine-room, where the machinery was busily at work in solitude without attention. The machinery looked unusual and very complicated; the engines resembled the Diesel type, but were not precisely similar. I began to feel creepy because everything was so deserted, and for a while I almost wished I could meet some bloodthirsty pirates.

I returned to the cabin I had selected, by means of the after hatch. The light was still visible under the door at the end of the passage. Again I opened several doors and turned my flashlight into them, all a-tremble at each that I would be seized and throttled, but I saw nothing, felt nothing, heard nothing. I stole quietly up to the door under which the light shone, and stood a considerable while before it, hesitating. Finally I picked up courage to knock. A chair grated over the floor, and the door was flung open. In it stood the aged and mysterious man, pale and frightened. When he looked me over, he appeared relieved.

"For God's sake, boy!" he exclaimed. "What are you doing here? How did you get here? You unfortunate man!"

"For the love of Pete!" I said; "who is running this ship?"

"Don't ask me that, boy. I cannot take you back. You are lost!" He said it with a groan, so that for a moment I actually believed myself sentenced to death. But, seeing no danger, I laughed.

"The only hope is," he said, "that we can put you off in a boat when we meet another vessel." He seemed to be thinking deeply about it.

"I won't go! I know you, and know of the mystery connected with you. Your friends are still worrying about you. I'm in this thing and you can't get rid of me so easily."

"Promise me that you will get aboard the first vessel we meet," he repeated. I shook my head.

"You are lost!" he said. "I know the courage of youth, but that will be of no avail. There is no human danger; there are mightier and more terrible forces, of which you have no conception."

I confess I was worried. The old man looked good and kind, and seemed very much concerned about me. I saw a tear fall on his white beard.

"You cannot talk me out of it," I informed him. "I am the nephew of your old schoolmate, Jerome; almost a relative of yours, you see. You seem to be in some sort of trouble, and I'm with you to the end. Just now, I haven't anything particularly important on hand."

For a few moments, his emotion would not permit him to speak. He was a remarkable looking man; a high forehead and deep eyes gave him a wise and stern look, like the pictures of Jehovah; but he also had a look of patience, as though he had lived through much sorrow.

"Go and find you a bed and sleep," he finally said. "We shall meet in the morning." He closed the door behind me.

My bunk was fairly comfortably made up; I lay down with my clothes on, having tied my 25 caliber pistol into the palm of my right hand with my handkerchief. The ship was quiet, except for the splashing of the water past its sides and the gentle hum of the machinery. For a long time I was unable to go to sleep. I was a little seasick, and I was tremendously puzzled. This swift, lifeless ship seemed uncanny to me. The old man's room was bare; He certainly took no part in navigating it. Finally I fell into a deep sleep. I awoke suddenly. I couldn't understand the bright sun shining on me through the porthole, and the pistol in my palm.

When I recollected myself, I stretched my muscles. Daylight made me considerably bolder, and I was tremendously hungry. Therefore, I again searched the entire ship; the bridge, the engine-room, the saloon, the hold; even the galley I found in its accustomed place; but nowhere a living being, nor even any stores of food. In the after part of the ship, usually occupied by the officers, there was a great deal of complicated and delicate-looking mechanical apparatus, of whose use or purpose I had not the least idea. Some parts of it were in activity, with a faint rustling sound. I was too hungry to examine it closely. Everything on the ship was clean, shining, orderly; there was a good deal of minor mechanical activity here and there, water running from a hose, a rotating anemometer, a pump sliding back and forth.

I found no food, and the old man did not appear. At 10 o'clock my patience gave out, and I breakfasted on chocolate and dried meat, beans, and cornmeal from my stores, and drank water from a little keg in the galley. Then I sat on the deck in the sun, in complete solitude. All of my efforts to ascertain how the ship was managed were failures. Old Kaspar appeared about noon.

"I must ask your pardon," he said; "I was unable to sleep until almost morning; and then I overslept. You must be hungry. I forgot. Come."

We went to the galley, where in a little chest in a corner were a few cans of preserved meat and soup. "I was not expecting a guest," the old man apologized; "there is hardly enough food for two. But we'll be there by evening." During the meal he asked me my name, inquired about my parents, and whether or not I had a wife and family. He looked relieved when I replied negatively to the latter.

"I suppose it is all right," he said, partly to himself. "One person more or less over there – what does it matter?"

All afternoon he sat on deck, unwilling to speak. I surmised that he was watching for a ship. Occasionally he spent a while among the unintelligible apparatus in the after part of the ship, touching buttons, moving levers, though I perceived no particular immediate result in the behavior of the ship. We met no vessels, though several times we sighted smoke on the horizon. Several times we also sighted land, sometimes high cliffs, and again sand with tropical trees. From our speed and direction, I made a guess that we must be somewhere in the Caribbean Sea. I gave up my attempts to engage the old man in conversation. He sat motionless, apparently sunk in deep thought. He did not seem to be in the least concerned about the management of the ship.

II.
The City of Beauty.

Toward six o'clock and the end of the strangest day I ever spent in my life, I sighted blue land ahead of us. Before it got dark, I made out tall, rocky cliffs, over which hung a canopy of dark smoke. When night came, the ship's searchlights made the cliffs ahead of us bright as day. We headed directly at the rocky wall, then turned quickly parallel to it, and in a moment there were rocky walls on both sides of us, and even behind us. There must have been a narrow passage among the cliffs, parallel to the coast line.

After some minutes of swift travel in this manner, the rocky walls sank; there were lights ahead of us, and we approached a dock.

The machinery on the ship was busy. I stood with my knapsack ready, and the old man gripped my arm till I trembled – for again it was night, filled with busy machinery without human control. We descended the gangplank, and a small brilliantly illuminated group of people advanced to meet us. They seemed quite indifferent to the clattering machinery and the great bales being swung from the ship on waiting automobile trucks. There was a little old lady, as old as my aged companion, two young men, and a girl of about twenty, of comely face and cheerful disposition. They greeted old Kaspar effusively, but looked in astonishment at me, following a few feet behind. He spoke a few words to them, and then presented me to them: his wife and granddaughter, and two gentlemen friends of the family. I surveyed them intently; they were elegantly dressed with taste that I considered exceptional; their manners were easy and courteous, and they all seemed happy. Only old Kaspar seemed sad and silent; among them he seemed more so than on the ship.

"We welcome you among us"Mrs. Kaspar said; "you will see many strange things here; also some wonderful people."

Two automobiles awaited us, of a rather unusual model; bodies hung low between large wheels, headlights set high, and broad hoods. The Kaspar family seated themselves in one of the cars, and I entered the other with the two young men. We sat down, and the vehicle started off, very smoothly and silently, and raced swiftly through the darkness. I sought in vain for the driver; one of the young men, a red-headed, Irish-looking fellow, moved a hand on a dial and from that moment, neither of them paid any attention to the machine. The one was named Ames; the other I have forgotten.

"I hope you will like it here," Ames said.

"What, and where is this place?" I demanded, curiosity overcoming politeness.

"We call it Fortune Island. It belongs in the West Indies."

"I do not know it. I never heard the name, although my knowledge of geography doesn't amount to much." They admitted that they also knew nothing of geography. I was surprised at their apparent lack of curiosity concerning myself and where I came from. The vehicle stopped at the curb on a brightly lighted street, lined with pretty homes, mostly of the bungalow type; it was paved and planted with tropical trees. I was to be a guest of the Kaspars; I entered with them, and was conducted to my room. My surprise grew. It was all so ordinary, familiar-looking. As far as my surroundings, the house, the furniture, the people, were concerned, I might be on a visit at the home of a well-to-do friend in Chicago or St. Louis. The family seemed to be rejoicing over the safe return of its head, and I left them to themselves, and retired early. I fell asleep quickly, much to my disappointment, as I had hoped to lie in bed and think things over.

I can say that the two or three days that followed were the pleasantest I ever spent in my life; never have I so enjoyed a similar period. I do not remember everything in its proper order. The beautiful city, the deep blue of the sky, the luxuriant tropical vegetation, the happy, cheerful inhabitants, apparently not very busy, all observed in the company of a beautiful and intelligent young woman, whose main concern seemed to be to entertain me – all of this had on me an effect of beauty and happiness, so that I forgot myself, forgot Galveston, forgot everything.

Most of the time was spent in looking over this extraordinary community. You see many beautiful buildings in our American cities, and even beautiful streets; but never have I seen a city in which all the buildings and all the streets so harmonized into one unified and beautiful whole. Not only was each separate building a work of art, but it was a harmonious part of a whole which was a work of art. There were no ugly structures; neither were there any ugly people, toiling in rags. Even in the people themselves, I saw only beauty, and culture. And all around there was an astonishing amount of ingenious and complicated machinery for doing all the rough work. As far as I could observe, the genial men, charming women, and pretty children occupied themselves with light athletic amusements, tennis, golf, and similar games which I did not understand. Dancing seemed to be especially in favor; everywhere people were dancing. I began to think that I had discovered some sort of a secret Utopia.

Miss Mildred Kaspar seemed to have nothing more important on her hands than to take me around and show me the wonders of her native city. In two days we were at ease together, as though we had always been friends; I attribute it largely to her naive ways. Her grandparents we saw only at meals, and they always seemed sad. In the evening we would find ourselves in the company of several aged people, extremely aged, seventy and eighty years old; and these did not seem to want to speak; they seemed sunk in deep and melancholy thought. The young and middle-aged people all seemed to be cheerful and happy, at times it even seemed to me frivolous. It was a little difficult for me to carry on social conversation with them. They spoke excellent English, but I lacked common interests with them, and when the weather was exhausted, and I had answered that I found their city a wonderful place, I was at the end of my resources. I could not comprehend why I was not questioned about the country from which I had come. They seemed to take a great deal of interest in my person; but it seemed that in some way they hesitated to question me. The few that I inquired of whether they had ever been in the United States, shook their heads blankly. Probably the first discordant note that I detected in this harmony was one evening at a reception, where there was dining and dancing. I overheard a conversation among a number of boys about four-teen years old. Apparently they were talking about me.

"What? Do you suppose that he will also have to watch the machines?"

"Machines! Machines!" cried a thin voice angrily; "that's all I ever hear; watching the machines! The devil take them!"

There was a sudden lull in the conversation, as though of astonishment or fear. Then an older boy's reproof:

"Fool! Lucky no one heard. Those things have ears everywhere. Don't you know that last month they got old Higgins for treason? Older than Kaspar, he was."

Then a small boy said, as though repeating a lesson committed to memory:

"Our first duty is to the machines."

Things at the reception were so lively the rest of the evening that I had no leisure to think it over. But it began gradually to dawn upon me that there were other uncanny things in this place. It was a creepy thing to see machinery do-ing work which one expects only of living beings with human brains. At first I had only a vague impression that they all seemed to be automatic; and then I began to observe carefully. Not one machine did I see driven or guided or di-rected by a human being. All of them went, like those first automobiles I saw, in which the people took their ease and did not in the least concern themselves about the machine.

Another thing that I could not understand was this. Miss Mildred showed me libraries, theaters, museums of painting and sculpture (their art was won-derful, as far as my untrained understanding could see), gymnasia, dining rooms, shops with marvelous goods, schools, conservatories of music, flow-ers – but industry? I saw neither workshop nor factory. Everywhere only amusement and ornament. There was not even a city hall.

"What sort of city government do you have?" I asked of Miss Mildred. She did not understand what I meant. There was no such thing as a mayor, or city council. They had no need of them, she said; the machines cared for the city and for the people.

"But don't you have thieves here? And murders? Quarrels? Lawless per-sons?" Even those things it was difficult for her to understand.

"Not that I know of," she said. "I only know of people like ourselves. We all have too much to do, to get into trouble; everyone is occupied with art, mu-sic, writing, athletics; and we take turns watching the machines."

I told her of the big world that I knew; of great cities across the sea, broad lands, of nations and states; of oceans crossed by countless ships. She listened with wide eyes.

"Why do you people not visit the rest of the world?" I asked.

She seemed frightened at the question.

"My father has advised me not to speak of this subject. It is dangerous."

But I could see that she was all eager to pursue the selfsame subject further. "I know where we can talk," she whispered, and ran out of the room to get ready for a walk. Seeing her heavy shoes and walking skirt, I also got ready for a hike, including pistol and field glasses.

We rode out of the city in one of the automobiles that drove itself, on a paved road. We reached the little harbor where I had landed a few days ago, from which, however, the automatic ship was gone. I had seen so many marvels that I was but little surprised when Miss Mildred turned a hand on a dial of the automobile, which thereupon turned around and rolled back into the city, empty. Then followed about an hour's walk, constantly upwards on steep mountainsides, along a barely recognizable path. Our goal was a bowl--like depression at the top of a high cliff. On one side, five hundred feet below, the sea pounded on the pink granite; on the opposite spread the City of Beauty. And between them, diagonally into the interior of the island, I could see a cloud of dark smoke. With my field glasses I could make out smoke-stacks, broad buildings, and huge machinery; and a wide, swarming road from the City of Beauty, straight into the heart of this smoking nucleus.

However, for the time, my attention was occupied closer at hand. Two wide-open eyes bent intently upon me as I told in vivid words of the great world and of my own struggles to amount to something in it stirred me, and made my heart run away with itself. For her, my talk was tremendously romantic, with the flavor of ancient knights slaying dragons. Her own world was sometimes unbearably tedious. For a moment I forgot the important questions concerning the secret of the island. For a moment, I rejoiced and was glad to be alive.

But on the way home, I thought of the mystery. I wished to visit the industrial city that I had seen from the mountain top. Miss Mildred liked the idea. She had never been there; the thing had never occurred to her. No one ever went there, except to watch the machines, which was terribly monotonous and unpleasant and offered no opportunity for observation. People did not speak of it. We would ask Ames to take us over there. She was gleeful over the idea. I would have preferred to go without Ames.

Her glee was short lived. We found Ames at home. He shook his head, and it seemed that he looked either frightened or ashamed. And when we returned to the Kaspar home, Mildred's grandfather took her aside for a moment. She returned with cheeks flushed, as though from something improper; and thereafter avoided the subject. I said nothing, but my mind was made up.

III.
The City of Smoke.

The trips with Mildred to the Gulls' Nest, as she had named her beloved resort, cling in my memory with a sort of hallowed glow. For a few days we went there almost every day. Her restless nature longed for the inspiring world of which I spoke to her, and I reached, by degrees, the condition in which I should gladly have taken her with me, back to that world. Those were wonderful talks that we had there together. And there we wrought the plan for our secret visit to the industrial city. She was full of fears, but also of half-awakened, hitherto unfelt eagerness to know. Her anxious hesitation to let me go, and her efforts not to show it, were very dear to me. Just for that, I should have been willing to go through thunder and lightning for her. I had my knapsack ready, and a car selected. I ventured a good-bye kiss.

Just at that moment, old Kaspar came up the path into the Gulls' Nest. We fell apart, and stood a moment in speechless surprise. Again I saw a tear fall on the white beard.

"Dear children," he said. "And you. Why did you come here among us? You are strong and brave, like the people in the good old world." He looked around intently at the stones, and into the distance, as though fearing eavesdroppers.

"I would implore you not to go there, but I know it will do no good. Those that have tried it, have never returned. And, they are getting harder and harder to deal with –"

"They! Who?"

"Forgive me. Some day I shall tell you. But if you must see the City of Smoke, you might take your turn watching the machines. That you could avoid if you wished; all of us must take our turns at it."

As time was fleeting, I bade them goodbye, and set out on my way. I found my car and set the hands on the dials as I had learned to do, and leaned back on the upholstered cushions while the car turned toward the smoky horizon. I rather regretted that a third person had discovered our Gulls' Nest. I rode swiftly along the smooth road, which was quite busy, the traffic consisting mainly of freight vehicles, and only an occasional passenger car.

Suddenly my car stopped; there was a grinding among its machinery; it jerked several times, and then flung itself around and started back in the opposite direction. I reached for the control levers, and stopped it. But I was quite unable to turn it about. Again it started off at full speed, away from my goal. The pesky machinery was too complicated for me to understand; and I stopped it and jumped out. I ran off the road and disappeared in the thicket

165

beside it, and from my hiding-place, I watched the car. Its machinery hummed and buzzed; it moved forward, stood still, and moved backward. Finally it turned toward the City of Beauty, and disappeared down the road.

My goal seemed to be about five miles away, and I did not consider that much of a walk. I made for the sea, as the coast-line was the shortest distance, and cheerfully set out toward the forest of smoking chimneys – and walked right into the trap. It happened in about a half hour. Some sort of a machine flung out of the woods toward me. I paid very little attention to it until it came rather uncomfortably close, when suddenly it threw out an arm like the beam of a derrick; a sort of loop or lasso was jerked out of it, and fell over my shoulders. The next moment I was swinging in the air. From my elevation I looked the thing over. It was a small automobile truck with a derrick on it, but, as usual, no person anywhere about it. I was lowered into a seat, and a little bar quickly snapped across my chest. I was a prisoner. The whole thing happened so swiftly, that before I realized it, I was speeding along a narrow road through the thicket, toward the smoky city. A small, swift apparatus circled several times around the truck in which I sat locked, and then took its place ahead, as though leading it into town. It looked somewhat like a very small motorcycle.

Apparently, then, I had not fooled "them" in the least, whoever "they" were. I exerted all my efforts to keep my wits about me, and not to lose my head from fright, but none the less I shook considerably all over, when I considered how cleverly they had taken me in, and when I recollected that I had been reminded that previous adventurers had not returned from this place. Nevertheless, I saw no real danger; I was armed, and had a good head and strong muscles; and I was going toward the goal I had set out to reach. The industrial city enveloped me with its smoke and its noise very quickly. It hardly could be called a city; it made me think of the Brooklyn Navy Yard, and of lower Pittsburgh. We passed coal mines and oil wells, steel mills and foundries, and no end of factory buildings, in which machinery roared; the sky was screened by a forest of cranes and beams and derricks, swinging and traveling this way and that, and huge loads sailing through the air; on the ground was a swarm of things on wheels, large and small, running swiftly in all directions, whirling like a dense crowd of people; and in places, complicated stationary machines were busily at work; everywhere machines, machines, machines, until I was dizzy from it; nowhere a living person. What was it all for? Who made it all?

Among the roaring, rumbling buildings, threading its way through the dense throng of busy, swarming vehicles, the little truck carried me, constantly led by the smaller machine (though there was no visible connection between them), straight into the heart of this huge mechanical hive. It stopped before a building, comparatively small in size, but architecturally a little more ornate than the rest, and with numerous wires and cables leading to it. "Some sort of an administration building," I thought. "Now I'll see the boss, and see what it's all about."

The door opened, but no one appeared. The little bar that held me down, snapped open, and the free end of the line that still hung from my shoulders was thrown over to the little leading-machine, where it caught on a spool. The cold chills ran up my back – the uncanny thing rotated its spool and wound up a piece of the line, giving me a slight tug; then it loosened and tugged again. It was very obviously a signal for me to follow it. I did so, with a mixture of fright, astonishment, and curiosity. It led me into the door, which immediately closed behind me; and before me I saw a little table with an excellent lunch, an orange, a fish, bread, and coffee. I could not resist it. It occurred to me that it might be poisoned, but I doubted it. These people had me too completely in their power to be compelled to descend to poison as a means for getting rid of me. Why did they constantly keep themselves hidden? So slow was I in grasping the truth.

While I ate, I examined the room in which I found myself. It was filled with tiers upon tiers of countless units of some electrical apparatus, all alike. It made me think of an automatic telephone exchange; the instruments looked that way, and the little rustling among them, now here and now there, sounded just like the operation of an automatic telephone exchange. I noticed several large lenses turned on me, set in stereopticon-like boxings; they stared at me like huge expressionless eyes. But I saw only the glass, the glass and enameled metal. The apparatus all seemed to be quite busy; it rustled and stirred, making me nervously apprehensive of some hidden presence. I waited, surmising that I was being scrutinized by some hidden person by the aid of these instruments. It ended with a tug at my line, and I followed the little motor out of the door, where a chariot-like vehicle awaited me, just about large enough to hold me. It sidled up to me, like some familiar dog. I guessed that I was required to get into it.

"Good," I thought. "Thus far everything is all right. I am still curious. When I get tired of it, we'll see. And if I don't see your faces pretty soon, I'll be getting tired of it."

I could not keep track of the direction in which the thing swiftly carried me. We crossed a broad, paved road, on which I saw a number of passenger cars containing people. "Are they the watchers of the machines?" thought I; "or the inhabitants of this mechanical city?" In a moment I rode into an immense pavilion, up an elevator, and out on a raised platform, from which I looked down on a strange scene.

In all respects it looked as though it might be the central control station of this huge industrial community. Rows and tiers of dials and meters, levers and switches, valves and gauges, covered the walls and numerous racks throughout the immense, auditorium-like room. For a moment I thought that these people were in truth working with these things, and directing the machinery, and that I now beheld the masters of this place. They sat at the dials and levers in little groups; from little towers and platforms they reviewed streams of vehicles passing them, in endless variety of size and shape. But I did not think so for long. These people, whom I examined closely through my field-glasses, elegantly dressed, lolling lazily on comfortable seats, with indifferent and bored expressions – they did not understand this apparatus even as well as I did. I recognized some of the individuals whom I had met in the City of Beauty. These amusement-loving inhabitants of that little paradise, were now taking their turn "watching the machines." What was the significance of this empty comedy, I could not imagine.

Several of them noticed me up on my perch, clamped in the three-wheeled chariot, and it seemed that their faces suddenly grew grave. Some of them recognized me personally, and turned pale and looked away. And about then I began to get a little tired of my investigation; I would rather have been out of this thing. I determined to resign at the first opportunity. I was still trying to formulate some plan of escape, when a gong began to strike somewhere in a slow, measured fashion. People took their hats and coats, and seated themselves in waiting vehicles, and the great hall began to empty out. My own conveyance also began to move, but did not join the stream of cars that was going out the great doors. My alarm increased at the thought of staying here alone among all these machines, away from all human companionship, at the mercy of the unknown terror.

I was held in my seat on the chariot by a bar across my chest and shoulders, and no amount of squirming availed me in trying to free myself. Nor could I understand the locks that held the bar to the sides of the car. I examined it carefully for some time, and then lost all patience with the thing; I drew my Colt's forty-five automatic, pressed the muzzle to the lock at my side, and bang! The explosion deafened me, almost stunned me. The car was still moving, but I was free. My hand was numb from the recoil, but I stuffed the gun into its holster, leaped out of the car, rolling over several times on the ground, and jumped up and ran through the darkness.

It was dark as a pocket; I could hear the injured machine emitting a curious combination of fluty whistles, which in a moment were echoed from a distance, and later from several points. In front of me I saw a lighted opening, and ran for it, emerging in a few minutes into the waning daylight. I was on the broad paved road, filled with cars which were taking the "watchers of the machines" back to the City of Beauty. Luck was with me; one of the cars passed me slowly enough to enable me to catch it and swing myself into it. It gradually gained speed, and in a few moments rolled out of a huge gateway, and I saw ahead of me the long road, the tropical thicket, the mountains, and the sea. I sank on the seat, beside the solitary occupant of the vehicle.

"Ah! You are the victim!" he gasped weakly. "Get off, I implore you. You cannot escape them. Get off, or we are both lost! Do not bring down their violence on me. I have done nothing!" He begged and wrung his hands, and finally pushed me toward the side of the car. In disgust, I flung him into the farthest corner, but his warning was not lost upon me. In front of us I could see the vehicles stopping one after another opposite a sort of trussed tower; after a short stop, they went on. They were being searched. I did not wait for that. I seized the lever, slowed the car, leaped out, and plunged into the thicket. I rushed pell-mell for the sea. I rejoiced that I was still cool enough to reason; for, thus far I had seen no living enemy; there were only machines against me. And I knew that these machines, driven by electric or gas motors, could not follow me into the water. The salt water would stop them at once.

For about a half an hour, I had the world to myself and my harrowed thoughts. Around me was the thicket, and ahead of me the broad sea; I began to rejoice that I had won the game. I emerged from the thicket, and started across the hundred yards of flat sand intervening between me and the water, when one of the little motor-cycle-like machines dashed out of the thicket on my right. I broke into a run toward the water, in the hope that I was unobserved, but the machine swerved to head me off. Its speed was so great that I had no hope of reaching the water ahead of it. And I had no desire for an encounter with the spluttering, whirring iron thing. Again I drew my forty-five automatic, dropped on one knee, coolly drew a bead on the middle point of its machinery, and fired three shots. I saw something crumple in the machine, and a number of little black objects flew up in the air. There was a sputter and a crash, and the machine fell and rolled over and over, throwing up sand, and clattering loose pieces. I dashed for the water.

When I felt my feet wet and the spray in my face, I stopped and looked back. Two bodies, similar to tractors had rolled out of the woods on the narrow road on the sand; they were lifting the damaged machine with a crane, and they turned back into the thicket with the wreck dangling from a beam on one of them. I waded out into the water to my waist, and for a long time toiled in the direction of the City of Beauty. But I was not molested further. In a half hour it was dark. In three hours I sat in the Gulls' Nest, panting and eating chocolate. I drank big draughts of water from the little spring, and fell asleep with a pistol in each hand.

IV.
The Old Man's Story.

I awoke, it seemed in just a few minutes, hearing voices near me. It was very dark.

"I fear there will be trouble. I must act tomorrow. How thankful I feel that I am ready."

"Oh, grandfather, why did we let him go there? Didn't we know that he could never escape that awful fate?" And sobbing followed.

"Here I am!" I shouted, and turned my flashlight on myself. In an instant I had the girl in my arms; and then the old man took my hand.

"We heard about the disturbance," he told me; "and we thought you were lost." They were eager to hear what had happened to me, and I related it to them. When I finished, old Kaspar said to me:

"You have been filled with curiosity regarding the mystery of this island. Let me tell you about it:

"When, as a result of a happy accident, I found myself the possessor of sufficient wealth to enable me to indulge fully my inventive and mechanical inclinations, I found that in our country, the possession of wealth also means endless tangles with politics and other public obstacles. I therefore searched for an independent island where I might carry on my work. When on this undiscovered one, I found deposits of coal and iron, copper, tin, and platinum, oil, fertile fields for the cultivation of food, cotton, and silk, I saw an ideal realized. The only thing that was lacking was rubber and a few unimportant chemicals.

"I moved my shops and picked assistants and workmen over here, and got to work. I was mainly interested in the perfection of automatic machinery. Already, during the past few years, I had worked out an automobile that automatically supplied itself with fuel, oil, water, and air, when these ran low. That was the first and simplest step in a long and intricate process. The next step was to make the driving of a car more of an automatic matter. The discovery of the selenium reflex enabled us to construct a car that automatically avoided obstacles. The whole principle of the vision of these machines, by means of which they see sufficiently for the purposes of their activity depends on the sensitiveness of selenium toward light, which increases its resistance to the electrical current. The next step was the construction of a machine for which is was possible to lay out on a dial, an entire trip ahead, and then send it on alone to accomplish it. This step did away altogether with the necessity of a chauffeur or driver. A much simpler matter was it to furnish a vehicle with means of repairing its own minor damages and accidents, and to give notice automatically of more serious requirements. You can follow, as I tell it to you, how we progressed in the working out of an almost living organism from an ordinary automobile; but at the time it was not nearly so apparent to us.

"In the course of time, we made use of these same principles in other classes of machinery. We made a truck which we could send after the desired freight, without a driver, which automatically loaded and unloaded the goods. We made repairing machines, for repairing automobiles and other machinery, so that the machine in need of repairs automatically, without human intervention, drove up to the repairing machine and was taken care of. We so organized our machinery that it required nothing of us, except that we find work for it to do. It maintained, repaired, and manufactured itself. It could do everything except reason.

"However, machines which have a sort of reasoning power, are common enough in the world. An adding machine, a bookkeeping machine, the automatic telephone exchange, a surface-measuring machine, – many of them can do their one little task for better than the human brain can. It is easy to make a machine that reasons on the basis of the immediate situation only; all automatic machinery does that. It was also easy to endow our machines with senses or perceptions by which they could register and be influenced by outside conditions, touch, vision, hearing; we have even given them senses which we humans do not have, the consciousness of various vibrations and forms of energy. We gave them means of communicating with one another.

"But true reason involves judgment; it demands that the decision of the immediate problem be influenced by past experience. Mechanical memory was what we needed; and when we found it, our machines were able to think and reason better than we ourselves. To be sure we found it. I had with me a dozen men whose brains were as good as mine, and hundreds of skilled artisans. We found the variations in electrical resistance depending on delayed oxidation of several metals.

"Our human community entered upon a Golden Age. There was little or no work, and much time to spare. It is a human characteristic to dissipate such free time and energy: but our community was picked from the most intellectual class of humanity, and it devoted itself to art, beauty and creation. But we engineers suddenly realized that we had created a race of beings, independent of us and working for us. As soon as we installed the mechanical memory, the machines made independent progress, rapidly and steadily. Without our help, they increased, not only in power and ability, but in numbers. They did not possess life in any sense of the word; – their work, and their improvement and increase depended on the supplies of coal and oil. And yet, what is life? Does not our art and love depend on supplies of wheat and beef? We feared that these cold brains of steel and electricity might reach a point in their logic where they would see it to their interest to throw off their bonds of slavery to us, and become a source of real danger to us. We therefore intentionally saw to it that each machine remained to some extent still dependent on human assistance. Of this service, for which the machines depended on human beings, there remains only a sort of superficial inspection. But they cannot be without it; they cannot do any work or carry on any activity without it; the necessity was built into them when they were manufactured. It is like an instinct in animals. These machines live their own lives, care completely for themselves, as well as for us, do all our work, feed us, etc., but they cannot do without our 'watching'.

"This requirement we considered our salvation from the danger of the machines; it has turned out to be the thing that betrayed us. The City of Beauty now contains the third generation, which feels no need of the struggle and effort to take care of itself, that is biologically necessary to keep a race from degenerating. It is pampered by the machines. These are not the strong, keen people that their grandfathers were, whom I brought with me to the island. They meekly submit to the compulsory ceremony of inspection, like domesticated cattle. 'Watching the Machines' was once a prerogative of the masters: now it is a symbol of slavery. The City of Beauty is the slave and the City of Smoke is the master, a master without a living soul!

"Now you can see why my heart is forever sad. These are my children. Both the people and the monsters are my children, but the people are weak and without prestige. They are numbed by comfort and beauty.

"I have been trying to make the last short remnant of my life of some service to them. I have tried to awaken them to a life of courage and effort, but in vain. Perhaps I may have the power to destroy all of these machines, but I lack that much courage. I have therefore made a dozen small machines, completely independent of all human assistance, and set them to go into the hall and take the places of the watchers of the machines. They are able to handle the dials and switches, and they carry wax dummies of human appearance. You understand, the watchers of the machines do not actually do any work; they are merely present. It keeps seeming to me like some primitive form of worship. I had intended to start my machines within a few days; your own courage has been an inspiration to me. They only need to be filled with fuel and oil.

"But is seems now that the machines in the City of Smoke intend some sort of vengeance. You must have irritated them in some way. I fear that by this time they have carried away a number of people."

"Can I be of some help to you?" I offered.

"I do not need you. And I do not want to expose you to any more danger." He looked at Mildred. "My shop is in the City of Smoke. I must go there alone. I do not think they will harm me; and what is the difference if they do? I am old, and cannot live forever."

V.
The Rule of the Machines.

We descended the mountain and rode back to the city. As we approached it, we saw a crowd of machines just outside the city, at the spot where the broad road led into it; there were all imaginable shapes and sizes, passenger automobiles, trucks, tractors, steam-shovels, motorcycles, paving machines, ditching machines; they swarmed and crowded, some slow and clumsy, others darting swiftly in and out among them, a huge, squirming blot at the edge of the city. Just within the city gates, brightly illuminated by the searchlights of the machines, shrinking in little groups, were people. From the distance of a quarter of a mile, it was certainly a dramatic looking situation. Again I heard the fluty whistling, up and down the musical scale.

"Where is the explosive man who wrecked two of us?" old man Kaspar translated to me.

"Do you mean that that is a machine speaking?"

"Yes. The people are answering, but I cannot hear them."

"And the machines can hear, and understand human speech?"

"Yes. Have you not noticed on them, the little crosses covered with copper netting? Those are their ears, working on the principle of a wireless receiver. But, I fear that you must turn back, and conceal yourself in your Gulls' Nest. The people are promising that they will turn you over to the machines."

"Well, the miserable wretches –" I said slowly in surprise.

"They are afraid. They know nothing of courage. Already, several of them have been carried away by the machines. A panic is beginning – the machines practice vivisection on their captives; they are studying life, which they do not have, and which they desire."

While he spoke, he was trying to stop the machine on which we rode. It jerked and swerved sidewise, and shivered and roared, but would not stop. Mildred gasped in fear.

173

"Wait!" I said, through partly clenched teeth. "I suppose this beast heard us say that we wanted to stop, and now it wants to tell where I want to hide. I'll show it a trick."

I pointed my forty-five automatic into the middle of the rustling machinery and fired. Mildred screamed. I fired again. The machine shivered and stopped, but not before a half dozen hoots had escaped it. We got off, and I put several more shots into various parts of it; and the crashing of metal and the tinkling of loose parts on the pavement satisfied me that it would tell no tales. Mildred clung to my arm, and soon I found my right one about her shoulders.

"You must leave the road, and work through the thicket to the Gulls' Nest. In a few moments there will be several machines here. I shall go to meet them. I do not know if I shall return from the City of Smoke. My boy, leave this island; you do not belong here. Mildred will show you our secret yacht –"

"Mr. Kaspar, now I've really got a reason for staying here." I took Mildred's hand and held it in front of him.

"Then take her with you. She will be happy, and now hurry."

Three huge lights were hurtling down the road toward us. In a moment we had plunged into the blackness of the thicket. I did not dare to use my flashlight until there was an hour of darkness and jungle between us and the wrecked machine. It was toward morning before we reached Gulls' Nest. We ate of my dried stores and lay down on the sand for a short rest.

Mildred wavered between fear for our own safety, and anxiety for her grandfather. We kept postponing our flight from the island until we spent four days up there. On the fifth day we resolved to venture over to the City of Beauty, she with the intention of going into her home, if such a thing were possible. I accompanied her through the thicket, and awaited her about a mile from the city. I waited for several hours, and a worse torture I never endured in my life. I was apprehensive that something might happen to her, and that she might never return to me. About me, twilight reigned under the broad leaves and tangled vines. At times I was heartily ashamed of my intention to run away from the island, and of my fear before those stupid hulks. Of what consequence was my insignificant life, that I should flee from this wonderful, stirring place, to save it? I really ought to go among this soft and degenerate people, and be their leader, and overcome this race of iron and oil, and make it again the slave of humanity. That would be a glorious war!

Mildred returned, staggering under the weight of a small, but apparently heavy package.

"Platinum!" she said. "It will make you rich in your world, where riches seem to be so necessary. Come. Hurry." And she burst into tears.

Dumbly I picked up the package. It must have weighed nearly a hundred pounds. How she managed to drag it that distance, I could not imagine. For an hour I staggered along at her side and all the time she wept.

"They returned no more for watchers," she said. "It looks as if there were an end to watching. Grandfather liberated them, and they are praising him with the hymns of a martyr. For he also did not return, and they know he will not return."

"You mean that he was – like the rest –?"

"I do not think so. I do not think they will harm grandfather. They need his help. And he is the creator of all the machines. I cannot imagine just what they will do with him. Perhaps there has been an accident; perhaps he is a prisoner. But I think they will be good to him.

"But the people have promised to give you up to the machines, because you stopped three machines. It is very difficult to start them over when they have once been killed."

"Poor, unfortunate people!" I said. "They do not know that they are doomed –"

"Can I not return, and lead them in a war against the machines? Could I not arouse them to action?"

She threw her arms about me and clung to me.

"Do not think of it! I know that it is not possible. They fear too much for their poor soft bodies against iron beams and chains. They have no courage, no bravery. At this moment they tremble under the threats of the machines that are searching for you for their vivisection.

"I despise them, those people of mine! I want to go with you into your world. Grandfather's yacht is waiting for us, and I know how to handle it. You can find your way across the sea into your city.

"Farewell, my wretched people. How long you will last, I do not know. And you, terrible monsters! How soon will we see you again, pursuing us –?"

She turned to me.

"Those are not vain words. They are constantly learning, constantly progressing, with astonishing rapidity. Their intelligence grows, but they have no feelings, no hearts. And they are immortal; worn parts can be replaced, and the individual never dies."

www.ingramcontent.com/pod-product-compliance
Lightning Source LLC
Chambersburg PA
CBHW040826010826
48978CB00012BB/618